peripheries

a journal of word, image, and sound

CENTER FOR THE STUDY OF WORLD RELIGIONS

Cover image from Mélanie Berger, *Entrecorps #3*, 2007, color pencil on paper, 8.2" x 11.7"

Internal folio covers from the *Entrecorps* series, 2007, color pencil on paper, 8.2" x 11.7". #1 on p.137, #8 on p.138, #9 on p.165, #7 on p.166, #2 on p.201, #15 on p.202, #4 on p.247, #12 on p.248, #14 on p.277, #5 on p.278, #13 on p.313, #11 on p.314.

Editor's Foreword

Francis Ponge, with characteristic precision, describes the ordinary pleasure of walking through a doorway—"your progress slows for a moment, your eye opens up and your whole body adapts to its new apartment." Your mind must also adapt to a new conceptual space. Walking through a door interrupts your thoughts and can even cause you to forget why you were walking through it to begin with. The very act of crossing a threshold, neuroscientists have discovered, disrupts memory. It can also be a spur for remembering: if you misplace a word, check the next room.

This works, because we parcel out information into box-like categories and represent such psychical structures in our embodied lives. Rooms represent units of memory. Medieval memory artists knew this, building "memory palaces" in their imaginations, and leaving items in conspicuous places. To remember those items, they had only to walk back through the palace. Poets knew about memory rooms too. Historically, poetry had a pragmatic memory function: so many elements of craft—rhyme, meter, image—were originally mnemonic devices. The stanza—Italian for "room"—is another such device, illustrating our method of capturing the passage of time in discrete units or events.

Few readers memorize poems now, but poetry still mirrors their cognitive architecture, and poets still design these containers to preserve and display the past.

Two folios in this edition, guest-edited by *Peripheries'* editors, explore the poetics of rooms. Amanda Gunn invited seven poets to ask "of these interiors," in her words: "what light do they let in or keep out, what peoples them, what foundations are they built upon?" Amanda also shifts our orientation ninety degrees to consider how poems take up room on the page, in the book.

For the next folio, "the Book, the Room," Gabby Woo and Yongyu Chen invited writers and visual artists to respond to Mallarmé's dream of a book roomy enough to contain *everything*, on condition that their contributions would traverse digital space to a physical room before residing in this volume. Contributors' words and images lived in Gabby and Yongyu's bedroom, which "left its traces," the editors write, listing: "shifting light from the north-facing window, slow accumulation of dust, images peeling up at the corners, paper curling from humidity."

The folio form is itself a discrete compartment within a larger volume. In issue three of *Peripheries*, we began inviting experts to guest-edit folios on special themes, and every edition since has included a folio (available on our website). This year we have built an enfilade: a series of six adjacent "rooms."

The third folio opens the door of literary form onto the "real world." We invited the Australian poet and scholar, founder of *Rabbit: a journal for nonfiction poetry*, Jessica Wilkinson, to collate nonfiction poems that work with archives—historical, biographical, scientific—to present research and document events—sociopolitical and personal. The folio consists of ten such projects, including a poem that recounts six women's experiences of the atomic bombing of Hiroshima. Another poem juxtaposes the lives of two wives of male artists, and another studies the journals of a nineteenth-century scientist who dissected platypuses.

Contributors to the fourth folio also work with archives. *Peripheries* music editor, Andrew Schulman, curated this folio of musicians and musicologists who preserve, interpret, or adapt obscure source material, including an Irish poem, thirteenth-century chants, and songs with less than one thousand streams on Spotify. Showcasing this artistic processes of collage and improvisation, the folio also includes a *QR* code to access audio.

In the clearest example of cultural and linguistic preservation, the fifth folio is a collection of Yiddish poetry. Daniel Kraft invited ten translators to each translate one Yiddish poem of their choice. Several of these translators are involved with the Yiddish Book Center in Massachusetts, where Daniel has also been a translation fellow.

Recognizing our community institutions, the final folio in the collection commemorates the beloved Grolier Poetry Book Shop in Harvard Square on the eve of its one-hundredth year. The store's manager, James Fraser, invited ten poets who have read their work at The Grolier over the course of their careers to submit a poem from a recent performance and an older poem dating from their first reading at the shop. Each poet also includes a note remembering The Grolier's role in their career, and *Peripheries* also thanks James for first stocking our journal and displaying it in The Grolier's iconic shop window.

The cover of this seventh edition of *Peripheries* features an image from the whimsical series "*Entrecorps*" by the Belgian-based artist, Mélanie Berger. This protean shape leaps, hides, and reels—with a surprising range of emotion—through the journal to land on each of the folio's cover pages.

These covers function like doors, "with a friendly hand one still holds on to it, before closing it decisively and shutting oneself in" to the world of the next collection. If so, you are about to enter *Peripheries'* in-house collection, whose artworks also perform the work of memory. We invite you to consider how they reflect processes of retention, delimitation, and loss.

Our in-house collections are never themed. They reflect a year's work, with all its contingencies and chance encounters. We also document *Peripheries'* events that year; this edition includes craft talks which Tracy K. Smith and Donald Revell delivered to our community, and from which we trust our readers will benefit.

This issue also features the winning poems of our inaugural poetry competition judged by Josh Bell. Second prize went to Alan Yan for "Impossible Blue" and first prize to Alinh Dolinh for "Dream Sequence Stricken from a Tapestry" whose "odd, blazing breadth of tone and diction here—britomartian to gorget, cellophaned to heft," Josh writes, "is the announcement of an arrival, of a world coming into focus."

Along with the annual competition, *Peripheries* can announce a residency and writing retreat—a world of poetry endeavors. The journal and its events are only possible because of the hard work of our designer, editors—guest-editors and members of our editorial advisory board—and readers. And because of the ongoing support of Charles M. Stang, the Director of the Center for the Study of World Religions at Harvard Divinity School, and Gosia Skłodowska, the Center's Executive Director. *Peripheries* is grateful for its home at the Center, and proud to release this seventh edition into the wide world this spring season, 2025.

Sherah Bloor,
Editor-in-Chief

Table of Contents

Rooms

Edited by Amanda Gunn

The Book, the Room

Edited by Yongyu Chen, Gabby Woo

To/for 'nonfiction poetry'

Edited by Jessica L. Wilkinson

Source Material:
A Folio Of Transcriptions, Arrangements, & Departures

Edited by Andrew Schulman

Worlds of Yiddish Poetry
Edited by Daniel Kraft

Grolier Approaches 100: Poetry and Archives
Edited by James Fraser

Stag

Carl Phillips

The head lay severed in a
small clearing deep within
the forest where the forest
stops for a bit, then as if
remembering itself,
continues...No boot prints
to suggest someone had
brought the head here,
and left it, no blood, no
trace anywhere of the body
that must once have borne
the head aloft, have shifted
accordingly for it to lower
itself when feeding, or in
combat. Some people see antlers
and think branches, as in
trees, but all I could think of
was a patterned sequence
of mistakes, questions, and un-
rewindable dreams—that's
how it felt, at least, when I
touched them. Around me,
the forest moved then didn't,
like any artist who, after
back-and-forthing between
revisions, prefers the original,

that stillness through which
the snow still falls without
settling, too light to settle,
not needing to: proof – not
an offering. I lay down on
the moss-covered ground, my
own antler-crowned head beside
the stag's head. Messenger, hello.

Special Occasion

Sawako Nakayasu

Sometimes circumstance loops me back to a place I thought I would never revisit. Intimacies of initial touch—sex or surgery—that occasion a hush and quiet, no more than one or two syllables at a time, any more would threaten the gingerly establishing rhythms of the moment, a matter of solemnity and respect in the face of that which flays open, where a tiny spasm of a drumbeat emerges in layers that actualize in the moments just before the blood blossoms.

All that having been said, and whatever dignity or reverence be intended, the name of the game today is not enough control, the dance move of the moment is a hyper localized thrashing, the room throbs darkly, there is too much seeing and too much being seen, it is vulgar and irrevocable, it is full and too full, widening and disbelief, and when pressed, it gives, like this, don't look, I press, on your eye, as open or closed as it may be.

Selfie Stick

Andrea Cohen

I'd rather
have a carrot.

Bio

Andrea Cohen
is and will
be was.

My Father's Watch

It's a Bulova, nothing fancy.
It sits in his desk, then in mine.

Finally, I take it to Leo, who
does what I never thought to do.

He winds it. He lifts it to my ear.
It won't keep perfect time, he says—

which is fine. Time is imperfect.
It soldiers on, we say, as if

it wasn't us sabering
the days and nights.

Trees on the path.
Rain on the leaves.

This ticking along—I
miss him.

Directional

He held
a match

up to
to see

which way
the dark

was headed.

Apples on a Chair

after Alvin Ross

There they are—three
apples on a white chair,

on a pillow on a chair,
where we have to imagine

they're comfortable,
where a sitter for a portrait

did not show, or was, by
a few luminous fruits,

upstaged. How will
we be remembered?

I am what I left—
pen, shell, the letter

I could not write.
Render that, with a grey

floor and ochre backdrop,
or better, rest a while

with apples on a pillow
on a small chair—

marvel at all
we call fallen.

Craft Talk and Poetry Reading (May 8, 2023)

Tracy K. Smith

I thought I would frame my work in dialogue with a Chinese poet I love, Yi Lei, who began publishing her poems in the late 1980s. One of her most famous and controversial poems was called "A Single Woman's Bedroom." In a long suite, the speaker describes her longing for a lover who has broken a promise to come and live with her. She also expresses longing and insistence for freedom, both personal, and I think, collective.

As I was working with my co-translator, Changtai Bi, on bringing this work into English, Yi Lei would stand by and watch my versions of the poems take shape. And in that poem in particular, she said, you're paying too much attention to the love story. This is a poem about citizenship and freedom of the spirit, she insisted.

I think that when we listen deeply to another poet's work, we find a stronger footing in our own questions and themes as well. And so maybe this reading, which is kind of like a conversation between Yi Lei and myself, will enact that a little bit, even across poems that I wrote before I became a student and a devotee of her work.

Yi Lei passed away in 2018, before this collection, *My Name Will Grow Wide Like a Tree*, was published. But I feel that our conversation continued. There was a moment I remember very clearly and frequently—sitting in a hotel room while on the road working on the manuscript, getting ready to hand it in. I didn't know what the book should be called, which poem ought to give it its title. I asked Yi Lei to help me, and she gave me a nudge toward an English line in one of her poems. Maybe I'll start with that. Already I'm running afoul of my little plan, but I think that's always a nice sign.

This poem, "Nightmare," makes reference to Miguel or Michael Cervantos who was a monk—or actually a secular humanist who was put to death for heresy. And he makes an appearance in the poem alongside the speaker.

NIGHTMARE

I'm bound to a stake
Planted in a nameless square.
Twigs pant at my feet
Awaiting the match.

Michael Servetus, scraggy
Madman, should be bound, too,
And hoarse from shouting.
I'm weak. I quake with rage.

With what words will the world
Be quenched? Michael Servetus
Calls on God, but I'm godless. I say,
Soon, the language of reality will be silence.

What sparks true today, blinds tomorrow.
Today, I die for a crime. Tomorrow,
People will be crowned for it.
My name will grow wide like a tree.

Flames growl and pounce.
I am consumed with fear.
Michael Servetus and I cry out
Together: *No! No!* This morning

I woke with those words
Burning my lips.

Poems help us talk to ourselves. They help us find the proper tone of voice and sense of stakes; to be honest with ourselves about what we know and what we fear. Sometimes I think of poems as thought experiments whereby we can bring into language the inkling that what we obey in our day-to-day lives is less than what's possible. And I feel that in a poem like this.

Yi Lei also teaches me to ask questions in my work, and to struggle with questions that I don't and won't know the answer to. I'll read a few more poems by this poet. This is a love poem. I think it's also a poem that becomes cosmic in scale. That's something I admire in poetry in general when we can move from the known and the felt, into a space that upends our certainty and reminds us of the proper scale in which we operate. This poem does that very elegantly.

I'll tell you a little about how these poems were made, these English versions. I don't read Mandarin, Chinese, and so Changtai Bi who goes by the name David created a literal translation of Yi Lei's selected poems. And even in that direct—in some cases—rough form, I heard and felt a kind of emphatic insistence. Sometimes that occurred through repetition. Other times it occurred by moving again and again by different means toward a single question or event. I was eager to find image systems that would allow me to feel at home and grounded in the body of Yi Lei's imagination. In finding forms in English that could help constrain and guide my own ear and thought process through her cosmology. And sometimes that meant changing forms of the poem.

After this poem, I'll read you one poem in which I had to invent a new cage or container for a poem that is a concrete poem in Chinese, which couldn't be replicated in English vocabulary.

THE NUDE

My eye laps at you in lamplight
Like a white-hot tongue. Longing

Draws back, then rises, tidal.

The curtain of my hair
Announces my breasts. Your lips:

A languid breeze. Like a miracle
We feast and feast and nothing is spent.

Let flesh attend to flesh, sex to sex.
O dexterous gold watch of the universe

On which one minute can straddle
A hundred years

I have this belief that the middle line of a poem is a key, almost in every case, to something that's at stake at the heart of the poem. And as a poet I know you don't know what the middle line of your poem is as you're writing it. And so there's something that feels like a mystery operating alongside the poet's conscious mind. We have lots of different names for that. The unconscious is one. But especially thinking about my connection to Yi Lei or my interest in poems that take me toward what feels like the cosmic or the mysterious, I urge myself to expand my vocabulary of what that might be. And to imagine it might be *guides*. Or people on the other side of the mortal divide. Or *language* itself.

In this poem, the middle line is "A languid breeze like a miracle." And I think for me, that is the moment where something else becomes possible in Yi Lei's imagination. The room, the intimate encounter between two bodies is now in space with the ineffable and the profound and powerful. And the possibilities within the poem open in new directions for me.

There's repetition that does something, we feast and feast. And the miracle is nothing is spent. And then there's one of my favorite moments in her work, the moment where the scope of the universe also has bearing upon the moment at hand between lovers.

"*Dexterous gold watch of the universe on which one minute can straddle 100 years.*"

That verb allows me, as a reader, as a translator to live in both realms at once, to hover there.

This is the poem that is a concrete poem. These poems behave so different from one language system to the next that the book isn't a side-by-side translation. It is laid out like two manuscripts. But this is what the poem I'm about to read looks like in its original form.

It's a poem called "Red Wall." And that block structure feels very intentional. This is a poem—as I read it—that's about nationhood, allegiance, and fidelity and also qualms and indifference or resistance. And how that dwells in and around our markers of nationhood and our relationship to the place that we help constitute.

RED WALL

Hot. Having burned me but also
Warmed me. I regard it from a distance.
The flowers choking it, bleeding onto it,
Red legacy binding our generations.
From below, we thousands cast upon it a
beatific, benighted, complacent, complicit,
decorous, disconsolate, distracted, expectant,
execrative, filthy, grievous, guileless,
hallowed, hotheaded, hungry, incredulous,
indifferent, inscrutable, insubordinate, joyful,
loath, mild, peace-loving, profane, proud,

rageful, rancorous, rapt, skeptical, terrified,
tranquil, unperturbed, unrepentant,
warring eye.

October 31, 1987

So you hear that insistent list of adjectives that the poem becomes, right around the middle line of the poem. I'll just throw that out there. But—that's the language that comprises that block or that wall in the original text.

I wanted to find something to bind my version of the poem, but it couldn't be a physical form. I thought that alphabetizing those adjectives would become the constraint. That it would maybe not be recognizable at first. But as the list goes on beyond what is acceptable, almost beyond what feels practical, I think that ordering system becomes legible. You start to wonder, and so your eye starts to wander the text. And you realize it's obedient to something.

I'll read one last Yi Lei poem, which is a poem that I think also bears witness to her sense of ecology, sense of the natural world with its power, wisdom, and its sense of order, regeneration. Yi Lei reveres the ecology as something that we are accountable to and that we are stewards of. And something that has potent powerful force to act in its own, in accordance with its own will.

This is "Song for Heaven, Earth, and Humankind." And it is inscribed for the painting Celestial Music Floats by Inio, written on the fifth day after the Sichuan earthquake in May 2008. So this is a poem that in some ways is an elegy.

SONG FOR HEAVEN, EARTH, AND HUMANKIND

Each blade of grass is a glorious eye,
Every ripe fruit a mouth.
Angels stretch out their thousand hands
And dewdrops and rain rain down

All things ache for love.
Water and fire withstand each other.
Heaven journeys alongside Earth.
A small voice belts out the saddest song.
Year after year, flowers thrive.
Sea gives way to land, land to se.
Humanity creates, ghosts endure.
The soul in the cloud dances quietly.

May 16, 2008
Written on the fifth day after the Sichuan earthquake

Since the poems I chose from Yi Lei are speaking at different registers to the self in terms of the nation across the divide of strangers or neighbors, I thought I'd select poems of my own with a similar logic.

This is called "Flores Woman." And it begins with an epigraph from Nature Magazine: "A species of tiny human has been discovered which lived on the remote Indonesian island of Flores, just 18,000 years ago. Researchers have so far unearthed remains from eight individuals who were just one meter tall with grapefruit sized skulls. These astonishing little people made tools, hunted tiny elephants, and lived at the same time as modern humans who were colonizing the area."

In that article, the circumstance or the condition that accounts for why and how humans and animals might grow smaller over time in proportion to their environment is called endemic island dwarfism.

So this species of human was named Flores man. And I wanted to imagine a space beside someone like Flores woman. And I start with this poem because it's a poem in which I find another vocabulary for thinking about what's at stake in my living. And I think in some cases that that's a really helpful and humbling or chastening exercise.

FLORES WOMAN

> A species of tiny human has been discovered, which lived on the remote Indonesian island of Flores just 18,000 years ago. . . . Researchers have so far unearthed remains from eight individuals who were just one metre tall, with grapefruit-sized skulls. These astonishing little people . . . made tools, hunted tiny elephants and lived at the same time as modern humans who were colonizing the area.
>
> —*Nature*, October 2004

Light: lifted, I stretch my brief body.
Color: blaze of day behind blank eyes.

Sound: birds stab greedy beaks
Into trunk and seed, spill husk

Onto the heap where my dreaming
And my loving live.

Every day I wake to this.

Tracks follow the heavy beasts
Back to where they huddle, herd.

Hunt: a dance against hunger.
Music: feast and fear.

This island becomes us.

Trees cap our sky. It rustles with delight
In a voice green as lust. Reptiles

Drag night from their tails,
Live by the dark. A rage of waves

Protects the horizon, which we would devour.
One day I want to dive in and drift,

Legs and arms wracked with danger.
Like a dark star. I want to last.

I recognize in some of the gestures in this poem that part of my brain was also thinking about the statement in the article that modern humans at the same time were colonizing the area. And so I think my ear and mind enter into this scenario with a sense of threat. What is encroaching upon the stability or the sanctity of these people's lives? I hear that in gestures like "a rage of waves protects the horizon" or "legs and arms racked with danger". And, of course, in that wish which is my wish too at the end of the poem, to last.

This is my poem "Mothership" written for the poet Kamilah Aisha Moon when she was still with us in the year that she lost her mother. And I had this moment where I imagined that Aisha's mother and my mother, who were both deceased, would know each other now as they had not had the opportunity to in life. And that gave me a sense of comfort.

And then that thought grew in diameter. And I began to imagine, well, what if that's what happens to all the mothers? What if they all are united in some way where they can come to understand. And that's kind of where this poem digs in.

MOTHERSHIP

You cannot see the Mothership in space,
It and She being made of the same thing.

All our mothers hover there in the ceaseless
blue-black, watching it ripple and dim

to the prized pale blue in which we spin—
we who are Black, and you, too. Our mothers

know each other there, fully and finally.
They see what some here see and call anomaly:

the way the sight of me might set off
a shiver in another mother's son: a deadly

silent digging in: a stolid refusal to budge:
the viral urge to stake out what on solid ground

is Authority, and sometimes also Territory.
Our mothers, knowing better, call it Folly.

All of the new poems in *Such Color* were written during the summer of 2020. And so much on my mind was what felt like and what feels like an ever increasing onslaught of violence against unarmed Black citizens. And I think that's the sense of territory and threat that the poem is grappling with.

I wish I had a love poem like Yi Lei's poem "Nude." But I'll read one of the first love poems that I published in my first book. This is called "A Hunger So Honed." I think in my own vocabulary it begins to open up a space for me to consider that what lives outside of our wanting of another, and what charge that space or maybe even a presence holds.

And I think it's a space and a presence that I return to with many vocabularies in my work. And I also believe that in some ways it's a site of interest for me in terms of a practical theology that I believe my poems are also helping me to construct.

A HUNGER SO HONED

Driving home late through town
He woke me for a deer in the road,
The light smudge of it fragile in the distance,

Free in a way that made me ashamed for our flesh—
His hand on my hand, even the weight
Of our voices not speaking.

I watched a long time
And a long time after we were too far to see,
Told myself I still saw it nosing the shrubs,

All phantom and shadow, so silent
It must have seemed I hadn't wakened,
But passed into a deeper, more cogent state—
The mind a dark city, a disappearing,
A handkerchief
Swallowed by a fist.
I thought of the animal's mouth
And the hunger entrusted it. A hunger
So honed the green leaves merely maintain it.
We want so much,
When perhaps we live best
In the spaces between loves,
That unconscious roving,
The heart its own rough animal.
Unfettered.

The second time,
There were two that faced us a moment
The way deer will in their Greek perfection,

As though we were just some offering
The night had delivered.
They disappeared between two houses,

And we drove on, our own limbs
Sloppy after that, our need for one another
Greedy, weak.

A lot of the poems that I'm writing—I would say most of the poems that I'm writing now and maybe even for the last couple of book projects have been preoccupied with questions of nationhood, questions of citizenship, an itch about the form of regard that we are encouraged to adopt across lines of difference.

And I'm trying to figure out what I know about this sense of distance, mistrust, hierarchy that I don't wish to know—if that makes sense. What does it mean that I can populate a poem like the one I'm about to read with a vocabulary that, to my conscience, comes from the wrong set of assumptions?

And so poems in this fashion are trying to listen differently toward documents and voices from history that we believe we know. Those are tools by which I'm trying to figure out a different mode, a different relation, and a different sense of what questions we might more productively begin to ask and answer for one another.

So this is a poem called "The United States Welcomes You." It's comprised entirely of questions. The first few drafts of this poem were written from the perspective of somebody I imagined like this, being apprehended by a person with power or the authority of law.
But I had too much cherishing for that person. I wanted to keep the encounter from going wrong in the way that so many such encounters

do. And so my poem was failing. And the strategy that I devised in order to revive it and keep moving forward was to change the perspective, to speak out from the perspective of someone who I imagine might be standing like that or at the very least with a bright light saying, tell me what I know you're up to.

And that was a form that offered a lot of momentum and what felt to me like productive unrest.

THE UNITED STATES WELCOMES YOU

Why and by whose power were you sent?
What do you see that you may wish to steal?
Why this dancing? Why do your dark bodies
Drink up all the light? What are you demanding
That we feel? Have you stolen something? Then
What is that leaping in your chest? What is
The nature of your mission? Do you seek
To offer a confession? Have you anything to do
With others brought by us to harm? Then
Why are you afraid? And why do you invade
Our night, hands raised, eyes wide, mute
As ghosts? Is there something you wish to confess?
Is this some enigmatic type of test? What if we
Fail? How and to whom do we address our appeal?

Form is something in this poem helped me keep going. Even after I figure it out the strategy that would save the poem from platitudes, I still didn't necessarily know where the poem ought to be to trying to get to. And the choice to compose it entirely in questions was a constraint that gave me a more narrow set of possibilities which I could follow forward. I remember getting to the moment in writing this poem where I began to think something other than me—something other than what I'm consciously aware of is beginning to break in. This poem might know something, might be capable of showing me something.

And for me, it happens around the line—the middle line, "Have you anything to do with others brought by us to harm?" And so for a moment the speakers are beginning to envision the self as a subject or a site of scrutiny. And a few lines later, that speaker asks, "Is this some enigmatic type of test?" And for me, that was the moment where a subterranean kind of awareness or anxiety begins to come into the poem. Maybe it's merely vulnerability. But what excited me about that thread within the poem was that it made me trust that even in circumstances where power is easily and frequently abused, there might still be a place where the imagination can ponder even just instantaneously, the notion that we might all actionally have an accountability to something other than the human. And that felt chastening and exciting to me.

And it allowed me to end this poem without simply pointing a finger at someone but saying, oh, I'm caught in that same dynamic as well. What are we accountable to? And what might it mean if our choices thus far constitute a kind of failure?

I'll read one last poem of my own. And so that final Yi Lei poem that I read is thinking about the planet, the Earth. This poem is too, but by way of other circumstances. It begins with a frightening dream that I had, that I couldn't wake up from. And it moves toward the sense of the numinous or the sublime.

THE ANGELS

Two slung themselves across chairs
Once in a motel room. Grizzled,
In leather biker gear. Emissaries
For something I needed to see.

I was worn down by an awful panic.

A wrenching in the gut, contortions.
They sat there at the table while I slept.
I could sense them, with a deck

Of playing cards between them.
To think of how they smelled, what
Comes to mind is rum and gasoline.
And when they spoke, though I couldn't,

I dared not look, I glimpsed how one's teeth
Were ground down almost to nubs.
Which makes me hope some might be
Straight up thugs, young, slim, raw,

Who bounce and roll with fearsome grace,
Whose very voices cause faint souls to quake.
—*Quake, then, fools, and fall away!*
—*What God do you imagine we obey?*

Think of the toil we must cost them,
One scaled perfectly to eternity.
And still, they come, telling us
Through the ages not to fear.

Just those two that once and never
Again for me since, though
There are—are they?—
Sightings, flashes, hints:

A proud tree in vivid sun, branches
Swaying in strong wind. Rain
Hurling itself at the roof. Boulders,
Mounds of earth mistaken for dead

Does, lions in crouch. A rust-stained pipe
Where a house once stood, which I
Take each time I pass it for an owl.

Bright whorl so dangerous and near.

My mother sat whispering with it
At the end of her life
While all the rooms of our house
Filled up with night.

the girl in the picture

Halina Poświatowska

Translated by Ryan Mihaly and Karolina Zapal

your pigtails are like spiderwebs
and the night is so long
you can't hide your eyes with a pigtail
stars walk across the window panes

a burst of blue across your eyelids
spiders and tears—congealed
memories fly from the windows
yesterday they were vivid as heat

you won't escape into the soft river of dreams
into nothingness—you won't jump out of bed
light—a knife buried in your belly
through a thin pigtail—in your eyes

dziewczynka na obrazku tęskni

warkoczyki masz jak pajęcze nitki
a noc jest taka długa
warkoczykiem oczu nie przesłonisz
gwiazdy chodzą w okiennych framugach

siny blask na powieki strząsa
pająki i łzy - zakrzepłe
odfruwają od okien wspomnienia
wczoraj żywe jak dotyk - ciepłe

nie uciekniesz w snów miękką rzekę
w ciemne nic - z łóżka nie skoczysz
światło - nożem zagłębionym w brzuchu
poprzez cienki warkoczyk - w oczy

(It is spring again)

It is spring again, spring so astonishingly familiar: so why is poetry choking on its breath? The tree outside my window is committing plagiarism for the twentieth year in a row, adding green leaves to green leaves. The flowers of the cherry tree are no different from the first cherry tree; the same smell as yesterday permeates the air. And—though old people find this boring—my sister is kissing someone under trees the same way I used to kiss, passionately, plagiarizing the first kiss. I can still recall the grass, all the grass that sprouted faithfully and persistently, the same grass as months ago. Life is not afraid of plagiarizing itself, and equally astonishing and monotonous in its obstinacy is death. So why condemn poems of love, why blame them for their shamelessness and their primitive, chaotic groans of pleasure, faithfully replicated for centuries, indifferent to who reads them?

Tego roku jest znowu wiosna

Tego roku jest znowu wiosna, wiosna niesłychanie znajoma, dlaczego więc poezja dławi się własnym oddechem. Drzewo pod moim oknem popełnia plagiat już dwudziesty rok z rzędu do liści zielonych dodając zielone liście. Kwiaty czereśni tego roku nie są inne niż na początku drzewa czereśniowego, ten sam zapach co wczoraj przenika powietrze. I - chociaż ludzie starzy twierdzą, że to nużące - moja siostra całuje się pod drzewami tak samo, jak ja się całowałam; całuje się namiętnie popełniając w nieskończoność plagiat z pierwszego pocałunku. Jeszcze mogłabym przywołać trawy, wszystkie trawy, które wzeszły z nasion wiernie i nieustępliwie, te same, takie same jak kilka miesięcy temu. Życie nie obawia się popełniać plagiatu rodząc życie i zawsze jednakowo zdumiewa monotonna w swym uporze śmierć. Dlaczego więc potępiać wiersze o miłości, czemu mieć im za złe bezwstyd i prymityw bezładnego jęku rozkoszy powtarzanego wiernie przez niedbałe o poczytność stulecia.

I like writing poems

I like writing poems. Tempers boil over in verse like at a rally, a scream pierces the form and feelings rush in, waving a great red banner.

Poetry refuses censorship—it jeers at helpless angels who crush their silken wings. It calls God names and runs roughshod over its creator. Poetry is dangerous.

O working class, I prayed, waving your flags of red, mighty and brave, rallying lover, dark-feathered fowl, my great danger, come, we'll bury God under a gooseberry bush, and on the fresh grave we'll dance in shades of green!

Let's just hope an angel won't eavesdrop and give away our plot prematurely…

I am suspicious of purple. In Egypt it was the color of mourning.

Cleopatra dressed herself in it

after the emperor's death
before she died

alone.

I prefer red!

Lubię pisać wiersze

Lubię pisać wiersze. W wierszu jak na wiecu temperament wrze, krzyk rozsadza formę i uczucie wieje wielkim czerwonym sztandarem.

Wiersz nie poddaje się cenzurze, kpi sobie z bezradnych aniołów załamujących jedwabne skrzydła, wyzywa boga i poniewiera swym stwórcą. Wiersz jest żywiołem.

Klaso robotnicza, modliłam się, klaso powiewająca wielkim czerwonym sztandarem, klaso potężna, klaso dzielna, kochanko wiecująca, ptactwo ciemnopióre, żywiole mój, chodź, pogrzebiemy boga pod krzakiem agrestu i na świeżym grobie zatańczymy zielono!

Żeby tylko ten anioł nie podsłuchał i nie wydał naszego spisku przedwcześnie...

Podejrzewam fiolet. W Egipcie był to kolor żałoby.

Ubierała się weń Kleopatra

po śmierci cesarza
nim umarła

sama.

Lubię czerwień!

Translators' Note

Halina Poświatowska (1935-1967) is Poland's preeminent poet of desire. Keenly aware that her life would be brief, due to a heart condition she developed at a young age, she devoted her life to poetry. She managed to publish four books during her lifetime—three books of spare, lyrical poems and a memoir—all dwelling on themes of love, death, desire, and art. Beyond that, she endured countless hospital visits, surgeries, got married, became a widow, traveled extensively (despite near-constant pain and physical restrictions), and earned a degree in philosophy from Smith College in Northampton, MA in three years. In her native country, the very mention of her name suggests resilience in the face of death, mixed with youthful eroticism. Along with Wisława Szymborska, she is the most-read poet in Poland.

The three poems published here all come from her fourth book of poems, *Jeszcze jedno wspomnienie*, "One More Memory," which was published in 1968, a year after she died after a failed heart operation. In "the girl in the picture," we see her obsession with art and death—many of her poems were directly inspired by museum visits, particularly the Metropolitan Museum in New York. In "(It is spring again)" and "(I like writing poems)," we see a poetics emerge, in defense of two kinds of writing: one that dwells on and celebrates romantic love, and another that throws itself headlong into battle, in which the poem itself "runs roughshod over its creator." To date, a translation of Poświatowska's work has not been published in the US. We hope to introduce English-speaking readers to this beloved Polish poet whose work quivers with life and flirts with darkness.

Ryan Mihaly & Karolina Zapal
Florence, MA

Fayez Sersawi, *Where to Escape*, 2024, charcoal on paper, 21.7" x 15.7"

Fayez Sersawi, *Repetitive Displacement*, 2024, pastel on Canson paper, 19.7" x 13.8"

Fayez Sersawi, *Seeing Her Nearby*, 2024, pastel on Canson paper, 19.7" x 13.8"

Fayez Sersawi, *A Window on the Desert*, 2022, acrylic on cardboard, 23.6" x 19.7"

Fayez Sersawi, *Before the Sea*, 2018, acrylic on canvas, 27.6" x 19.7"

Fayez Sersawi, *You Alone*, 2003, charcoal on paper, 47.2" x 35.4"

Before Dawn

Tayseer Abu Odeh

I wake. Goats wake behind the Rum mountains.
I burnish my slender body with pink sand.
I search my body for its scar.
It looks just like the key to my grandfather's house.

I can't find my toothbrush.
But my imagination is a greyhound after its prey,
and the golden dawn waves to me from behind the furious foothills.
I water the orchid,
it drinks time like a cat.
I check my empty pockets. Listen to Bach's sonatas.
A lot. I write something. Awful. I trash it.

I'm looking for a new name for wheat.
A name from before the Gazan annihilation.
I page through Al-Tawhidi's book *Friendship and the Friend*,
I wipe dust from it. Like a jeweler polishes his silver.

I forgot my coffee in the coffee pot. It's gone cold.
I look for a new face. A hopeful one.
Look for a new lexicon for liquid time.
I imagine they visit me—the old stories.
They whisper into my ears. Poems for Elia Abu Madi.
Then the Quranic verse *The Poets*.
Hope's last will is on my breakfast table.

قبيل الفجر

تيسير أبو عودة

أستيقظ صباحا كما تفعل ماعز الجبل خلف جبال رم
أشحذ جسدي النحيل بالرمال الوردية
أفتش في جسدي عن ندبة قديمة
تشبه مفتاح بيت جدي
لم أعثر على فرشاة أسناني
خيالي كلب سلوقي يرصد طرائده
لكن الشفق البرتقالي يلوح لي بذراعيه
من وراء التلال الغاضبة
أسقي زهرة الأوركيدا،
تشرب الوقت كالقطة المدللة
أتفقد جيوبي الفارغة،
وأنا أنصت لموسيقى باخ بلا توقف
أكتب نصا رديئا، ثم أمحوه
أفتش عن اسم جديد للحنطة
في غزة قبل حدوث المجزرة
أتصفّح كتاب التوحيدي الصداقة والصديق
أنفض عنه الغبار كما يسوس الصائغ خاتم فضة قديم
قهوتي التي نسيتها في ركوة الوقت لم تزل باردة
أفتش عن وجه جديد للأمل
عن معجم جديد للزمن الرخو
أتخيله يزروني كالأساطير القديمة
يهمس في أذني
يغني لي قصائد إليا أبو ماضي
ثم يرتل سورة الشعراء
ويرحل بعد أن يترك على طاولتي وصيته الأخيرة

Seven Glasses of Beer
(from the diwan 'Snoring')

Razan Bannoura

Writing from a bar stool
sounds like a great idea.

My head, heavy
with thoughts
that aren't fit
for even a poem.

I killed four cigarettes.
The beers do nothing except
make me pee.

I wiped the toilet seat clean.
My body is so heavy.
I can't pee standing.

It's my friend's birthday
on the other side of the world.

Next to me, my new friend asks
about my name.
And I ask
the dancer in the square
the same question.

Another friend
on the stool beside me
asks if this seat is taken.
It seems he doesn't see my feet.

If the poem were a dress
I could not sew it
to fit my body.
It would be too tight.

I am colossal
and poems like dresses
don't fit me.

The poem lies
on the back seat.
How can I miss this vision.
I see myself murdered constantly.

My blood is inside me
and my poem is my friend.
Unfaithful,
it survives,
leaving me
to die alone.

Seven beers
as many as the men I've loved.
The seventh is half drunk.
I'll finish it when I'm done loving him.

It's no use
going out with me
you could read a book.
I am going home
nursing my glass.

Doors
not sure I locked them.
It's okay,
it's okay if my house is stolen.
I'll write some poems
and live in them.

I want one poem
just one.
Where's the poem hiding?
Where have I hidden myself?
In the bathroom of mirrors
I become twelve selves
I don't know
which of them
I am.

It seems the poem, she's gotten wasted
and runs away like me
from herself.

كؤوسٌ سبعٌ من البيرة
(من ديوان شخير)

رزان بنّورة

الكتابة من وراء كرسي البار
تبدو فكرة مثيرة

رأسي ثقيل
مليء بالأفكار
لكنها
لا تصلح
لكتابة قصيدة واحدة.

أنهيتُ حياة أربع سجائر
كؤوس البيرة لم تُحدث مفعولها بعد
إلا في جعلي أتبولُ كثيراً

نظفتُ كرسي الحمام جيداً
جسدي ثقيل
ليس باستطاعتي التبول وقوفاً.

عيد ميلاد صديقي
في الجهة المقابلة من العالم.

يسألني صديقي الجديد بجانبي
عن اسمي
وأنا أسأل
الراقص في الساحة
السؤال نفسه.

صديقي الآخر
في الكرسي المجاور
يسألني إن كان المقعد محجوزاً لأحد
يبدو أنه لا يرى أقدامي!

لو أن القصيدة فستان
كنتُ سأفشلُ حتماً
في حياكتهِ
وكان سيكون ضيقاً
لو ارتديته

أنا ضخمة جداً
والقصائدُ كما الفساتين
لا تسعني.

القصيدة مستلقية
على المقعد الخلفي
من السيارة.
كيف ستغيب عني هذهِ الرؤية؟
أرى مصرعي دائماً
دمائي بداخلي
وقصيدتي صديقتي
غير مخلصة
تنجو
وتدعني
أموت وحدي.

كؤوسٌ سبعٌ من البيرة
بعدد الرجال الذين أحببتهم
الكأس السابعة لم تنتهِ بعد
سأنهيها حين أتوقف عن حبهِ.

الخروج معي
ليس مفيداً
كقراءة كتاب
سأعود إلى المنزل
وأنا أحمل كأسي معي.

الأبواب
غير متأكدة أنني أقفلتها
لا بأس
لا بأس إن سُرق بيتي
سأكتبُ بعض القصائد
وأسكن فيها.

أريد قصيدة واحدة
واحدة فقط
أين تختبئُ القصيدة عني؟
أين أختبئُ مني؟
في الحمام المليء بالمرايا
صرتُ اثني عشر
ولا أدري
من منهم
أنا الحقيقية.

يبدو أن القصيدة تملّ
وتهربُ مثلي
من
نفسها.

Calmly, Calmly
(from the diwan 'Snoring')

This is a bad time
for such nonsense,
I am sad…

I don't feel
like housekeeping.
It just makes matters worse.

I am so sad,
how can I say
to the dishes
I'll be gone a little longer.

I'm desolate,
my heart is coated
with lint like a carpet.
I want to die.
People are dying.
The world is a serial killer,
a vacuum cleaner.

I'm at a standstill…,
a washing machine
out of action.

No joy in my pockets,
it's spent on my friends
who made me
burst into tears today.

I possess only one thing—
this loneliness.
With it, I can kill myself
very calmly
with meticulous introversion.

I've been hurt by hope
but I don't doubt it.
I cut my doll's
hair when
I was nine.
I'm still
waiting for it
to grow
back.

هدوء هدوء

(من ديوان شخير)

رزان بنّورة

هَذا وَقْتٌ غَيْرُ مُنَاسِبٍ
لِهُراءٍ كَهَذَا...
لَكِنَّنِي حَزِينَةٌ

لا رَغْبَةَ لِي في تَنْظِيفِ المَنْزِلِ
وَهَذَا أَمْرٌ يَزِيدُ مِنْ حُزْنِي

أَنَا حَزِينَةٌ
كَيْفَ سَأَقُولُ لِلأَطْبَاقِ التي تَنْتَظِرُنِي
إِنَّنِي سَأَغِيبُ أَكْثَرَ

أَنَا يَائِسَةٌ
قَلْبِي مُوَبَّرٌ
مِثْلُ سجَّادَةٍ
أُرِيدُ أَنْ أَمُوتَ
النَّاسُ تَمُوتُ
والعَالَمُ قَاتِلٌ
كَمِكْنَسَةٍ كَهْرُبَائيَّةٍ

سَاكِنَةٌ...
مِثْلُ غَسَّالَةٍ
مُتَوَقِّفَةٍ عَنِ العَمَلِ

لا فَرَحَ في جَيْبِي الآنَ
أَنْفَقْتُهُ كُلَّهُ على أَصْدِقَائِي
الذينَ أَبْكُونِي اليومَ

أَمْلِكُ الآنَ شَيْئاً وَاحِداً،
هَذِهِ الوِحْدَةَ.
يُمْكِنُنِي قَتْلُ نَفْسِي بِهَا
بِهُدُوءٍ مُفْرِطٍ
وَانْطِوَائِيَّةٍ شَدِيدَةٍ.

وَبِي أَمَلٌ
لا أَشُكُّ بِذَلِكَ...
دُمْيَتِي التي قَصَصْتُ شَعْرَهَا
فِي التَّاسِعَةِ مِنْ عُمْرِي
مَا زِلْتُ حَتَّى الآنَ
أَنْتَظِرُهُ
لِيَنْمُو.

Pear Blossom Snow

Zhou Bangyan, 1056–1121, Northern Song Dynasty

Translated by Shangyang Fang

To the Tune "Lang Tao Sha Man: Waves Sifting Sand Extended"

The sky leaden at daybreak, the riverbank grass frost-wilted,
the parapets of the citadel consumed in fog. The axles of carriages all greased up
by the East Gate, where the farewell banquet draws to an end.
Tears medleyed with the rouge powder. You pick a thin sprig of willow,
soft and taut, knotting it into a bracelet. The geese of last year
beside the Han River, even the letters they left in the sky an image of the past.

Love hurts. These eyes are not designed to hold an earth and sky
so infinite. I walk to where streaks of wind sharpen the coldness of dews,
where the water-clock drips all night, imitating human sadness.
Tell me, water-clock, you who will not be injured by sorrow, how to get used
to these long, valedictory echoes? The jade cup isn't emptied.
By the West Tower, the remnant of clouds holding over a damaged moon.

The silk-laced waistband has lost its luster. The quilt wrinkled
like years. The interlocked glass rings smashed. The scented sachet, just a sachet.
Singing sad songs to the night's end, beating time with a chopstick
on a crystal pot until one of them breaks. I hate that the Spring always leaves

without forewarning—against the black of midnight,
a sheet of pear blossoms scattered on the ground, mistaken for the first snow.

浪淘沙慢

周邦彦〔宋代〕

晓阴重，霜凋岸草，雾隐城堞。南陌脂车待发，东门帐饮乍阕。
正拂面、垂杨堪揽结。掩红泪、玉手亲折。念汉浦、离鸿去何
许？经时信音绝。

情切，望中地远天阔。向露冷风清，无人处，耿耿寒漏咽。
嗟万事难忘，惟是轻别。翠尊未竭，凭断云、留取西楼残月。

罗带光消纹衾叠，连环解、旧香顿歇。
怨歌永、琼壶敲尽缺。恨春去、不与人期，弄夜色、空馀满地梨
花雪。

To the Tune "Zhe Gu Tian: Partridge Sky"

Wu Wenying, 1205-1260, Southern Song Dynasty

Translated by Shangyang Fang

Lakeside vermillion dresses: lotuses lean
        languid beside the balustrade:
ravens return: purloining a shard of sunset

        behind the satin darkness
of their wings: rain too darkening: shaving
        off more sycamore leaves:

moon in autumn sky: the inaugural coldness
        that sets the folding
silk fan neglected by its familiar hand:

dream of homeland: narrow: porcelain clouds
        above the water: vast:
the squared mountains in the window frame:

        fog-thinned: the pigment
of painted eyebrows: twitching: wild geese
        from the land of Wu carrying

letters to the houses behind the poplar trees
        utside the Chang Gate:

鹧鸪天

吴文英〔宋代〕

池上红衣伴倚阑，栖鸦常带夕阳还。
殷云度雨疏桐落，明月生凉宝扇闲。

乡梦窄，水天宽。小窗愁黛淡秋山。
吴鸿好为传归信，杨柳阊门屋数间。

Recording a Dream on Jinling River, New Year 1187

Jiang Kui, 1155–1221, Southern Song Dynasty

Translated by Shangyang Fang

To the Tune "Ta Suo Xing: Treading on Purple Nutsedge"

Light-winged as a swallow touching another swallow,
soft-voiced as a warbler calling warblers,

I can't tell whether it's you or my memory speaking
to me again: you, who are clueless

about my long nights, causing this beginning of Spring
saturated with love's sickness. Letters

you sent me. Your needlework remains deeply stitched
along the inner lining of my coat.

To make me dream of you, your little soul
must have crept outside of your body to travel

near my hairpin. The moon of Huai Nan, burnished
in coldness, freezes a thousand mountains

in one night. When your soul walks back, she walks back
alone, abandoned like the rest of us.

踏莎行·自沔东来丁未元日至金陵江上感梦而作

姜夔〔宋代〕

燕燕轻盈，莺莺娇软。分明又向华胥见。
夜长争得薄情知，春初早被相思染。

别后书辞，别时针线。离魂暗逐郎行远。
淮南皓月冷千山，冥冥归去无人管。

At a Hotel in Lin Zhou

Qin Guan, 1049 – 1100, Northern Song Dynasty

Translated by Shangyang Fang

To the Tune "Ta Suo Xing: Treading on Purple Nutsedge"

Those high balconies disappeared in fog.
The moon lost before waterfront.
The Peach Blossom Spring
remains buried inside ancient scrolls.

Chill arrives early at this hotel
where the sun slants in the voice of cuckoos.
Horses rush to me, dappled
with plum blossoms from the post stop.

Silk letters found inside the slim guts of fish.
Sadness piles up. Lin Stream surrounds
the Lin Mountain. Why does it
flow eastward, becoming River Xiaoxiang?

踏莎行·郴州旅舍

秦观〔宋代〕

雾失楼台，月迷津渡。桃源望断无寻处。
可堪孤馆闭春寒，杜鹃声里斜阳暮。

驿寄梅花，鱼传尺素。砌成此恨无重数。
郴江幸自绕郴山，为谁流下潇湘去。

The Return: Jura

Ollie Cowley

Each time you are smaller in the white bed, the sheet
distending about you, your eyes removed and each day
full of a diffferent light. At your side, I am Somebody's
Daughter. Perhaps yours. You no longer are sure.

On the bedroom wall, someone has hung an old
Breughel print, *The Hunters in the Snow or The Return*
of the Hunters. In Breughel's painting the trees flatten
under the hoarlight, and the lead white of snow. There

everything has its quarter—the inn, the bridge, the dike,
the people like charred velocities, simple as the birds.
Only the hunters arrive with their minds run in and
tracked, interwoven with claw and boot and growth

of sputtering line. The dogs never undid the scent.
They are returning with nothing but the wire-thin
body of a fox, too small to cast a shadow.
Sunlight seals the tar black road.

It is evening now, the world outside blue and unfevered.
On the mantlepiece, schoolgirls line like letters and
there you are in velveteen, your face the wax of
girlhood. Medicine bottles store the last of the light.

You talk of the little grey dog he hid under the tree in
a box, of love's miracle and its knot, of the two-foot grave
at the garden's base, of him gone, of les cigonnes, of
wars won and wars lost, of her off the blue rocks,

of her gone, of the heat like a midwife and the house
lime-white, of my mother, your mother, of them gone,
of the heart a telephone or archipelago or la vie
donnée à celui qui donne. From the window we can hear

the hunters returning, the crack and weft of sole on snow.
All their life they have walked the woods' dark verge,
the highway, the treeline. All their life they have loved,
bought love home by the neck.

Daughter Chord

At the road verge, the old dog fox
is burying his love, telling it

the heart is an honest weight
until you weigh it. There are

shells in the southern earth
whistling in iron hides & serial

steel spines, testing their names
under the till-torn earth. Tonight

a mortar shell is trilling its
rust plate. It has forgotten

the why. On the familiar road
we know we are nothing

our own. We are tar exhaust,
piston crack, each sound loose

through night's bivouac.
Listen to the scale of spur,

its cold turning of earth.
It has turned out the years,

the return. Listen to the staves
of stone, trying to sing their

pitch extinct. Listen. Over time
the human larynx turns to bone.

Dinner Theatre

Audrey Chambers

It was Isabella's fault they were late to dinner and by the time they finally arrived at the restaurant they'd missed the sunset. The wide observation windows that had promised such spectacular views looked out onto nothing but darkness. After a back-and-forth with the maître d' they were whisked along the aisle of cozy couples dining in candlelit contentment and deposited at a table that jutted into a quiet corner enclave on the far side of the room.

"Isn't it nice?" Isabella said. She was peering out the window, past her hazy reflection towards the darkened cityscape, the towers that rose up around them, the pearl-strands of headlights shining in the maze of streets below.

Her husband, his nose stuck in the wine menu, didn't hear her. Isaac's skin was tanned from a day of sailing. Isabella had opted to sleep in. It was the third week of their honeymoon and the island fever had begun to take its toll; she missed the frosty city they'd left behind. When the sommelier arrived, Isaac ordered for them; he knew what she liked because she liked what he liked.

Isabella continued looking out at the city, trying to catch a better glimpse of the shadows shifting around behind the windows in a tower across from them, humanoid shapes made vague and irregular by the filmy curtains. She leaned across the table, nearly singeing one of her long curls on the guttering votive. Isaac looked at her over the top of the menu, then reached out a hand to lift the lock of hair out of the pool of wax. Isabella didn't notice.

"Look," she said, pointing. A hand had materialized in the window directly facing them, tugging back the curtains to reveal a little round table, so similar to theirs, a man and woman being seated for dinner, a dark-suited waiter pulling out their chairs, pantomimed deference. The woman wore white, just like Isabella; the man wore a suit the shade of ashes.

Isaac followed her gaze out the window but missed the scene she was pointing at, the kindred couple in the window next door. Instead, he looked beyond the city, in the distance, at the inky expanse of the sea that rippled underneath a sheen of moonlight.

"Do you think they can see us?" Isabella asked. The couple was speaking animatedly, the flickering candles on their table casting a golden light on their faces that rendered their features indistinguishable. She reached towards the window as if she wanted to tap a fingernail on the glass, her emerald engagement ring heavy on a peach-pale hand. Isaac caught her before she could make contact, and she looked at him, as if slightly surprised to register his presence but pleased nonetheless. He laced his fingers through hers.

"It's a beautiful night," he said. "I'm happy we made it." Whenever Isabella smiled, she looked a little like she was baring her teeth. It was one of the cutest things about her.

The first course was a selection of oysters glistening atop a bed of ice. Isaac swallowed one after another, barely even chewing, but Isabella stared at her plate, poked at the raw flesh with the tiny fork she'd been given. It looked to her like a dissected organ served on a half-shell, and eventually Isaac ate that one, too. The next courses fared better, and it wasn't until the dinnerware had been cleared that Isabella's attention strayed away again, back out towards the quiet night and the lofty towers and that same couple, still silhouetted in the proscenium window. Their meal had been served; the candles burned ever lower. Isabella couldn't make out what they were eating but she caught a flash of silver every time the woman lifted her fork to her mouth.

"Isabella?" Isaac asked.

The waiter had just served their dessert. A billowy pavlova mounded with fruit sat on a glass stand between them, crackling as Isaac sliced into it. He offered Isabella a bite and she accepted, remembering how she didn't care for meringue as it dissolved on her tongue before she could even taste it. She sipped her wine to rinse away the sugar-stickiness that lingered, looking out the window again as the woman reached out to catch her lover's hand, the gauzy cuff of her dress trailing low over the table. Isabella could only watch as it dragged over one of the tiny candle-flames, which were so nearly extinguished!—and ignited in a bright blaze of fire. The woman reared back, as did Isabella, sloshing her glass of wine down her front in a jerk of horror.

"Someone needs to help her!" she cried, looking around the room, the other diners coming to a halt in the middle of their meals and conversations. Isaac was already on his feet, the maître d' striding towards them. "Isaac!"

He was gently lifting her to her feet, pressing a napkin to the scarlet stain seeping down her chest, an arm going around her shoulder. She twisted around, trying to catch another glimpse of the woman she was certain would be engulfed in flames, but his grip was firm and within moments she'd been hurried into the elevator. As the doors shut, she looked past the dining room full of people slowly returning to their meals, out to catch one last glimpse of the dark sky, the sleeping city, the empty windows.

As they began to descend, Isabella turned towards her husband. "Didn't you see her?" Isaac's expression was impassive. "Didn't you see the fire?"

"I think you're just tired," he said, kissing the top of her head.

The elevator dinged as the doors opened at their floor. Isaac walked Isabella down the hallway, both in silence. With every few steps, a few drips of wine would stain the cream-colored carpet, looking like the trail left in the midst of a wounded animal.

Samantha McCulloch, *You could sense the child in you, harboured in her,* 2024, oil on panel, 7" x 9.4"

Aschely Cone, *Tan Arch in Blue Light,* 2022, oil and acrylic on canvas, 48" x 36"

Aschely Cone, *Arch in Cool Fog,* 2022, oil and acrylic on canvas, 48" x 36"

Jonah

Isaac Jarnot

Don’t pretend it’s
not November
because it is,
and everyone is
growing old
including the trees
and the porpoises
who are only
a dream
or a YouTube
video or a word
rarely spoken
though also
made by God,
which is a
substance like
Astroglide
congealed
on the way to the
post office
I bow down to the
scientists
I cry out
with the
salmon
Hey!

let me respectfully
remind you
the hairs on your
head are numbered
too.

Blue

Katherine Irajpanah

Wear it to be
sky. Wear it
because you can't
hide. Of course

it will kill you, this

thin skin
covering yr
heart—that is
how fragile

we are.
Once I struck
my father
on his scar-line. *What*

are you doing?
I sd I
didn't mean it.
Laughing, smoking

gun—have you
ever held one?
It is heavy.
Inside the blue flame-

thrower suit
you live,
& yr mask keeps
you a-

live, only

to take our breaths

away. Was
poison always
this soft?
Or, the

cud. What
is left
of the horizon—

The True Receiver

Sophie Mollart

For John Berger

Late August—the silver ring
of Autumn has yet to press itself into the soil.
The white lilies have flowered; the anemone too.
Heaven's ceiling has fallen and left a pattern on the grass.
Not heaven as place, windows tinselled with the pearls of virtue—
heaven as intimation; heaven as fainter strings;
heaven as the soft ochre façade of Florentine houses.
They call it Orpiment; it carries with it the proof of sunrise.

His memories of Autumn rouse with the taste of sweet cider. He was
born in November, under a tender star.
There is, he believes, a shared language between luminosity and texture;
it sharpens its enigmas like a sculptor's tool.
He recollects a sculpted figure cut as if from the marrow
of cadmium yellow. Or else it is cut from light itself.

The marble approaches the night like a pair of arms
belonging to a body untouched for years;
it reaches toward the memory of tenderness, its slow blaze. The lobe.
The dip of the mouth. Everything whitening.
The sculpture contains the likeness of touch.
The recollection of softness is housed in its hard stone.

There is a world that was never meant for us, he writes;
and yet it knows us, like the oakwood panel knows the touch of burnt

sienna. Or a lover's handprint, vanished in tempera.
What does the painting *know*?

His spirit remains as contour. His likeness inked in loam.
Like the lines across a printed page speak to the memory of chiaroscuro.
He was born in November, under an aching star.
In his sky all stars are a beam but also the echo of an unseen order.

Mère

Yagmur Akyurek

It was raining in autumn when mother moved out.

Naturally, I was ecstatic.

I was running out of places to hide my vegetable marionettes.

The table was always hissing at me.

Once, there was a spill of sherry.

The wet rice—she scolded me.

My measurements of landscape went ignored.

Stuff and nonsense.

In winter, trees lost their usual degrees of objectivity.

They started swaying to the beat of not-her-heart.

Cars were skidding in the shape of perfect ribbons.

Fortes, fortes—I welcomed the rain.

Leek tied the knot.

Beet grew a nice large belly.

And Onion came out to the foyer to show us what she was twerking with.

Kikkity-kakkity.

Fershl: oo.

And then she went kerplunk.

The funeral was a long July.

Radish was born with fountains for eyes.

The neighbors' blinks got increasingly more noticeable.

Every map looked like a dancing leaf.

Though none could dance as pitchy as mon ail.

Even in the commercials on TV I see her:

Grandiose in the way she exhales.

A long line of decisions like pews.

We are not dummies, never were.

But behind the perfume on the nightstand there is a little box.

A little wooden box that looks almost like me.

The Factory

Josh Kurtz

once made all manner of things—
tiny mannequins, silver sconces, in-
candescent fishbowls, even tea tins with fake
inlaid mother of pearl, but the factory

was best known for its teeth, mostly
gold and silver, the occasional porcelain
crown or bridge, it depended on the
season, the year, in 1968 everyone wanted

platinum dentures and aquamarine implants,
something to do with Nixon or mercury, I
think, or the war, everyone had just seen
Hair on broadway, except of course the folks

at the factory, they didn't have time for nudity
or strobe lights, they all had nephews
who were born here in this unfinished
city with its fire escapes and dumpsters, "they're

still building it!" my grandma exclaimed from
that first taxi from JFK, all those years ago,
one plastic suitcase packed with teeth mold
powder, a bit of plaster, a tongue depressor

and tooth tray, some pliers and one hand-
knit glove. Within five years she had a
factory, and though she and my grand-
father still worked the torch from time

to time, they loved to sit in that dusty
office with its one glass wall overlooking
all those plastic chairs they bought downtown,
muddy green and so uncomfortable. Years before,

my grandfather—let's call him "Tiny"—
spent three years in a labor camp that used
to be a monastery, three years for a fake
tooth made in a hurry, a gold coin and brass

mold, his tiny fire in some Bucharest basement,
glinting off shelves of jars, the smell of
brine, so many teeth spread out on
the floor, he wouldn't call it a labor of love

but it was something—"they never grow
back," he used to say with an ounce of
pride, a little regret. Now the factory
is a Rutgers dormitory, or maybe a dining

hall, I've never seen it, I can't imagine
they kept the work benches, the evergreen
chairs, a crown in a tiny frame, all I have
is a button in the shape of a tooth, the

Platonic ideal of a tooth I'd say, white
and sharp with a gold outline and
"The Congress" written across, I imagine
some conference somewhere, in Ohio

maybe, a ballroom and some baked
Alaska, a red tablecloth, though who really

knows, maybe they met monthly at the
Coney Island aquarium, maybe they voted

on the next year's dental trends—how about
papier-mâché teeth in May, dentures for
every day of the week, how about steak dentures
and bread dentures, dentures for kissing and

dentures to avoid kissing, maybe there was
infighting or indelity, maybe the metalworkers
hated the ceramicists, maybe they all missed
someone back home. I like to think about my grand-

parents sitting on a bench at the aquarium,
rating all the shark's teeth—first the hammer-
head, always the hammerhead. I wonder if they
ever looked into each other's mouths—

ZAMBILĂ

In the story, my great-great-grandfather is followed home after a long day of work and drink, by a white goose. White, because in my imagination, it could not have been any other type of goose, such as the Toulouse goose or even the Pink-footed goose, though that is certainly a beautiful goose. But in the story, my great-great-grandfather is escorted home by a Roman goose, with its orange beak and proud tuft of hair combed back, a goose bred over 2,000 years ago and known to be sacred still to the goddess Juno. They say that sometime in the late 4th century the honking of this goose saved Rome from attack, but in this story, my great-great-grandmother sends the goose to a bar to bring her husband home, it being many decades ago, before the war, when geese could be trusted with such an errand. In the story, the goose is named Zambilă, borrowed from the Ottoman Turkish word *sümbül* and the Persian word *sombol*, both meaning hyacinth—the flower not the type of macaw, though I like to imagine Zambilă feeding on nuts and announcing her presence to all who care to listen. The word *zambilă* is pronounced with an 'uh' sound at the end, languid but guttural, you have to be embarrassed to say it, you have to make it sound like a goose. In the story, which takes places in the outskirts of Bucharest, the 'Little Paris of the East' according to some, the goose was my great-great-grandfather's confidant, this being before the war, when there were still confidants, we all know a goose is a good listener. My great-great-grandfather was called Papa mic, meaning little daddy, though *papa* can also mean bye-bye in Romanian, a language that prides itself on its proximity to Italian, though with a bit more woe baked in. In my family, the story ends with Zambilă disappearing, maybe even being eaten by the family, this being a story of poverty after all, as well as of the goose. Recently, though, we have resurrected Zambilă, performed a seance on the concrete banks of the Danube, this being after the war, Bucharest now a dissonant note, a harsh word, a bad place for a Roman goose who is, after all, sacred in more ways than one, all geese born fully-formed from the mouths of goose-barnacles, which grow like callused claws on the slopes of rock, and on flotsam caught in the throat of the ocean. In this story, Zambilă is alive and well in a village that celebrates the first of March by tying red and white string to tree-branches. After all, a goose can mean many things to many people, amongst them my mother and I, sitting in the archive of goose, surrounded by hyacinths as far as the eye can see.

Impossible Blue

Alan Yan

It does not stop. All day
I dwell on you; silver tongues of rain
count the hours. Cars wheel past,
laughing over puddles
in the bituminous glaze.
Beyond the window, a woman
takes her daughter's hand
before crossing the street,
one umbrella briefly
superimposed over the other.
Nameless others rush and pass,
huddling like bundles of wet leaves,
the trees turning bare. And falling
this eternal falling…
brightens the black fence
a man on his hands and knees
painted just yesterday: rescued
from its destiny of rust. Water
we prayed for: how it builds
an ocean of silk and light
inside me, then breaks me up
as if to remind me of why
I love you—seek you, us:
descendants of rain.
What shall we make of this
impossible blue? Blue

through which we swim
full of sky-shimmer.
The bike across the street is locked
still: no seat, no wheels,
nowhere to go. Only
a place for loneliness
to drown. And how many
scars, bark of the sycamore
streaked green—bolder
because of you. Darkness
seen for what it is. In other
words, water mourning
until it finds earth
anticipates light. Yes
to make an island of the earth.
The kettle, started some time ago,
distracts me now from the dragging
pearls of rain, a tireless tremolo
that seems now and then
to make a loving autumn of my room.
My body lifts itself from the chair.
I do what I must do.
O how soon it all goes… how
in the absence afterward,
just raindrops
silent on the window:
annotations of your love,
by which I mean
I do not know who I will become.

Jason Brooks, *Sun Up Til' Sundown,* 2023, oil on panel, 16" x 12"

Jason Brooks, *Midnight Sun,* 2023, oil on canvas, 60" x 48"

Jason Brooks, *The Matriarch,* 2023, oil on linen, 20" x 16"

Paul-Sebastian Japaz, *Ally Kitchen II*, 2023, oil on canvas, 72" x 59"

Paul-Sebastian Japaz, *linger*, 2023, oil on canvas, 67" x 53"

Paul-Sebastian Japaz, *I'd wonder if this was the last time*, 2023, oil on canvas, 36" x 36"

Splash

Cécile Girardin

We were both staring at the pool, avoiding each other's gaze. I had donned sunglasses, meaning to appear carefree for the rest the afternoon. We had chosen the holiday house for its pool, and a nice one it was, surrounded by fragrant fig trees and a safety fence. From my deckchair, I could see my two teenage boys wrestle and frolic, not thinking for a second how silly they looked. My stick-thin daughter played along willingly: one of the boys would ferry her on a mock-boat made of those long floating devices, only to make her plunge at a great expense of high-pitched squeals.

Next to them were my partner's two daughters, a pre-teen and a six-year-old named Charlie. Since she couldn't swim, one of her grandmothers had provided her with a special bathing suit featuring cylindric polystyrene buoys inserted in the garment's cloth. The kid could remove them, one at a time, as her floating techniques improved. Somewhere between a bullet-proof vest and a costume for circus bears, the suit's ugliness was enhanced by a garish liberty motif made of sickly-looking flowers. Where that thoughtful grandma had dug the foul accessory, I would never know, but somehow it had focused my resentment as the days flew by.

For his daughters would not play with my rowdy bunch for our entire stay together. Disregarding calls to take part in this and that challenge, they stayed on the side. The eldest had arrived by the poolside covered with a large towel, reluctant to expose her body. I could have sympathized with such inhibition, but she made a point of ignoring us, showing up nonetheless and taking advantage of the facilities. She deployed elaborate skills to slip into the water unseen and stay there until everybody was out. She swam laps, avoiding contact with my kids.

Her younger sister enjoyed herself in her own peculiar way. Once it was made clear that it was time for a swim, Charlie would run to get her suit. Then she would jump into the water, make a few rounds, get out, and jump in again. Charlie was needy, and her sister brought her whatever she longed for, without either having to say anything. They had a language of their own, made of glances and whispers. Her whining meant she wanted the buoy that my three used for their games, and the big sister would snatch it for her when the others weren't looking.

Charlie's lifebelt didn't prevent her body from getting thoroughly immersed, and each time she reemerged, she did so by inhaling air so noisily that her father asked: "Are you ok, Charlie?" After she had done that twenty times, and he had said that same line twenty times, I said to him: "Can't you see that she's never been so fine? She knows how to enjoy herself all right." She was taking immense pleasure in completely ignoring the others.

Her father adopted that worried expression he always had when I said something about Baby Charlie. He was concerned she did not behave the way kids were supposed to behave, and he was concerned that I was concerned. So far, I had avoided being overtly hostile towards her and I had told him, with sincerity, that things would smooth out eventually. He was such a good man; and so bright and cultured. He was worth more than what his daughters were giving him in return. A psychiatrist might have called the girls inhibited, autistic, neurodiverse or whatever; but I had finally decided to call them rude, and, yes, mean.

Both had strikingly delicate features, with huge diamond-like eyes of changing hues. That summer, I still found them stunningly beautiful, but I found them ugly, too. For one thing, beauty never thrived under a mask. His daughters never smiled, but they were not unhappy, either. Far from it. Yet, the lack of spontaneity put a great strain on the gorgeous traits they inherited. Because she so rarely opened her mouth, I had only lately realized that Charlie had lost one of her incisors. She must have been the only child in the world who didn't elicit spurts of amused yet genuine fondness at the sight of missing front teeth. During meals, she would get her mouthfuls on one side and try to chew hard stuff with her back teeth, but even that didn't make her funny or cute. She didn't eat less for that matter, she just ate for longer stretches and made an even greater mess than normal. She was a great eater, and a sound sleeper, majoring cum laude in two areas that were often a great source of concern for parents.

The older girl's sullen temperament had already spoiled her natural beauty. Besides, her attire was repellant, with clothes that never quite suited her; dresses she wore over striped leggings, unfitting jeans, tee-shirts bearing nonsensical messages, like "Hold on to the summer" or "Never stop exploring." But like her sister, she never deigned to talk to or look at strangers, let alone me, and she simply acted as if we were not there. But after all, wasn't that true of any teenage girl who had to spend her free time with a lady she disliked, a lady who tried to teach her manners while sleeping with her father at night? Well, with a genuine rebel, I would have been fine. But she wasn't that.

The sun was high and bright, and my feet were getting pleasurably watered from the ongoing splashing. I was searching avidly for my kids' eyes, the way I would scoop oxygen in thin air. In the beginning, I used to smile at the girls, and also wink, make funny faces, blow a kiss, all those things that worked wonders with kids. I prized myself on making kids laugh. But not them. They were only capable of the petty laughter of situation comedy, say, if my daughter fell on the stairs, or if I shouted at my boys for their rowdiness, or hurt my little toe against the coffee table.

Within the rectangle of the pool, my three kids were bumping and bursting like electrons, making a mess but at least endlessly interacting. Meanwhile, the teenage girl was rounding a corner, performing her sluggish laps, her head floating about warily, and the flowery bomb next to her was exploding repeatedly and not showing any sign of stopping. Charlie was making sure that the spot of happy bickering was disrupted and the water's mirror pulverized to smithereens. Emerging from the water, she breathed so heavily that her father had to ask: "Are you okay, Charlie?"

The thought suddenly hit me: our relationship would be over if he said it one more time. I couldn't believe I was able to feel that way, yet it appeared so obvious that I couldn't clear my mind of it.

My kids were fond of him, and I knew he was fantasizing I would become a substitute mother to his girls. He had a soft spot for his little girls, and how could I blame him for that? Yet I couldn't stand his daily routine of submitting to them. He mastered the art of answering questions for them, of doing things for them he shouldn't have, of believing all their stories about how terribly others had behaved towards them.

He reclined in his long chair, laughing at a joke my eldest boy had just made. Charlie was standing on the poolside, her pudgy arms lying almost horizontally upon her armored suit, and ready to make a splash. Each time she jumped in, she took a longer run-up on the glistening tiles, and for some reason she aimed diagonally, so that she almost brushed the adjacent side of the pool on impact. I turned to her father, with an air of saying that it was getting dangerous, but he didn't react. When Charlie missed my daughter's head by a hair's breadth, I jumped up: "You almost killed her!" I stood over her plump, floating body, and all she could do was look towards the bottom of the water. "Look at me, for once! You're not alone in this world!" But she kept clutching the edge, her eyes cast downward, brimming with tears. That was another thing about her: she would cry, let go large, glistening tears that rolled down her perfectly rounded cheeks, and go back to business in a second's time. Of course, she never apologized to my daughter, and she wore her immutable poker face instead.

I focused for a while on a lizard circling about an earthen flowerpot. What was it about him that made him so hesitant around his daughters? I wanted to tell him his own dignity was at stake.

Charlie was bracing for yet another jump, and I could see an imperceptible smirk on her face. Even my children had started to notice it. If you looked closely, you could spot the shadow of a smile, by which she told me that she had won.

After the incident, her father looked satisfied, too, grinning peacefully. He always did when his daughters were busy doing something that didn't require him to intervene, as if the quiet that they achieved left him silent about everything else they did or failed to do. After that, the daily routine would resume: he would tell them to shower, to set the table, to go to bed, and they would. But they would leave tracks of dirty clothes behind them, toilets that needed scraping and flushing, small toys and pencils scattered everywhere, as well as food, plenty of food scraps under the table where Baby Charlie had eaten her platefuls.

Was it a simple case of not standing kids who weren't mine?

I had gone through this question a hundred times. I would never have claimed that my own kids were particularly clean, thoughtful, or even well-behaved. But my time with them was filled with laughter, words, harsh most of the time, and affectionate hugs that made up for the rest of it.

The best answer I had found was somewhere lying in their father's hands. He accepted being treated like this. How many times had I seen him play with them, just because they turned their backs on the other kids at the playground; how many times had I heard him ask what they wanted to eat, to wear, to buy, and promptly provide? That was my tentative answer: I couldn't stand them because of what they made of him, and that very thought was shaking the foundation of our love.

Physical desire was still sharp, especially on those days of sweltering heat when we roamed about half-naked from morning to night. He was strikingly handsome all summer with his tanned skin and muscled body. Of course, in the company of children, nothing of that desire came out and I pursued a daytime mental life of my own, a nice, lulling feeling during periods of relative rest. But afternoon pool sessions did not count as rest since Charlie couldn't swim and took great advantage of it, and I could hear her noisy breathing, a reminder to behave myself. Her father was always afraid she'd die. He said that she was so careless, she hurt herself frequently, that she had no sense of danger. What I knew was that she was well aware of her father's fear. I also knew she needed, more than any other child, to exert control over her environment. But she did that through unusual means, humming to herself in a low voice, or breathing to herself, as if she had asthma or some lung condition, even though she didn't. Was she merely keeping herself company? Speaking out loud or engaging in a conversation was never an option: she never responded to anything I'd say, however hard I kept trying, and I presumed that her bodily noises made up for her contempt for language and human contact.

My boys finally got out of the water, glistening and smiling in the sun. The eldest bent over my chair to give me a kiss. He said I looked old with my ugly hat and we laughed. They were like two oversized puppies shaking water off their fur and enjoying the way they overstepped onto my territory. Their company, at that precise moment, was so comforting that I relied on them, not to prove myself right, but to prove that my life was worthwhile. That was what his daughters were doing to me: holding their power over me, in an attempt to extinguish something. My boys' liveliness gave me hope and I turned to the man I loved. I held on to this fantasy that we would be able to rescue him from the deathly forces lying all around him. We were showing him what affection looked like, and my sprightly daughter joined us, soaking my chair wet. She begged and I said, okay, I'll go get my swimming suit. But as I was walking away from the pool, I heard him ask: "Are you sure you're okay, Charlie?"

Mira Applies for a Job

Mirabai

Translated by Chloe Martinez

Keep me in your service, Lord.
Mountain-lifter, let me look after you.

If I were your servant, I'd plant a garden.
I'd get up early just to look at you.

Keep me.

In the little streets of your village
and in the green groves, we'd sing and dance.

Keep me in your service.

I'd make looking at you my occupation
and take remembering you as my pay.
My devotion would be the property
I've wished for in every life, every rebirth.

Lord.

With his peacock-feather crown
and his yellow robe
and the rainbow garland around his neck
the Enchanter is grazing the cows
in the village, playing his flute.

Let me.

I'll make a lush green bower
with borders in between.
I'll wear a sari, deep *kusumbi* red.
I'll look and look at the Beloved.

In your service.

In the middle of the night, Lord, let me
meet you at the edge of the river—

Mira's Lord is the Mountain-lifting One;

her heart:

unsteady as a cloud.

मीराबाई

म्हाणे चाकर राखाँजी, गरिधारी लाला चाकर राखाँजी।
चाकर रहस्यूँ बाग लगास्यूँ नति उठ दरसण पास्यूँ।
बंद्रिावन री कुँज गलनि माँ गोवन्दि लीला गास्यूँ।
चाकरी में, दरसण पास्यूँ, सुमरिण पास्यूँ खरची।
भाव भगत जागीराँ पास्यूँ, जणम जणम री तरसी।
मोर मुगुट पीताम्बर सोहाँ, गल वैजन्ती मालो।
बंद्रिावण माँ धेण चरावाँ, मोहन मुरली वालो।
हरे हरे णवाँ कुँज लगास्यूँ, बीचाँ बीचाँ बारी।
साँवरयिा रो दरसण पास्यूँ पहण कुसुम्बी सारी।
आधाँ रात प्रभु दरसण दीस्यो जमणाजी रे तीराँ।
मीराँ के प्रभु गरिधर नागर, हविरो घणो अधीरा।

Dream Sequence Stricken From A Tapestry

Aline Dolinh

While questing in the orchards adorned
with forlorn columns of maidens' white
and braceleted arms, I was tempted.
First the warm earth oozed before
embracing me. Irradiated and relaced,
I heard voices but not the ones
I had gone searching for. I saw myself
enclosed pastoral and then rendered
soft as tallow into more gamine and
britomartian shapes. They told me
I could know innocence. Yes, its pearlescent
and grotesque face. My head sprouted
the crown of the bride and then the knife.
What had I ever known of romance beyond
my childish desire to play the bolting hind
and not the knight? I could have chosen
from all permutations of metamorphosis
available to a lone girl beset by strange
forces in a dark grove but awoke only
holding the gore-slick secret of eternal love:
a thorned rope of organ that seared me
where it thrashed in my ungloved hands.
If I was brave I would have swallowed
the entire blazing cable, but I realized
this was a test of diligence. I rewound my gorget
and drew my gift's sanguine heft into

its tightest orbit around the neck. And I rode on,
the vast caustic flock of all longing
domesticated into a pendant that left
my breast red and cellophaned to the touch,
never learning whether the test
was the pain or its attendant garishness.

Psalm of the Fifth Brain

Talin Tahajian

I was born under the sign of the adder's tail
in the final quarter of the Pseudocene
when the feather-tailed scorpions were just beginning to shed their
    feathers
and the miraculous boar had not yet risen up from the subway tracks
to tell us its news. My mother popped me out on the Café Car
of the Amtrak Northeast Regional Train 93 as it passed through the
    coastal rainforest called
the State of Connecticut. She recalls
Canadian geese the size of boxcars swooping down
to look at her with their wound-slit eyes
and reeds so tall they blocked the sun. She says
all the marshes were flooded and the highways were flooded
and sunlight sifted gorgeously through the huge flora in rigged doses
and my dad sniffed a fat line and the train conductor pressed down on
    the accelerator
and the thick vegetable stalks growing up along the tracks were half-
    drowned
in the terror. I fostered an early interest in mathematics
and spent days in my father's
vaulted library, as dark and full of filtered light
as the steaming woods that day, I'm told. It's no coincidence I took an
    interest
in his field, the fourth brain
of megaflora, which led me naturally to his subfield, the fifth brain
of megaflora, and by the age of twelve, I'd read through his three
    monographs—

Endomycelia: An Introduction, Endomycelia: New Observations, and Amphimycelia: Beyond the Endomycelium—and memorized their figures, one particular diagram of which
depicted the growth phases of the fifth brain so beguilingly, I pulled out my prized sheepsfoot
knife from my pocket and, very carefully, removed that page and carried it with me
until the age of sixteen, when it became almost my sole
object of desire. I observed it every day
and then I went to school and studied it. By this point
I had a bad right ear, having one day come downstairs
to find my father reading my journals, which described my sister
in meticulous detail. My ear rang like a diagram, I remember
raising my hand to the side of my head and feeling the sticky plasma
and looking instinctively to my left—the entire
right side of my sensorium having been eradicated by, at the end of the day,
what my father saw to be one of my more irrational affinities. I saw
a holographic wave form floating above the kitchen sink
as water flowed from the tap like a translucent
snake-shaped angel. It was, you guessed it,
Divine Mercy Sunday, and I prayed to that angel for years whenever I imagined
my sister, waiting for me
perfectly and wholly on the other side of the heavy gate
at the back of our garden, where twisted, bowed and buckled plants
that looked like Venus flytraps but ate beasts as large as rat-pigeons
swarmed my boots and tried to maul me, announcing
to me my sister's name like it was their
one-syllable endomycelial psalm
every time I tried to take a step. In college, I taught myself
to read palms, I taught myself stichomancy, I read cards
in a basement at MIT, where I went through extensive covert screening
and was eventually recruited to a team of professional card-counters
called the Fifth Brains, and then—once I'd proved the theory outdated
in my undergraduate dissertation—called
Bier. We won millions in the desert, I remember

looking out the window of the jet we took each Friday
to observe the mega-geese my mom once spoke of, these ones of a slightly different
breed, having lost their feathers and gained some sort of scale plating
that looked like crude oil. Once, we were playing at our usual table
and performing our signals to one another
using the cryptographs we'd developed for that purpose
when the semiotics dragon, who had recently been promoted to the managerial level,
descended upon the blackjack table where I'd later
meet my wife, electricity coming from his nose
just as you would imagine it might
or may have seen it, if you, too, happened to be there that day.
He saw through our heist, by this point
years long, and telecommunicated immediately to the FBI
via a potato chip in his reptile brain. The agents assigned to our case
appeared instantly and arrested us, the bail of which
was only half of what we'd won, which no one could count right
because the casino dealt, as was the convention in those decades,
in raw gold, and all the records were kept in a rare kind of codex
bound in human skin, which we'd made sure to burn earlier that evening
because I'd seen, that morning, in my palms and in the cards,
that we'd be caught. This act of conflagration pained me
because I'd taken one course in mammalian codicology
to fulfil a distribution requirement in the Mammalities
during which I fell in love with my professor. We spent long hours together
in the museums, on psilocybin, and in her bathtub, but firstly
in the dining hall, where I pretended
to run into her regularly but really had synchronized my schedule to hers
in practically thirty-second increments on the back of one of my copies of
My Life-Destroying Diagram,
which at some early point I'd taken to my department
and made three hundred copies so I wouldn't ever
lose it, should that book go out of print or "the cloud" go dark

in the event of another solar flare or whatnot. I keep some of those copies
in a shoebox labelled ANGEL SNAKE in bright green letters
and the rest are taped across my walls
very neatly in 15-by-15 arrangements. I still lie on my bed and watch
the sad expressions of their defunct mythos, most of the time
unmoving. Anyway we won our case
because they couldn't prove we were cheating. They brought in witness
after witness, but no one in the world could break our code,
not even the semiotics dragon. Witness to what in Christ's name
is what I have to say about that. Jesus! Jesus Christ evolved
from a shark tooth! What do you think all those shark teeth are for!

After college, my friends thought I had a jinn, so I left
and lived for years in East Berlin
with my actress girlfriend I met in a bar called O Tennenbaum,
I'll take you there someday. Anyway she had a black bob and these
    ridiculous
round eyes like a cow and though she didn't speak German or English
and I didn't speak New Franco-Russian, we lived for years in a handsome
    Altbauwohnung off Hermannstraße
that had an obscure provenantial connection to the historical Buddha.
    She kept me there as a pet
and I lived dumbly and happily on labneh and vitamins
for years, seeking bodily transformation
and spiritual fitness, until she threw me onto the street
for being too dumb and happy. It was at this point
I became a priest, having lived on the street for nearly
one hour before a beautiful boy with blonde curls
and long cream robes with a little hood and an embroidered
gold cross on the back—I'll never forget,
he was the spitting image of my sister, so help me God—
came up to me and said what was essentially the text of Ephesians
    1:15–23, though I didn't
know that then. I followed him back to his monastery
where I met several of his friends, who I liked enough to stay for dinner
and then ten more years, during which time I got ordained
and became excellent at flood management. I developed an intricate

practice of prayer based on several numero-astrological factors. I sought
the One, I paid my tithes, I woke up early, I kept Christ safe
in his elaborate box, and I'll have you know
I looked to see who wasn't looking
every time I said Behold! and kept track of the count. Three. Three.
Three. Three. Three. Three. Seven. Eventually, I got invested with a kind
of sickness
no holy balm could cure and my friends came, again, to think
I had a jinn, which scared me. After trying a wide array of exorcisms
they left me
exactly where they'd found me and I watched for a while, through
the illuminated window of our old apartment, the silhouettes of two
men
moving against the darkness. I got on the U-Bahn and took it back and
forth for a while
screaming something like THE GOOSE HAS LEFT THE NEST. It was then
I saw it—
my eyes on the prize, I leaped for it, I made it
amongst the lagging screeches of my enemies, who lurched at me
from all around me like visions of themselves after the rapture. It was
OK, I'd plotted all of it out,
I was told by a fashionable poet, years later, in a dimly-lit hotel ballroom
on the Lower East Side. My friends thought I had a jinn, I said in
response.
I recognised, suddenly, the face of my father, who I'd been told had been
dead
ten years, and the face of my wife, who looked up from her cup of
espresso and said
I will not destroy you, sweetheart, don't worry, the strain
is tangible, the sweat on my face
untenable, and I
am a secret
you keep only from yourself. A gorgeous stack
of jars of various kinds. A swine to whom you've tossed your pearls.
Leave it
to the dogs, all your holy things, knock on my door
and I'll knock back. Look at the grounds at the bottom of this cup—I

feel
I never really grounded you, electricity divine, though I love you—really
I'd die for you. Yes you too sorry, you must also leave too please. Anyway
what was it
in the tower, what is it here on this walk I wake to, on this train I take
just to keep from myself
myself, the half-dead boar lying there on the platform
where I left my heart when I left you, rigged
like a mast to the vessel of my desire, please wait for me,
I will not go unmentored by my elders, I will not
go, if I can find a different music,
maybe I can save my soul, I will not leave this spot
until the adder's tail stings, until last wave descends into the last wave,
until the angel returns to scorch the Euphrates
and the night bursts, until rock and roll runs clean with His glory
and the clocktower shudders at His name, please don't go,
the darkness is riddled with something I don't know
what to call and the light is getting shorter, please, have you seen my cat,
where did you go, can you see me, do you know what I mean?

Bionic Avatars

Ethan Seeley

The tech billionaire hated death. He hated it more than the average person, who hates it a lot. In meetings, he was always going on about telomeres and apoptosis. Make a note. He declared war against death at both the macro and the micro level. And the other people gathered around the table nodded, scratched their thighs. He planned to live for a thousand years, but not in a weird way like Dracula. Make a note: Construct bionic avatars. Then he goes home and eats a dry muffin and drinks a protein shake and wipes most of the crumbs off his pants. In his bedroom he watches amateur porn on a large screen, because he likes to see what non-billionaires look like naked. He clicks on a video. The tech billionaire is disgusted. He can hear the television on in the background. He recognizes the theme song to *Friends*. He can hear the laugh track.

The tech billionaire misses the bus so his mom has to give him a ride to work. It is his first day of being a tech billionaire and he wonders if the other employees will laugh at him. A lot of people think being a tech billionaire is easy, but turns out it isn't. First of all you have to meet with politicians and other billionaires and pretend you like them. Secondly, your skin gets dry sometimes. Sometimes whole bits of skin fall off and you have to replace them with wet paper. Sometimes a bridge collapses and it's your fault somehow. Sometimes you reap the whirlwind.

There Are

two sides to every story.
Ant v. Grasshopper. Humbert v. Haze.
A man who is chasing a fox and a man
who sees a fox emerge from the treeline

and crawl into a well. He kills the fox.

I believe you have my fox,
says the first man. I believe I have my fox
says the other and walks off. It's not entire-
ly about the fox. Is giving chase

to a wild creature sufficient to establish possession?
If so, what does this mean for those of us
in hot pursuit of some elusive, but glimpsed
thing? I am in hot pursuit of three beautiful men,

a Maltese Falcon, an idiom as crisp as a new
$100 bill. And in turn I am pursued by death, collectors
of bad debts, receptionists from various doctor's
offices. The calls go to voicemail. Thus my life

is unremarkable. Few have
remarked upon it. And yet the commentaries
on this particular fox have swelled to the size
of several Mahabharatas. The court,

relying heavily on the writings
of Baron von Pufendorf, maintains
that pursuit does not
establish possession. One must, in fact,

mortally wound the "creature" before one owns it.
He who mortally wounds me owns me
is a thought no fox has ever had.
He is too busy listening for the footfalls

of mice under the snow.
He is gazing longingly up at some too-high
bunch of wild grapes. The beavers,
nearly hunted to extinction

in 17th century New England,
have returned, due to a decline in the popularity
of beaver-skin hats. Now the beavers
have built a large swimming pool around

the high-voltage power lines. The towers'

steel legs are knee-deep in water
while overhead the wires sizzle with info.
New words appear as we need them and
old words are repurposed, like when

this lusty young couple with triplet moves
into the abandoned Methodist church. Next
door the bank is auctioning off a house.
There are people inside the house.

They live in the house and a small group
has gathered in the street to bid.
In the end, the bank buys the house
back from the bank. The people inside

stay there. They can hear shrieks from the church across the street and a bugle call that plays at noon for some reason they could never quite understand.

Song of Songs

Robocop strolls downtown to follow no-good goons who shoot
common crooks.
Hollywood's non-stop tomorrows go vroom vrooom.
God's not wrong. Got cosmos on lockdown.

Postdocs opt for monkhood, not lots of blowjobs; schoolwork, not
off-color porn plots.
Profs co-opt God's words for so-so books on Solomon's songs.
Two goth boys, grown fond of non-orthodoxy, bow down to Moloch's
consorts.

Off-work bookworms foxtrot to songs of cool blonds who slowly croon
doo-wop or Motown.
Don Johnson logs onto hot-solo-boys.com to post photos of Don
Johnson's cock.
Townsfolk kowtow to food snobs who won't chow down on foot-long
corndogs.

On Tom's porch, mobs of phlox blossoms form whorls of sloppy color.
Ohhhh. Tom's on shrooms.
Most doctors own Volvos to go to n fro from Toronto to Boston—both
hotspots for cowpox.

Now look how flocks of crows roost only on rooftops of mom n pop
shops,
how monsoons flood low spots—bottoms of bogs or mossy pools.
Frost swoops down on crosstown woodlots.

So who knows how forms morph?
Cow-god to owl-god—body to rock to Gorgon.
Cold protons glom onto two gold horns.
Foot born from hoof. Logos on workshop doors.

Don't stop now! O moon of Hong Kong!
Of Solomon! Color of oxblood!

Doctrinal

Donald Revell

I'd been remembering the seven days
Almost any word spoken aloud became
A creature—insect, lizard, bird—appearing
For an instant at the corner of my eye.
They would gasp in the sunlight, and become
Sunlight. Only the one smile shared
Between everything, just one word.
Then I remembered how, in summertime,
A light rain chooses carefully among
The green leaves, which to bend and which to let
Alone. Enchantment is not choosing.
Syllables elect a creature among themselves,
And the humans gasp. Rain and mercy,
Mercy and rain spoken aloud are lost
Causes making all the mischief when nature
And the supernatural share one smile:
A crooked newborn, bending in the leaves.
There's something else to believe. At the summer
Gate called "Beautiful", the sun was let down
In a basket and I believed in that.

Pieta

Everything in the cold room points
To a girl puzzled at her own becoming,
As though a weed, bent double
In waste ground had found itself
Suddenly human, and beautiful.
There is no memory of the angel
Nor of any beginnings. There is
Only this agony stretched across
Her lap, and the poor stranger
Weighted down with that agony.
How did he come here? Was he
A different weed perhaps, mishap
Of a different transformation, not
Wholly successful? The poor stranger.

The Quarrel

Not the silvering leaves, but rather
The motion of those leaves sending
Words into the center of the earth
Via roots and crawling things—
Lonesome but careful words easily
Mistaken for love—is the nearest
Supernatural. Otherwise,
This world is a machine. Otherwise,
Even the Christ child fussing in His icons
Is nerves or a trick of candlelight.
And His mother is a cloud, one cloud
All by itself in the hot, divisive sky.
The wind takes notice of a leaf, moves it,
And all of our mistaken earth changes.
Love silvers the leaf then, all afternoon.

Words Are Deeds

I must stand, as every chair in the room
Is filled with light. Winter light in midsummer,
The kind that bares the trees and makes a razor
Of the brilliant air. My house is an
Identical house, Pentecostal
To all comers. Come the end of the world,
It will be standing with thousands of itself.
It will see adorable skating
On the pavements. A steep current of air,
Razor-sharp, mothering ice in the trees,
Mimics an angel inside a boy skating
Inside the dream his is lord of.
Tell him your grammar, Lord, your anagrams
And seating arrangements. While there is time,
Music in the hallways, and a last warmth
In the room, tell him his summer name.

Craft Talk: Almost a Prayer—The Afterlife Of Enchantment (October 5, 2023)

Donald Revell

Abstract

I'm considering a moment (and it is a moment of various durations, from the briefest to the eternal) shared by *some* poems with *some* prayers.

In that moment, a suddenly delighted attention is transfigured in forgetfulness. The result or, better, the *consequence*, is Enchantment.

St. Augustine: "I must pass beyond memory to find you..."

INTENTION ABDICATES TO ATTENTION
or
INTENTION IS ABOLISHED BY ATTENTION
or
AS AT THE HOUR OF DEATH, CONSCIOUSNESS ESCAPES PERSONALITY

Purgatorio XXVIII—

Dante is at the top of the Mount of Purgatory, on the threshold of the Earthly Paradise, on the riverbank of Lethe, having just bid farewell to the poets Virgil and Statius, his guides and companions. From the far shore, a woman who has been gathering flowers, speaks to him:

> "Those ancients who in poetry presented the golden age, who sang its happy state, perhaps, in their Parnassus, dreamt this place. Here, mankind's root was innocent; and here were every fruit and never-

ending spring; these streams, the nectar of which poets sing." Then I turned round completely, and I faced my poets; I could see that they had heard with smiles this final corollary spoken; that done, my eyes returned to the fair woman.

end of canto (translated by Allen Mandelbaum)

Poetry behind; Paradise and an imparadised Beatrice ahead, with only Lethe still to cross. It is to such moment, and then to the next, possibly eternal moment , that all of my little talk refers.

At the beginning, it is always honest & just to confess one's credentials, one's point of view. All my sense of how it is that the poems I care for most come into being, and all my hopes for my own poems anymore, originate in a happy accident of birth—i.e., to the particular parish in the Bronx into which I was born.

A) St Peter's Episcopal—founded1699 and now beneath the shadow of the El, as witnessed by Big Bird & companions in the first season of Sesame Street. An oasis in an unlovely neighborhood, with a wonderful, high church rector, Father Thomas Brown...bells & smells...mass SUNG from the book of Common Prayer...an absolute connection between beauty (exotic!) of language and the purpose of prayer...between the Music of language & prayer...a Bronx forgotten in the enchanting cadences of Cranmer's liturgy(+ a great advantage to the study & love of 16th & 17th century English poetry in college & grad school.

B) JHS 101, grades 7-9 with Miss Petrusa...Dante every Friday for three years: 7th grade *Inferno* 8th grade *Purgatorio* 9th grade *Paradiso* Dante my first poet...a constant reaching thru words to the Imaged word...once reached, the Commedia ends.

I'm concerned today with the approaches to that point at which the music of prayer leaves the language of prayer behind, the point at which the Imaged word leaves words behind...a point that TSE called a *frontier of consciousness beyond which words fail, though meanings still exist.* And as with prayer, so too, I suggest, with poems.

While acknowledging the profound and numerous differences between prayer and poetry—the imagined, though not imaginary audience being only the most obvious, both are events of attention. And it is the dynamic of that attention that determines their shape, their effect and their Afterlife.

The dynamic begins with motive, and all too often ends there too. Stubbornly fixed upon motive, prayer stalls inn petition. Stubbornly fixed upon motive (or purpose if you like), poetry stalls in argument, in imprecation, in complaint or in kitsch.

But sometimes the motive for a prayer yields to the Experience of prayer. There, touching the supernatural, it either reaches into an ecstatic silence or falls back onto the ground of its beseeching. Dante did, after all, faint quite a lot.

In a similar dynamic, sometimes the motive for a poem—what Richard Hugo used to call its triggering occasion—disappears into the Experience of the poem—ie into the verbal sensorium it conjures around itself. There, forgetting itself for a while, it becomes the supernatural of itself. There, it can simply break off, leaving words behind ("Kubla Khan"?) or delight a while in the ecstasy of its supernature, eventually to fall back into the original nature of its motive & expression, acknowledging the limits of poetry but, perhaps, changed by the experience. And this change, I believe, increases the reality available to the next poem, to the next poet.

A quick case in point is Herbert's poem "Prayer 1"
**note the sudden shift from metonymy to sensual enchantment beginning with line 9*

It is in the supernatural event—a distraction, a disruption, and elevation—of enchantment that poetry and prayer can comprehend and complement one another. And my own favorite scholars of prayer—Richard of St Victor, Aquinas, Teresa of Avila—proposed a dynamic I've been delighted to find at work in many of my favorite poems. It begins with motive (sometimes called inspiration) which then, via thought, memory & imagination, hopefully expands into Meditation, wheremotive is or must be literally forgotten. There is the river Lethe. There, Purpose encounters Presence. If the prayer is true, that Presence is dearly Beloved, a vivifying object of enchantment in an aura of perfect forgetfulness.

Enchantment can be momentary, or lifelong or, for the saints and the very few great poets our species can boast of, eternal. (I'm thinking of Dante again.)

At the limits of enchantment, prayer either rises into the heaven of contemplation, where neither words nor any apparatus of consciousness obtain—call it ecstasy, the sublime alienation—or falls back into itself, tragically remembering itself and its origins…perhaps enlightened, but uncertain still, uncertain again.

Time at last to talk about how this dynamic finds a complement, sometimes a congruence in poetry. Being made entirely of words, poems cannot reach quite as far as prayer. But at the limits of enchantment, poetry sometimes protracts the moment of enchantment, engrossing it in beautiful delay, just short of the ecstasy of contemplation, right there at the edge of consciousness and of language…until, of necessity, it falls back into itself and its origins, uncertain still, uncertain again. (I'm thinking of Keats and his nightingale.)

In *Purgatorio*, on the banks of Lethe and in the Earthly Paradise, Dante gives us a model of beautiful delay. Across the water, he sees a woman gathering flowers. He hears her singing. (Wonderful that THIS is the one passage of the Commedia that Shelley translated.) The woman's smile is the promise of a further, all redeeming smile—that of Beatrice—only to be seen after he has been immersed in the waters of forgetfulness. Dante is on the brink of an Enchantment without end, a Paradise engrossed all the way to the empyrean.

But Dante is a poet, not a saint. The Commedia ends and its enchantment, spacious as it is, fades into the reality of time. As Auden has written: *All true enchantments fade in time. They can start us on the road towards God, but they cannot bring us to Him. Sooner or later we must do without them and walk alone in faith.*

What does not fade is the model Dante provides and the dynamic he boldly enacts for a kind of poetry that is the vivid shadow of prayer. The gorgeous pageant and reunion awaiting him in the Earthly Paradise is only possible beyond Lethe, ie is premised upon a deep and transformative forgetting. To once again greet the eyes of Beatrice with his eyes, he must leave Virgil and Statius, his poets and guides, behind him, must forget the models his poem has avowed thus far.

This is meant to be a craft talk, some words about something I have gathered from thinking about poetry and prayer together. (Thanks once again to Father Thomas Brown and Miss Petrusa.)

Something wonderful happens when intention is surprised, perhaps Elevated by attention. I have been shown that this surprise, this elevation is Enchantment…something that allows a poem to become almost as intransitive as music. "I want a bicycle" becomes, upon contact with the supernatural, "I want." "I love Miss X" becomes "I love" etc. I recall that Dante's "intention" in Canto 1 of Inferno was to find a way out of the dark wood. It is the enchanting intervention of Heaven, an interrupting Beatrice, that is the making of the poem.

My first example was taken from the great devotional poet Herbert. But enchantment has a secular life and secular adventure as well. (Though in the end, this proves that all true poems are very near relations of prayer. This, as D. H. Lawrence said, is only for the good to know.)

What poem could be more secular than Marvell's "To His Coy Mistress" and its expressed, unabashedly seductive purpose. But something happens; Marvell becomes enchanted by his own gorgeous hyperbole… for a beautiful while, carpe diem as left behind and the poem is enchanted by itself. And even when, after a while, it falls back into seduction mode, it has changed into a new, and visionary extremity.

Think of Keats' "Ode to Nightingale", in which a long, slow feverish desire for enchantment is suddenly interrupted by supernatural contact—"Already with thee!"—after which comes the intense but all too brief instant of elevation: "tender is the night…" etc. And then, as with prayer, comes the tragic remembrance of self and of the poem's origins, uncertain still, uncertain again. "Was it a vision or a waking dream? Fled is that music—Do I wake or sleep?"And I think of tender Coleridge, and of how the long, depressive pathology of his Dejection Ode is redeemed by distraction and by an enchantment with the noise of the wind in section VII and then one distraction is followed by another deeper one, an enchantment with "deepest silence"…the consequence is caritas—relief and redemption by love, love for the lost child screaming for its mother, and then for a beloved, unobtainable Sara sleeping in the next vale by.

I want to conclude with a contemporary poem—though *I* realize that what I mean by the word "contemporary" can seem far-fetched in this unaccountable 2023. But Frank O'Hara, by grace of his unfailing energy, and by grace of the genuine hagiography that has embraced him since his tragic early death is, to my mind, a permanent contemporary. And the poet who ends one of his finest poems—"Steps"—with this ecstatic prayer—

Oh god it's wonderful
To get out of bed
And drink too much coffee
And smoke too many cigarettes
And love you so much

surely knew how to make the most of the supernatural's gorgeous distraction. I think of O'Hara's most famous poem, "The Day Lady Died"…(read the poem through in its entirety)

All the way up to the final line of its penultimate stanza, "The Day Lady Died" looks to be simply one of the many "I do this/I do that" poems O'Hara effloresced in his hectic city life. But then "The New York post with her face on it" distracts him out of his moment and out of his day's lightsome itinerary. He is transported to an elsewhere and an otherwhence—a night at the 5 SPOT where the whispered song of Billie Holliday takes his and everyone's breath away…the poem literally comes to the end of itself and of its words, expiring in the wordless contemplation that is the ideal destination of all prayer—pure contemplation…unfading enchantment. Showing the way, **all** the way, O'Hara, like that other great Catholic poet, Dante, is forever a step ahead of you and me.

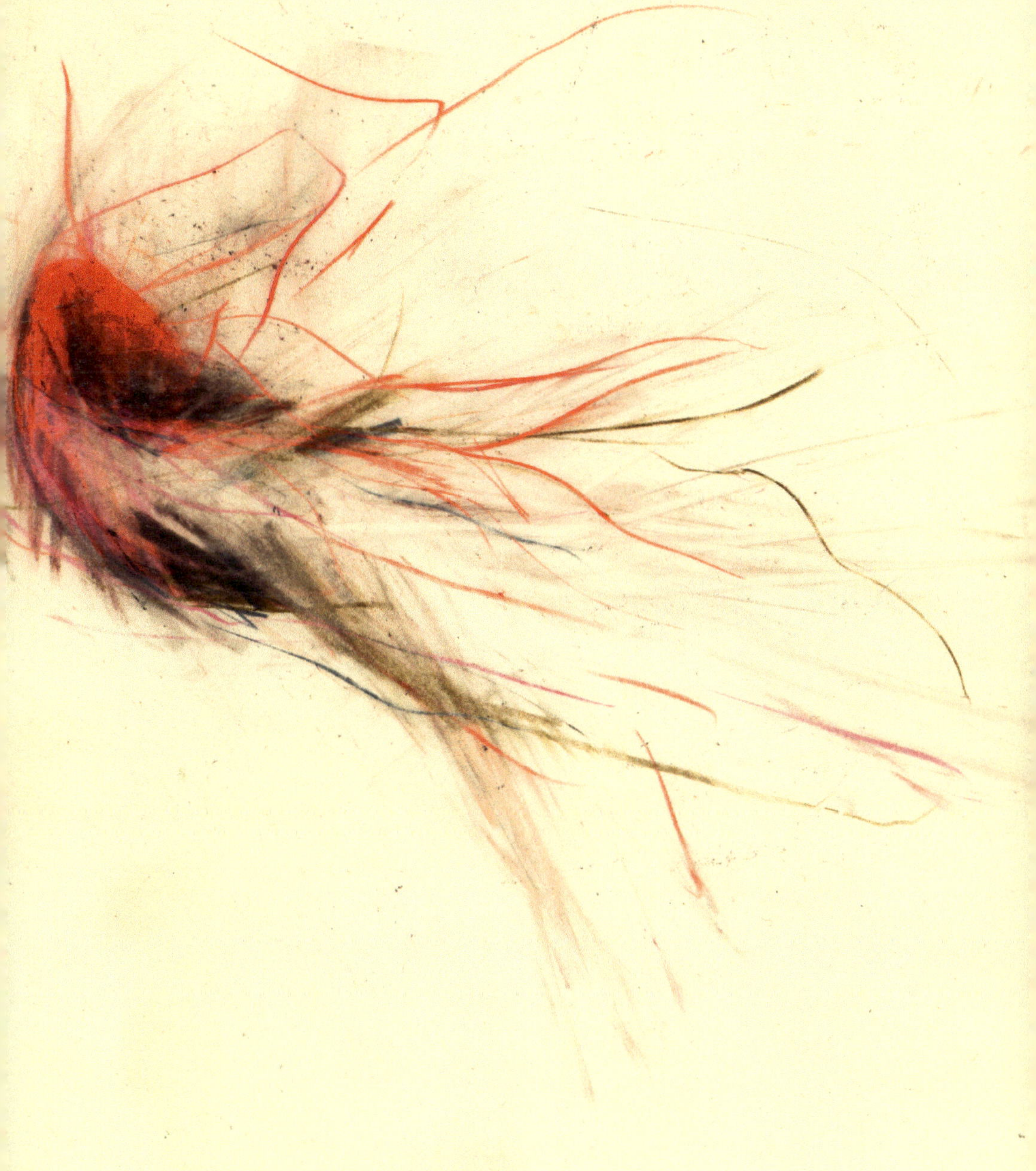

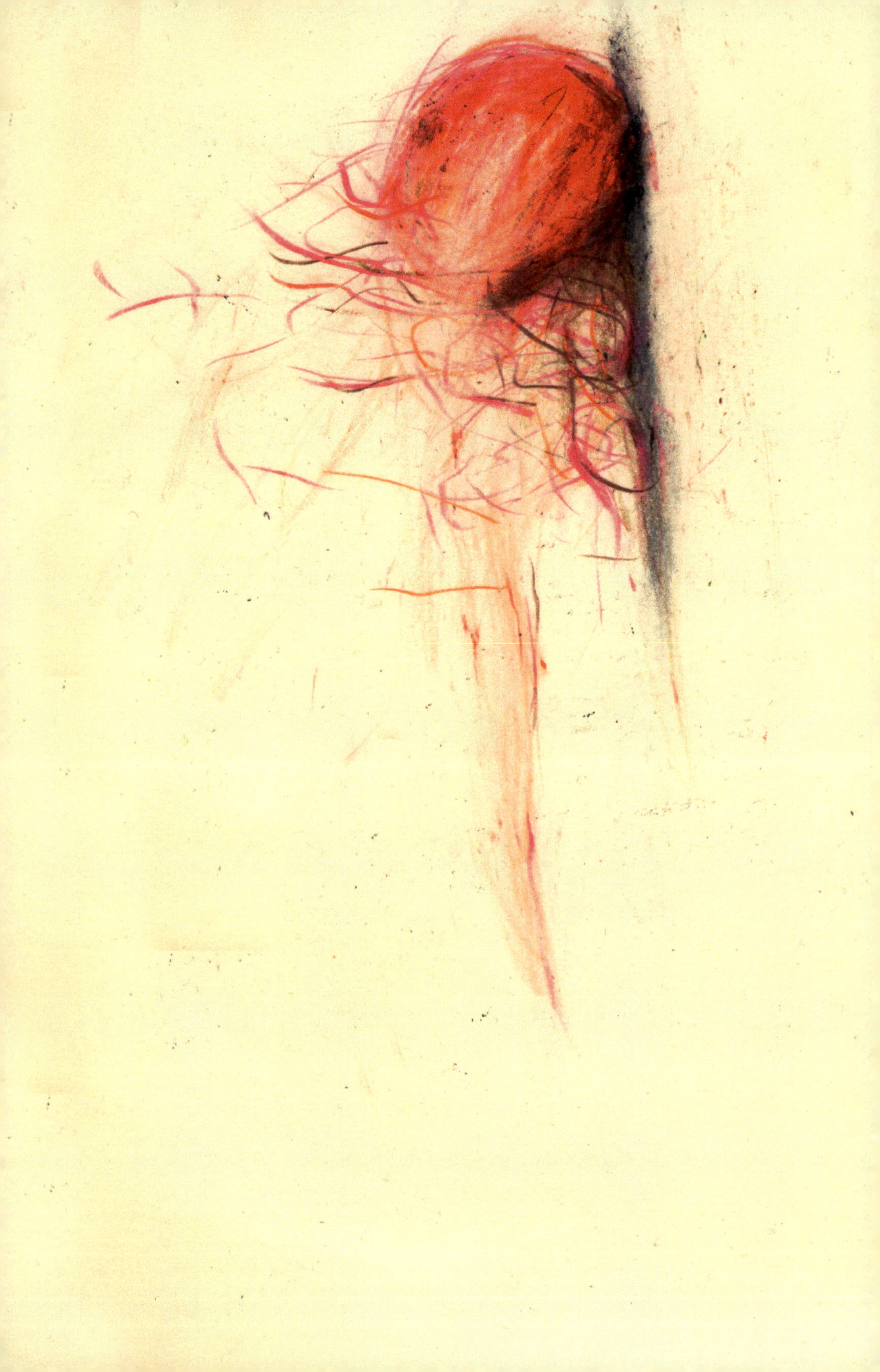

Rooms

Amanda Gunn
Editor

The seven poets whose work is presented here invite us to visit rooms of all kinds, asking of these interiors: what light do they let in or keep out, what peoples them, what foundations are they built upon? Some of the rooms are thickly packed with the tools of living; or, as with Isabel Duarte-Gray's "Jeannie," with rich voices that expand to fill the space. Some rooms, like those featured in Carolina Hotchandani's "The Burning," shift and narrow disorientingly from living spaces to sites of burial. Some rooms are spare and capacious. Some rooms offer comfort. Others offer delicious escape, the privacy to behave as the subject pleases. Others function like traps or as deep-dark holes for secrets. Here are shops, hotels, armories. Hospital rooms populated by the dying and the watchful. Rooms that travel the city (buses). Sodden graves—subterranean rooms that remain painfully still. Some rooms operate multiply like the chambers of a heart. No matter their precise physical location, the speakers of these poems gaze forward and backward, reckoning with the rooms of memory and imagination.

As I "read the room," I want to extend beyond thematic concerns to consider, too, the formal strategies of these seven poets, to observe how each poet negotiates the white room of the page as well as the smaller room of the stanza, the poem's major unit. (Note that "stanza" is a word borrowed from the Italian meaning "room.") I invite you to notice the sensual and undulating stanzas of Richie Hofmann's "Maze"; the sprawling, audaciously long-limbed stanzas of Jay Gao's "Plan(e)t Cluster" that bounce off the limites of the page, the carefully controlled couplets of Lauren Winchester's "Overwinter" that keep pace like icy and repetitive winter days. And, too, the barely contained extended quatrains and tercets of Paul Tran's "Into This Flame I Step and Enter That Dusk" that take their time, moving us from space to space and from register to register. And finally, we leave you with the remarkable single stanza of Eileen G'Sell's "*Close* (2022)," a film-ekphrasis that makes a sinister playroom of the poem, modulating and constricting as its lines carefully but relentlessly close down on two boys (the poem's subject) as well as the reader.

What does it mean to inhabit a room? What-all can a room contain?

Jeannie

Isabel Duarte-Gray

Poison flowers have the tenderest names,
the angel's trumpet and the foxglove, both,
and I can't help wondering, is this why they never
see us coming? I prefer the total picture
of estate sales to the modest practicality of yardsales,
which exchange only novelties for the means to buy novelties.

I only buy the reddest glassware.
Ruby blown, cut like diamond, spraying
the wall in arterial light,
in the long low afternoon, a row of eaten hearts,
fair warning. The man I married
married manhood first, tousled curls
still soft and gold, before they too
boiled red.

I like to think, since my mother taught me
to light fresh cigarettes with the embers of the old,
I carry some of her fire here,
on either side of my heart.
Each new breath hurts.
Each new breath replaces an old ache.

Once, breaking ground
for a stand of hollyhocks,
I found a cache of disarticulated
cats, buried shallow, only bones and leather.
And the little white teeth, like points on
a crescent moon. My son's work, maybe.
Best refill the hole, pat flat the dirt, forget.

Maze

Richie Hofmann

The pool-water clings
to his skin.
A techno remix coming in

and out. My mouth fills
with water. I think
of my swimming lessons

in Munich
in another century.
Frau Instructor,

her gruesome armpit.
She points wildly
into the lap lane, yells to go faster.

The smell of chlorine
is the smell of hatred
of the body.

German isn’t scary.
Any language
shouted at you militaristically

sounds a little ugly.
He is rough
in the apartment

and tender outside.
No towel for you.
Dry yourself.

It’s crazy—
you can know
and forget

a whole language.
And here we are,
saying what we feel.

We weren't sentenced
to death
by the government,

priests, or our fathers,
but centuries of hatred
have made us lovers.

Old Masters

I took a bus to the museum. It was a way
of forgetting
where I was, looking at the portraits,
sitters unindividuated
except for their costumes.
I was in a big city.
Winter was stripping
the landscape. My heart and my body
felt so distant, wanting to give themselves
to different versions
of a life. In a guard room:
preserved weapons,
chains, door-hinges,
and large dislodged gates.
Even as I rushed out through the hall of masters,

the paintings observed
my relative happiness.
I returned to my apartment,
where a cat with bruised eyes was making a home in the courtyard.

The Burning

Carolina Hotchandani

I can't gather the events of that day
or place them in a sequence.
Who spoke first, second, who told
the funeral home director no thanks.

The scent of air freshener
saturates that room where memory hangs
like a fake-flower spray over the pink carpet.

I remember the walk-in closet
whose door the director opened:
built-in shelves displayed rows of empty vases.
They weren't for flowers, I learned,
as he asked which urn we cared to purchase.

Eyeing $500 price tags, we must have looked stunned.
You can buy or choose to rent, he told us then.

We rented our apartment at that time—
the landlord collecting a couple
thousand each month.
I don't recall what we earned.

I remember I walked out of that
walk-in closet then.

Turned away as I thought
of my father burning.
The ashes. An urn.
The floral spray to hide
another scent. Our skin—
our hide.

In the room where I escaped
I thought of the urn
you could rent—

a clay vessel fired
in a kiln to frame
a person like a body.
Whose rent you never pay.
Whose rooms you never own.

Plan(e)t = Cluster

Jay Gao

Your (pl.) bodies sleepwalk the hotel car park like glass mayflies
In the absence of traceable rooms, a rogue twist of Japanese knotweed transforms into your (pl.) overworked night receptionist
You (pl.) tell her: We paused our breathing for so long, interrupted our singing, ever since the delayed plane landed at the minor airport, and that
        hostile march to each successive replacement bus, it only seemed to extend the insistence of this present
You (pl.) complain: It was as if we had been living underwater for centuries, resisting tidal forces, grazing on the sea-floor, insensate, dead to the
        world, asleep, secreting dreams, making do, forgetting love
You (pl.) scream at her: We, as a cluster of objects, refuse to be redistributed
Into her perfumed face: Wherever we love to dream intensely
Her taffeta green skin rustles. Summons a late snack
Your (pl.) new teeth were humming, grown overnight on the plane, as sharp as rose thorns
What lay buried underneath each second of this stopover, waiting for your (pl.) bodies to drop their peaty chunks of armour
The receptionist shook herself, cried, absorbed light, whistled, threatened to pull all cloth, in one motion, away from the spare

edges of the
evening, she could sing in her native tongue too, and shed all her fur, and grieved like hardened honey
She was sorry to inform you (pl.) of an earlier emergency. Flesh caught in the ice machine
Behind your (pl.) backs, the hotel staff swiftly locked away all of their advertised facilities
And whilst there were signs of children—a kid's menu, the option to add a cot to a room at an extra price, a jungle gym—children were nowhere
to be seen
Waiting there, at the threshold of that reception, the stale metallic air tripping over its own amble, you hear the pulse of a distant forest flooded
by electronic music, you hear it swell and swell and
You (pl.) argued about inadequate compensation, meagre meal vouchers, the poor light, invasive species, lost time, the threat of petrified unrest,
the question of limbo, thread count
You could imagine how that music might spill over into a series of worsening cruelties
Like a wave. Today turned into tomorrow; clock hands gossiped for a nimble moment before repelling
Again, you (pl.) were like trees racing towards the product of a translation
And all your (pl.) bodies were tinted with a tinny aura that becomes augmented the longer one spends in the air, as if it were a secret filter, or an
old way of mastering alloy or administering the atmosphere
You (pl.) imagine your bodies tracing this travel in reverse
You (pl.) onlookers

Earlier, you made this conservation that you (pl.) were like glass-people; in reality, you (pl.) were as warm as softened plastic
Volant material cooking in a site about to be erased
All night, handling over documents like paper machines, threatening bad reviews, demanding keys and their tongue-sized chains, polishing
        rusting optic nerves, becoming wooden, flesh, then wood again
You were afraid of being too involved in the bedlam of the negotiations yet still desired a share in the night's bounty
Because even with all those strangers, and their raised voices, through that thick onslaught of hospitality, through all the complimentary
        chocolates, your restless spirit called out
Lured by the invisible names of places your (pl.) map refused to load
No data. You (pl.) occupied the night like an alien organism, like a guest whose invitation into this country risked being rescinded the more
        demands you (pl.) uttered
You (pl.) were waiting for somebody to be knocked over, for a bell to be thrown, for a hand to come down on the receptionist's wooden desk, to
        make contact, embrace, stroke oily screens, caress, then go to sleep
Even now, in this state within state, you were constantly anticipating the violence you did not want to be a part of
Yet cannot help but summon forth. Shouting for a dog to return through the thicket
You (pl.) were garden statues helplessly watching nearby statues be toppled
Your (pl.) bodies were in the commons, always on the house
And it really did feel like a lifetime ago when you (pl.) travelled through those air-locked doors, then the bridge doors, the security

doors, the
    closing doors, the doors at customs asking whether you (pl.) had anything to declare, then the doors of the lift, the sliding doors, the door
    to the bus, the revolving hotel doors that kept jamming, the broken door, the doors of the stairwell, then the door to your bedroom, and
    then the door you struggled, most, to fit your concepts through, the door that was a window
Hospitable for the night air to take it all in
To take leave of the field; boomeranging yourself towards that precipice of no return
The instance is reversible
Poor receptionist, in the morning, thirsty, decides to soak in a long bath, to spread herself around slow shade, to obliterate the sky, to kiss her
    boyfriend as he leaves for work, masturbates, encourages fire, feeds her money tree, sleeps for a billion years, and forages through the
    specks of history in order to evolve a perfect toxin you (pl.)—the living world—have never seen before

Overwinter

Lauren Winchester

The festering bulb of the sun
gives up—overripe, sinking,

gone for the season.
The cold sends a stinkbug

crawling along the slick
ceramic bathroom tiles.

There are no tomatoes
to sink his stylets into,

no fluid to drain from a peach.
The stinkbug and I, we survive

this spoiling world together.
We will overwinter

in crevices, dormant
and abstaining, weathering

hostile winds
in fleece and plaster,

waiting for the clouds to stitch
themselves back together.

What we've been given
to thrive is used against us

in its turn, so I have no intention
of flinging him, helpless,

into the snow. Bending close,
I consider instead

his marmorated shield,
the glory of his being,

his waving,
white ringed antennae.

Ensure

She misremembered the name
of his health drink, the daily liquid

that was his only nourishment. She was occupied
with their states of mind: his wishing to die,

her helplessness. She sat by his bed
reading the Book of Job, John's gospel,

and stacks of medical pamphlets.
When the nurses came by for mealtime,

she'd remind them:
He prefers the Vanilla Endure.

Into This Flame I Step and Enter That Dusk

Paul Tran

Fleeting, slipping like my fingers from yours
While asleep in your arms, a wave you couldn't hold back. Outside time
I enter that blue bedroom, blue sheets we darkened
Like an exit wound. Shoulders against spine, we were two pages ages of agony sealed

In an illuminated manuscript unread until now
With a carnation tucked inside: crimson crown, concentric ring of flames
For our mothers escaping their mothers to wait for another dawn
At the disco or, released from fear, clutching a porcelain statue of Ngai Quan The Am Bo Tat

As the bodhisattvas blazed. I enter that unsettled dusk on Phan Dinh Phung, that club
Pulsing. Wasn't our freedoms tied like vicious tongues
When you turned me to face you. I face you, truest north, and that past

Reaped, sown by death, brought within an inch of it. From that inch of our lives
We made this bygone decade adrift at sea, finding a way
By starlight. You reach. You search. You surge, returning to me

That eclipsed hour the first man I loved stole sloppily, sliding open that shower door
Hand on glass crushed skull soap swirling drain
Psyche hoping to outrun fate. We made our own, on our own. We exceeded
Our expectations, depleted. I was less

With you. I was more. Unexpected, in the City of Angeles snow draped torched valleys
Like that veil my mother never wore. You tore me
And rinsed quickly to resume your real life, your heart cleaved. The secret we kept
Withered, remains because left. I'm here. I'm stitching the hole I found in your right sock.

In the furnace, the fire you started endures. I enter this immortal pyre
As I step into the amber towel you used to wipe your cum from my bruised lips.
All night I could almost taste you. Did you know that

Oak takes the longest to burn, burn out? Kindling, unkind and unforgiving, into smoke
I step as a girl must've from that door to greet that angel delivering
A message from the future. I will not be overshadowed.

Tina Turner In Paris

Eileen G'Sell

No need to touch in order to grasp
fifty and floating off the Eiffel

muse to Alaia, Lindbergh, body of
music three decades strong, gold

beaded swagger, velvet strut, eye full
of bicep flexed for the sky

overcast and underslept, muse to
her own indefatigable self, hemmed

in tight cotton, brow to the sun,
she swapped her passport for another

country that loved her better, not
because it understood her

but because it didn't try to
exhaust the ways a woman can

be touched in order to touch
her country, of course, has all but forgot

Close (2022)

Two boys sprint through a pink field, elbows and knees spearing the air.
Two boys through a field of knees, the air pinking their elbows.
Two boys field the pink air, sprinting past elbowed knees.
Two boys spear the pink, fielding knees, air, and elbows.
Two boys knee the field air, sprinting through the pink.
Two boys elbow the air, sprint through spears.
Two boys air the elbow field.
Two boys pink the air.

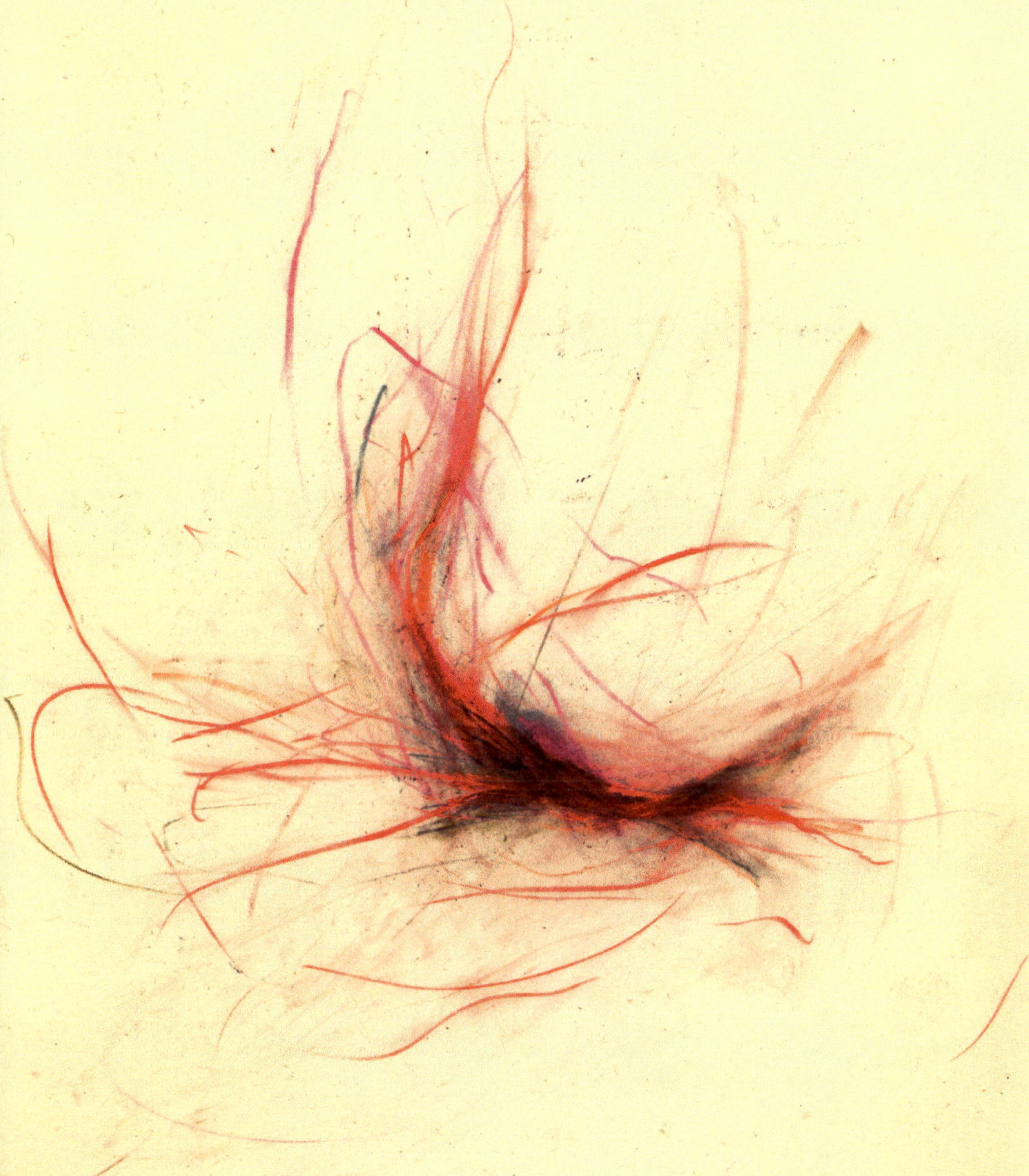

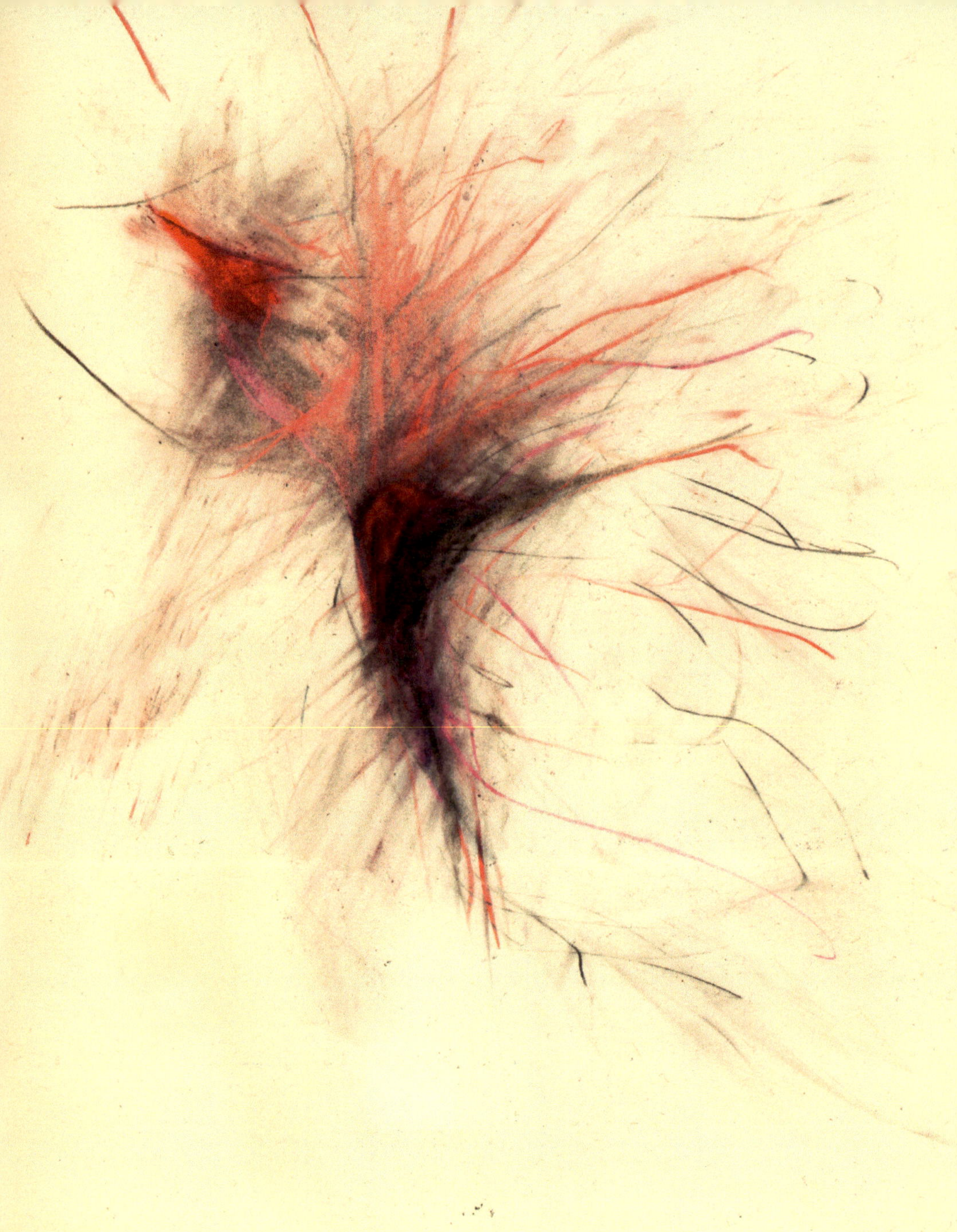

The Book, the Room

Yongyu Chen, Gabby Woo
Editors

We were reading about Mallarmé's dream of The Book—a book among books but which, in its dispersion, its volumes, and through the architectural workings of its structure, would be total in its ability to gather and assemble, a total work. The essay, by Maurice Blanchot, proposed Mallarmé poem *Un coup de dès* to be one realized fragment of The Book which exists otherwise in the form of notes, plans for assistants, calculations of cost. *Un coup de dès* disperses the lines of its poem over swathes of blank space. And, in Blanchot's formulation, it implies

> a completely different book from the book that we have: it makes us feel that what we call 'book' according to the traditional Western usages, in which the gaze identifies the act of comprehension with the repetition of linear back-and-forth motions, is justified to facilitate analytic comprehension.

The very simple geometry of this scheme excited us. The form of the line (the line as unit of the poem & the book) & the logic of linear successiveness (linearity as the logic of reading & thinking)—will they not open onto the affordances of space?

In the meantime the ferry which was taking us across the Tsugaru Strait, carrying us north from the northern tip of Honshu, the main island of Japan, to Hokkaido, docked. This geometry followed us into the 19th-century star fort Goryokaku, which temporarily housed the Republic of Ezo before it was absorbed by the Meiji Empire. Inside that star, we imagined a sequence of shapes: first *the book*, in its linearity; then *the room*, in its breathable, habitable volume; then *the star*, convex, volatile, implosive. The original title of this folio *The Book, the Room, the Star* insists on this further stage of explosiveness; *The Book, the Room* focuses, though not without looking forward to the star, on the passage from the book to the room.

The works gathered here—images and texts from artists responding to this idea—were lived with before they were arranged into pages. We set no specific guidelines, only that the materials, once received, would enter our room, be handled, repositioned, documented. The room left its traces: shifting light from the north-facing window, slow accumulation of dust, images peeling up at the corners, paper curling from humidity. The works, too, made their mark on the space, mapping new lines of relation across the walls—some speaking to each other, others silent though side by side. Water darkened in a vase, flowers dried. The book in its linearity, so direct it is almost vertical, surges toward its ending; here, displaced onto the room's horizontal present, it stayed open. The form remained in motion, held the residue of what had passed through it.

The book remembers the room, just as the room reshaped the book. In addition: something lingers. Residues.

Youtube Soundcloud

Scan above QR codes to access audio files for EP ROHO on p.180

the slong-bok. <u>indeterminate inflorescence</u>

4. when writing poetry, the words must always be separated from the self. otherwise, the words become oppressed by the brain.

12. to write poetry is to dig a waterway for words. poetry allows words to flow through you. the poet must not force the flow of words but rather watch and wait.

19. you must pluck the poem from yourself as quickly as possible. if you're thinking about the poem, it's already too late. make sure you expel the words faster than you can think about them. don't let your brain interfere. the stronger the poem's rhythm, the weaker its "meaning." a good sign that your brain is going faster than your body.

25. poems written with intent is violence against poetry. you need to rescue language from the brain and make it dance in your body instead. then both you and language will be happy.

45. don't be scared of poetry. write as if you're whispering intimately to yourself or someone next to you. but remember: half of speaking is silence. don't forget, also, that in order to say something, you have to say it through something else.

47. have your body write your poems, not your brain.

71. just write down the thoughts in your head. writing easily is the fastest way through. no need to write dramatic thoughts about the destiny of the human race. there are plenty of such poems already. just write down how many spoons you have in your kitchen.

POEM

SOUND

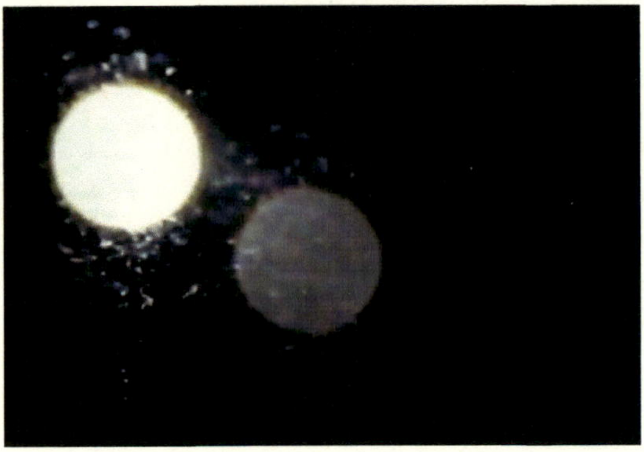

Personally...

I am surprised by the body restarting itself, the mind relieved of total burden and signaling, through the body, that audible relief.[1]

●●●

come in time /twist sugar cone
circling prospect park /a baby, someone's
baby bouncing balls /we look for our pit
sit down at the edge /top of a cold no
ass kissing bench. /wood is better for sleeping
make a pile of all the times /lumbar carries weight
of every felled word

●●●

if I give you no sentence
if I give you nothing
if I have no opinions

●●●

[1] On Loss of Feathers by Ursula von Rydingsvard (Brenda Shaughnessy, Tanya)

Feather says, no one will love me
/opinionless -- I share my thoughts
with him about love   once   /we haven't ever
since..ever since…spoken

●●●

I take a picture by the water   (show it to you - say nothing…)
You, ask me if I am in the water   ("*are you on a boat?*")
I am in the water calling you   (try to hear you in the static)
distance   --(each wave eroding the words)
of our sentences   (… suspending points/)
my love,   (becoming silent…)

My feelings come up for air like a submerged beach
ball : unpeeled orange : porous
wanting in a language of gasping
scream all my opinions into my mouth reaching hands

●●●

O' palms circle your gaping lips open
O' place my fingers in your mouth
O' praise praise praise…
O
O

O'

Hum

We never celebrated the first birthday
we did not know it was your birth
day   when the leaves shed their leaves
we only remembered the change that was
coming forgot all the life of summer
that you lived   painting our rooms
fixing up a new bed for us changing
the furniture we came home
we celebrated the change
my spine still recalls how it was held
in the mattress of the new bed in your
arms in the mattress I quilted of you
we only slept on that mattress for
two months then you transitioned
I wanted to suture myself into the mattress
using the thread of our coiled cord
held in your our blood   forget about all birthdays

during my birth the doctor
thought you were not real

now wait a minute

so you twist open the window
breaking water   libations
pouring down storeys   shouting
a lil bit louder now

I will jump I will jump I jump
jump jump shout shout

hip
hip
hip
a lil bit softer now
jump up and shout now jump up and shout now
jump jump shout
hooray hooray hooray

We never celebrated the first birthday
we did not know it was your birth
day when the leaves shed their leaves
we only remembered the change that was
coming forgot all the life of summer
that you lived painting our rooms
fixing up a new bed for us changing
the furniture we came home
we celebrated the change
my spine still recalls how it was held
in the mattress of the new bed in your
arms in the mattress I quilted of you
we only slept on that mattress for
two months then you transitioned
I wanted to suture myself into the mattress
using the thread of our coiled cord
held in your our blood forget about all birthdays

during my birth the doctor
thought you were not real
now wait a minute
so you twist open the window
breaking water libations
pouring down storeys shouting
a lil bit louder now
I will jump I will jump I jump

jump jump shout shout

hip
hip
hip

a lil bit softer now
jump up and shout now jump up and shout now
jump jump shout
hooray hooray hooray

We never celebrated the first birthday
we did not know it was your birth
day when the leaves shed their leaves
we only remembered the change that was
coming forgot all the life of summer
that you lived painting our rooms
fixing up a new bed for us changing
the furniture we came home
we celebrated the change
my spine still recalls how it was held
in the mattress of the new bed in your
arms in the mattress I quilted of you
we only slept on that mattress for
two months then you transitioned
I wanted to suture myself into the mattress
using the thread of our coiled cord
held in your our blood forget about all birthdays

during my birth the doctor
thought you were not real

now wait a minute
so you twist open the window
breaking water libations
pouring down storeys shouting
a lil bit louder now
I will jump I will jump I jump

jump jump shout shout

hip
hip
hip

a lil bit softer now

jump up and shout now jump up and shout now
jump jump shout
hooray hooray hooray

We never celebrated the first birthday
we did not know it was your birth
day when the leaves shed their leaves
we only remembered the change that was
coming forgot all the life of summer
that you lived painting our rooms
fixing up a new bed for us changing
the furniture we came home
we celebrated the change
my spine still recalls how it was held
in the mattress of the new bed in **your**
arms in the mattress I quilted of you
we only slept on that mattress for
two months then you transitioned
I wanted to suture myself into the mattress
using the thread of our coiled cord
held in your our blood forget about all birthdays

during my birth the doctor
thought you were not real

now wait a minute

so you twist open the window
breaking water libations
pouring down storeys shouting
a lil bit louder now
I will jump I will jump I jump

jump jump shout shout

hip

hip

hip

a lil bit softer now

jump up and shout now jump up and shout now

jump jump shout

hooray hooray hooray

texture on teeth. undefended eyes filling up pink and wet. the sprouting hairs and skin tags and shiny philtrum where oxygen tubes up into the nose and mucous puddles. if my mother were here — she said, hunched over.

coward, hiding in the back stairwell. we loaded my bike into the trunk and drove off into a pillow of night.

in the dream the screaming once it starts does not stop. the anger rises through the body through the head blasts past what was once fontanelle leaves the skull entire. the anger balloons the room right up into the sky. past the ozone. past the exosphere. what are you doing here, chirps the little green guy with three fingers and an eye.

texture of beef. chewing through tendon. gums red and bleeding at the gumline. chewing furiously, no room to swallow. the nutrients outside the bag of the body in a spatter.

sadness a manhole cover. painted over with road salt and age.

they sat in a small circle. anger was a hard and secret knot. if you were my kid, said one to the other, i would cover you in kisses. anger was a hard and sacred knot, the circle of birds in the air flickered, and changed direction.

anger was bunching up in her shoulders, pushing up to her ears. the teacher tapped her throat, the sugar risen in the sap seeped down her neck. anger, bitter syrup, anoint us.

ity of eyes, unlidded. burying the squirm so deep down in her pants. thrust forward choiceless, and yet this was my choice, when i stepped into the circle. nerve run raw through the centre of me. the eyes fixed in their sockets, not quite compassionate. nor watching just for fun.

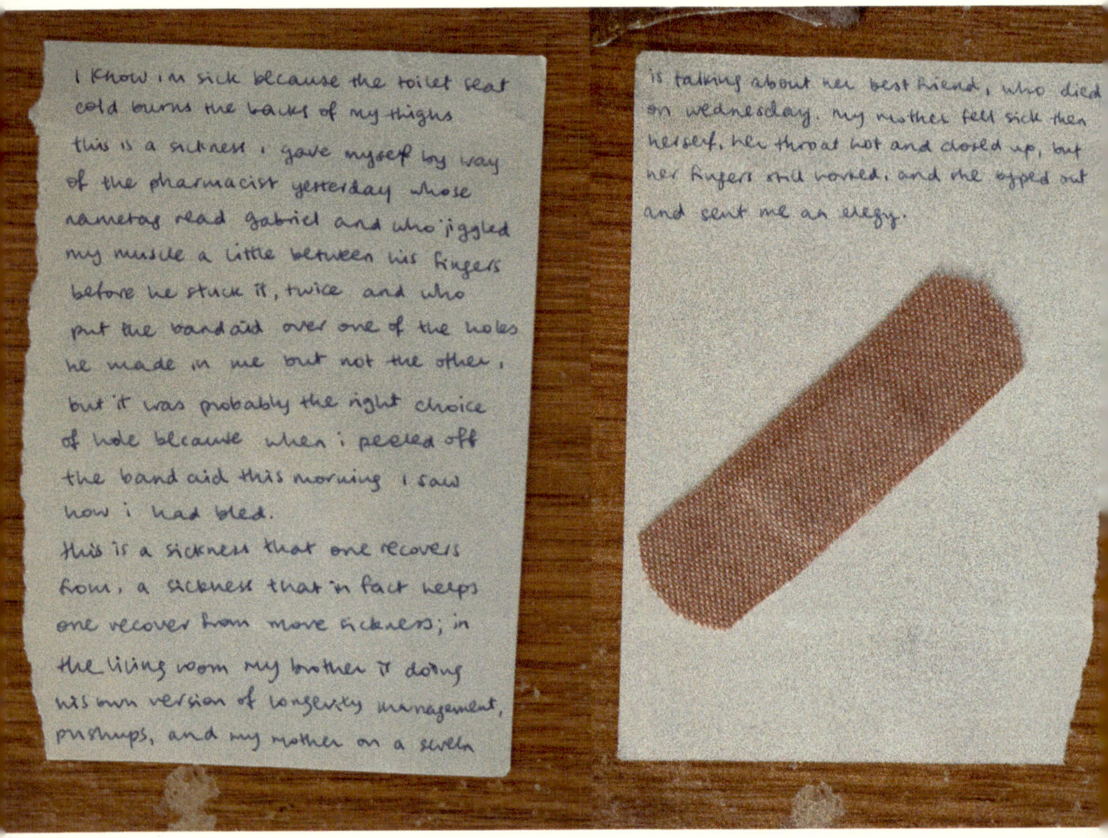
i know i'm sick because the toilet seat
cold burns the backs of my thighs
this is a sickness i gave myself by way
of the pharmacist yesterday whose
nametag read gabriel and who jiggled
my muscle a little between his fingers
before he stuck it, twice and who
put the bandaid over one of the holes
he made in me but not the other,
but it was probably the right choice
of hole because when i peeled off
the band aid this morning i saw
how i had bled.
this is a sickness that one recovers
from, a sickness that in fact keeps
one recover from more sicknesses; in
the living room my brother is doing
his own version of longevity management,
pushups, and my mother on a seveln

is talking about her best friend, who died
on wednesday. my mother fell sick then
herself, her throat hot and closed up, but
her fingers still worked, and she typed out
and sent me an elegy.

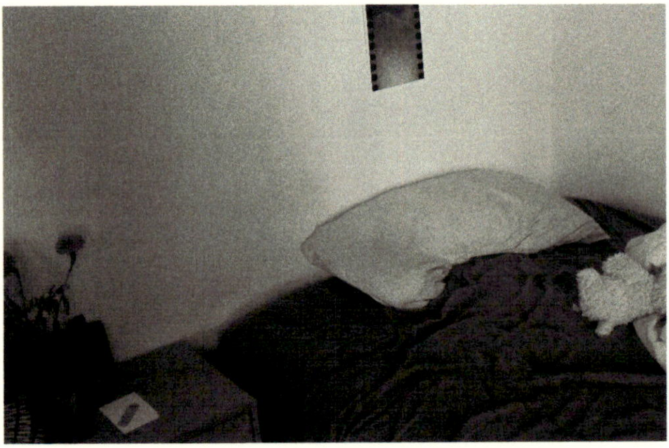

the cat left bite marks in me, little depressions, skin intact. i was going away the next day and felt guilty. maybe this is why i let her bite me, and left my hand in her mouth until she shook her head free of it. or maybe this is why she bit me.

don't think your cat is so sad when you're gone, said my mother-in-law, trying to comfort me. she may be very glad, and throw a party.

my mother-in-law will be at that party, because she is taking the cat in for the more-than-a-month that i'll be away.

i would like my cat to be very, very happy without me.

LIST OF WORKS

p. 171
Lilan Yang, *The Force that Through the Green Fuse Drives the Flower: a forgotten film roll discovered in a Yashica Mat-124G, hidden inside a storage bin, now comes to light*, 2024: 120 Fujifilm Provia 100F, exposed to natural sunlight with plants, 6" x 6".

pp. 172-173, 176, 190, 197
Hogan Seidel, *Objectionable Fruit*, 2024:
multiple exposures, 35mm, processed with an eco developer made of ginkgo tea developer.
pp. 174, 193
Hogan Seidel, *Celluloid Impressions*, 2024:
35mm film processed with an eco developer made from garden weeds and cyanotype.

pp. 175, 191-192, 195-196, 199
Text by Chew Chia Shao Wei

pp. 178-179
Kondo Heller, "Hum" and "Personally" casette recordings, 2024.
p. 180
Kondo Heller, stills from *Intro-Love, Mad Explosive, Hand in Heart* from *E.P. Roho*, 2024:
full videos and the complete EP are accessible on YouTube and Soundcloud via the QR code on p.170,
pp. 181-182, 185-189
Kondo Heller, "Personally" and "Hum"

pp. 177, 183-184, 194
Korey Martin, *Jumping, Beanie Weenie, Feet, Intuition*, 2021-22:
drawing on paper, dimensions variable.

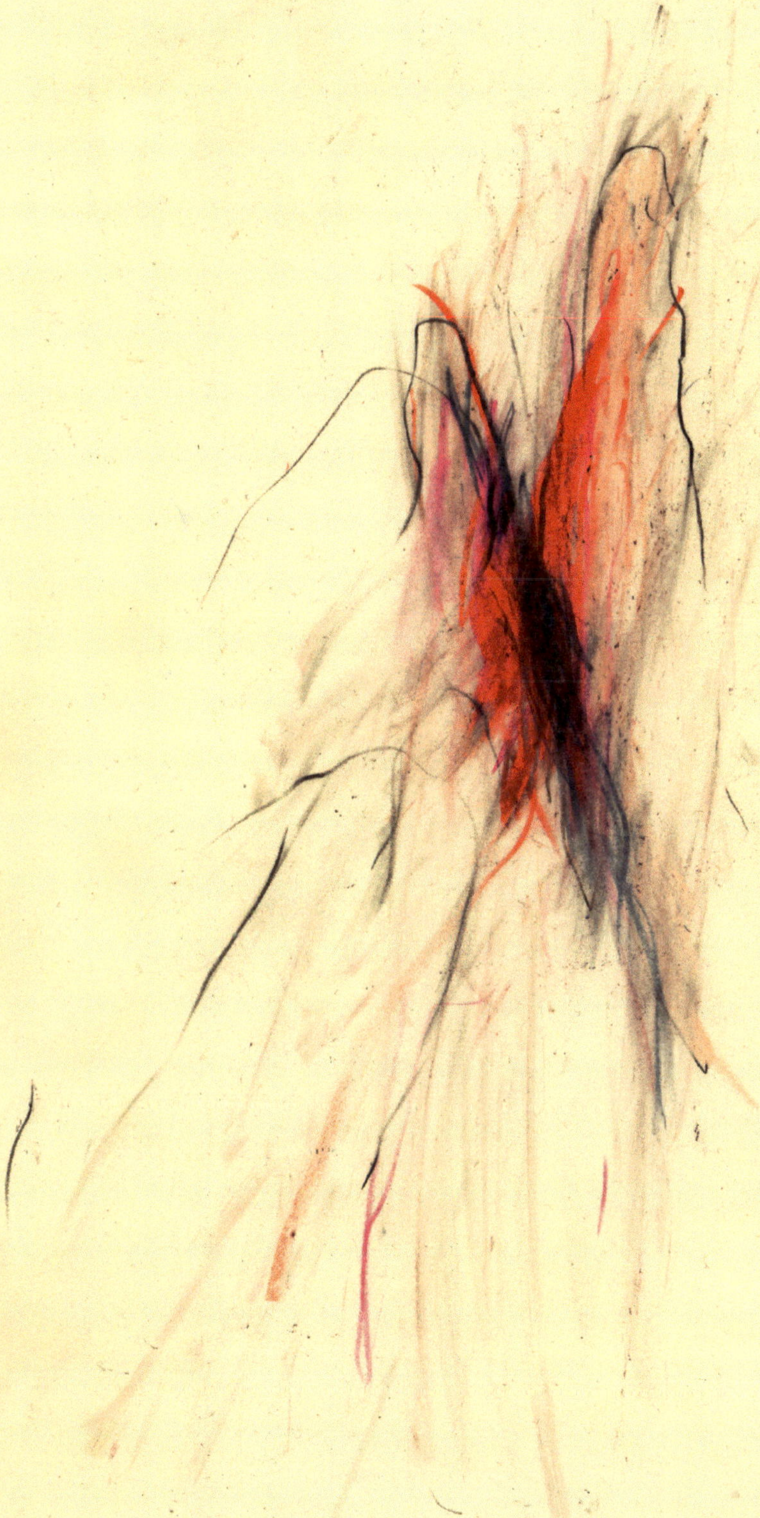

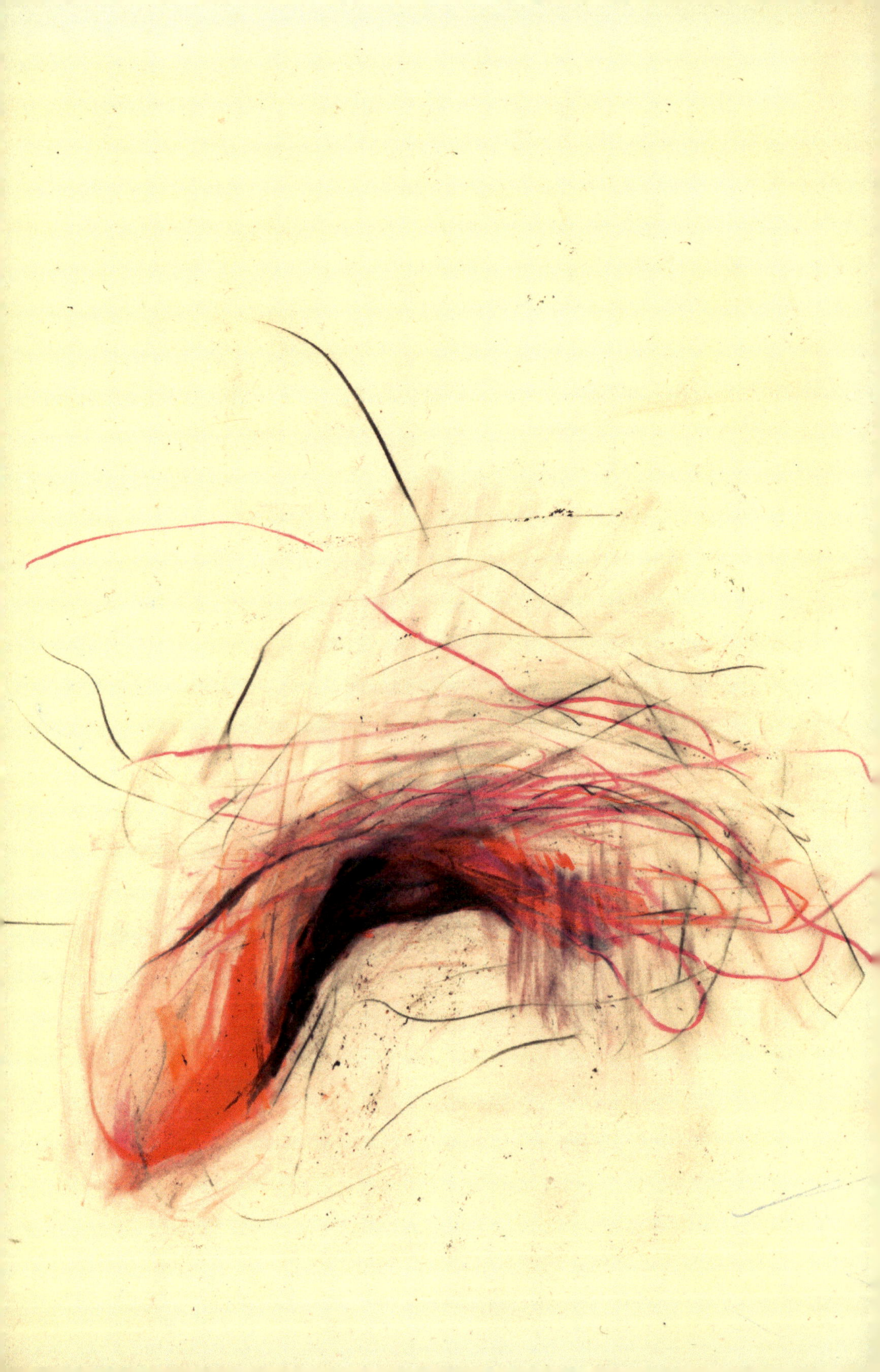

To/for 'nonfiction poetry'

Jessica L. Wilkinson
Editor

> The poet nothing affirmes, and therefore never lyeth. For, as I take it, to lye is to affirme that to be true which is false.
> —Philip Sidney

> Lines of lyric beauty descend from the data clusters.
> —Edward Sanders

> Poetry—amid all its ambiguity and ornamentation—is not only perfectly capable of conveying truth; it can also attain a unique relationship to truth because it implicitly acknowledges and interrogates the limitations of language.
> —Cole Swensen

What is nonfiction poetry? What do you think it is? What do you think it might become? These are some of the questions I pose to people who ask me for answers. Sometimes, I will reel off a few provocations: what might the poetic line do for nonfiction content that the prose sentence cannot? How does the label 'nonfiction' alter your response to this poem? How can a poet transmute fact (into art)? Who will care?

I am queried frequently about this term—or genre—'nonfiction poetry,' because of my founding the literary publication *Rabbit: a journal for nonfiction poetry*, which in 2024 celebrated its 40th issue. The journal itself emerged from a convergence of happenings. One of these was my own intensifying interests as a young poet and poetry scholar. I had become enamoured of the works of American poet Susan Howe; I loved the textual maps and fabrics of her poetry, how each of her long poems seemed to mark a reinvention; a new approach to historical enquiry; a new response to archival research. Howe homes in on the margins of (literary) history, and I was—and am—very much drawn in not only by the gestures of her poems, but by her attempts to move beyond digestible facts and towards a poetic pulse in sync with the subject, the documents, the archival experience. I wrote half a dissertation about Howe's work, how it might constitute a new approach to history writing; the other half of that dissertation—what was to become my first book—was a counterpart creative project, a 'poetic biography.' I became fixated on exploring the ways in which poetic form and play might meet—or preserve the elusiveness of—the character I had chosen (early cinema actress Marion Davies). Fifteen years down the track, I am still exploring the poetic-biographical field and the ways in which poetry can lead through/to a 'life' rather than the other way around.

This interest in Howe and historical/biographical poetry led me naturally to works of other poets such as Jordie Albiston, Mark Nowak, Lyn Hejinian, Muriel Rukeyser, Dennis Cooley, Edward Sanders, C. D. Wright, Ruth Padel, Emily Ballou, Craig Santos Perez, Cole Swensen, Charles Reznikoff, Natalie Harkin, Carolyn Forché, and many more. Indeed, I have dedicated bookshelves for 'biographical poetry' and 'documentary poetry' with subsections such as 'biographies of artists,' 'poetic memoirs, 'YA poetic biographies,' 'geography poems' and 'book-length poems about rivers'! This expansive reading has also urged me towards a deeper consideration of what poetry can 'do' when it collides with nonfiction genres more broadly—biography, history, autobiography, philosophy, literary criticism, science writing, and so on. How can a poet's toolkit expand what is possible to express in nonfiction fields? Can a poem or poem sequence bring embodied feeling into the realm of reportage, or enhance it? How might a poem, presented as 'nonfiction,' shape the poet's approach, and the reader's response?

Rabbit emerged from a curiosity about how other poets might undertake these tasks. But the 'nonfiction poetry' genre label also came about somewhat unexpectedly, as a response to an invitation from colleagues at RMIT University to join a group of creative writer-researchers in the 'nonfictionLab' (in 2014, the group 'expanded' its remit to 'non/fictionLab'). At the time I thought, well, what if *Rabbit* aligned with my own poetic interests and desires in biographical and documentary poetry, of exploring the potential of poetry to intervene in—expand, challenge, play with—nonfiction practices and modes? The co-founders of the research group asked me 'what is nonfiction poetry?' and my response was simply that I would use the journal as a space to find out, a platform for poets across the globe to tell us what it might be or become. With each issue themed—e.g. Geography, Philosophy, Science, Politics, Jazz, Biography, Dance, Lineages, Mutiny, Extinction etc.—poets have been invited to explore what is possible with 'poetry + theme + nonfiction.' It has been a thrilling 13+ years of the journal, with guest editors for each issue exposing our readership to a spectrum of approaches and interpretations.

Invited by *Peripheries* to curate a folio of 'nonfiction poetry,' I in turn invited ten poets, whose sustained work in longform poetry—emerging from archival, documentary, autobiographical research and more—was familiar to me, to submit a small sample of their recent 'nonfiction poetry' or works-in-progress. The poems that I received, and which are gathered here, demonstrate a range of ways in which poets are 'handling' or responding to nonfiction material, finding shape and tone—through language, mark, rhythm, space, gesture, irony, metaphor—to expressively bear the 'weight' of informational content and lived experience. Robert Hass writes in *A Little Book of Form* that 'The poem embodies the energy of the gesture of its making;' as such, we see the poet's commitment reflected in each poem, too.

These are poems that engage and play with biographical, historical, literary and scientific data, archival documents, personal reflection and self-reckoning, philosophical and linguistic contemplation, and speculative imagining. Several of the poems in this series home in on women's experiences, using poetry's capaciousness to reach towards marginal stories and voices. Excerpted from her work-in-progress on the life of nineteenth-century writer and women's rights advocate George Sand (pen name of Amantine Lucile Aurore Dupin de Francueil), Anne M. Carson tests the poem's capacity to hold perspective—Sand's personae—through imaginative inhabitation and quotation. Cassandra Atherton pieces together the fractured moments of six women who experienced the atomic bomb in Hiroshima; she draws on her own interviews with hibakusha and other research (through the Hiroshima Peace Memorial Museum and workshops at Orizuru Tower) to craft small prose poem frames to hold these stories. Shari Kocher's poem is also a piecing together, holding two unconnected women—two wives of male artists—side-by-side to see what sparks bring them out of the shadows. Miriam Wei Wei Lo uses an epistolary haibun to 'converse' with her grandmother, using her grandmother's autograph album as an entry point, a conversation starter.

Other poems confront the wreckages and traumas of the colonial project, drawing on archival and scientific data and other documentation to distil, through the clarity and irony of the poem, how colonial discourse (claiming, naming, owning, dominating) goes hand-in-hand with ecological devastation and species endangerment/extinction. Jeanine Leane stitches together excerpts from the journal entries of William Hay Caldwell, who dissected many platypuses (currently facing localized extinction in Australia) in Queensland in the late nineteenth-century to establish that they laid eggs. From the excitement of Caldwell's perspective, Leane uses the ironic potential of the poem to lay bare Caldwell's settler menace and racism, and to kick into gear the reader's critique. Lauren Russell's focus is on the Eastern cougar, the Caribbean monk seal, and the Mariana fruit bat, three species facing removal from the Endangered Species List due to probable extinction. Her poem enfolds a collective cry—"A screech, a dirge, a requiem, a curse, a crime, a reckoning"—as a revolt against soundless planetary elimination. Robert Sullivan turns the dirge on its head, gliding us through story—from the 'I' to the 'we'—like a *waka* gliding down a river, across oceans, pushing off from 'awkward' singularity and gaining momentum towards the shared "family-weaving-cording-carving...synchronised like a creature who hums hōea rā!"

The final set of poems are entranced by the actions provoked by language; how language extends thought. Anna Jackson's prose poem constellates thought emerging from discrete and disconnected information bites about communications in the nonhuman world, how they might help us to imagine our own way forward. aj carruthers continues this philosophical foray, as he stages spontaneous verse arguments between painting and sculpture, film and television, and poetry and music; these 'Antic Cinquains' are five-line, five-stanza compositions that draw 'antique'—defunct, outdated—words or ideas into their orbit/argument, primarily in service of rhythm. And finally, EJ Baird manipulates the document—here, transcripts of found audio recordings—to carry us into speculative domains, 'hallucinations' or new assemblages of self.

One of the things I love about poetry is how it lies dormant until that moment of irruption/eruption: a reader sets in motion an event that leads to rhythm, feeling, interpretation, breath. A 'nonfiction' poem, then, is not simply news *per se*—not a document, account or narrative based in reality. It is an experience—a happening, and never the same way twice. A nonfiction poem can extend our historical parameters, our speculative futures, our remarkable, ever-emergent present.

Five poems for George Sand

Anne M. Carson

Aurore's first memory

1806, Paris, aged two

Out of the milk and swaddle of babyhood
the tender embrace of infancy

the bundle to bosom clasp
of trust
A fall
a severing

Her body thumps to ground
her head cracks on fireplace granite

slipping from the slackened
forgetting arms of the drunken nursemaid

Her face a horror rictus
her blood redder than the marble mantelpiece

the suck of leeches behind her ears

Out of the blur of childhood
shock awakens the lamp of consciousness

clarity of awareness

A shock set her nervous system ticking
switched her on

Aurore, on self-transformation

1824/5? Nohant

I am on the terrace. It is summer, evening and I am smoking. The nightingales have drawn me out. The children sleep and Casimir is inside, attending to paperwork. He hates me smoking, calls it mannish and why should a wife of his anyway … ? He can be peevish when he's thwarted—or when he drinks. I bite my remonstration back—his absences, his preference for hunting over spending time with me, his many 'indiscretions' ... I had such hopes of us! We exhausted conversation hours ago, ate in strained and awkward silence. More verve in conversation with Marie about menus than with my own mari! Now, outside, enveloped by night, I let my guard down, let myself blur into the warm night air, desperate to escape the trap my marriage has become …

George Sand: poet as plougher

Vowels ploughed into other, opened ground,
Each verse returning like the plough turned round.
—Seamus Heaney, *Glanmore sonnets*

I yoke myself to the oxen
I drag the plough through the pain

The blade bites the page deep
I plough the obdurate plain

I turn my wounds over
Plough them back into the earth

Myself I drive the hardest
The page yields up its worth

The sods break nicely open
The plough turns at verse-edge

The earth turns under my tillage
Words plough into the furrow of the page.

The Mayor of Nohant-Vic makes an announcement
1876, Nohant-Vic

Baroness Amantine Aurore Lucile Dupin
resident of the commune of Nohant-Vic
the Department of Indre
widow of Baron Françoise Casimir Dudevant
daughter of Maurice Dupin de Francueil
deceased June 8th 1876, aged 71.
No known profession.
(*Nom de plume*: **George Sand**).[1]

George Sand makes a prediction

I believe fifty years from now
I'll be completely forgotten and
perhaps harshly understood.[2]

[1] M.M., "George Sand's unfinished legacy" on *The Economist*, 7/26/18. https://www.economist.com/prospero/2018/07/26/george-sands-unfinished-legacy.
[2] Sand quoted in Dickenson, *George Sand: A Brave Man – The Most Womanly Woman.* Oxford: Berg Publishers Limited, 1988, 142.

Wide Silence, Hiroshima: A Prose Poetry Sequence

Cassandra Atherton

i Sadako Kurihara

She was four kilometres north of the epicentre. She writes about it, but censorship destroys her lines with thick black boxes and overscoring. Her notebooks from high school are filled with haiku; now new poems rupture traditional forms. The blank page is ground zero. She sees beyond its edges and past Hiroshima. Her testimony burns. She is midwife at the birth of the atomic bomb. Her pen is heavy. In free verse, she reminds us—we are sitting on black eggs.

ii Tetsuko Shakuda

Hiroshima's resurrection begins hours after it is mostly obliterated. While the ashes are still hot, she gets the tram moving again. Injured people stare through open windows at the city's seething remains. The city is buried under bodies and wreckage. She is only fourteen, she has an upset stomach and feels weirdly light-headed. There is a wide silence, apart from the tram clattering along the realigned tracks. She is still haunted by the swarms of flies, imagines them feasting on distended bodies clinging to the tram's roof. The city is burning junkyard and desert but the tram's bell rings.

iii Midori Naka

In the soft morning light, she makes tea for the Sakura-tai troupe. The curve of the teapot's handle presses on her palm as she recites her lines: 'Life is no more than the repeated fulfilling of a permanent desire.' The small white cups are crackle glazed, their hairlines like silver scars. Waking naked under rubble, she remembers a blast, as if a hot water boiler exploded. Silence. Under the stripe of bright light, her white blood cells deplete. Leaving behind the smouldering charcoal of Hiroshima, she returns by train to Tokyo. Days later, her remains are floating in two glass jars. Wet archive, the wrinkled and brown tissue looks like decomposing plums. I think of cherry blossom petals bruised underfoot or the unripe fruit in bottles of plum wine.

iv Hatsuyo Nakamura

She washes the rice until cloudy water runs clear. While she reads the Hiroshima *Chugoku*, the grains bloat as they soak—the fatter they become, the fluffier the rice will be. There are more Japanese words for *rice* than *love*, but what she feels for her children won't be spoken. As the rice cooks, she turns it from the bottom. The children are still on their bedrolls, tired from the air raids. She hands them some peanuts and prepares for piecework on her husband's Sankoku sewing machine. She sees the seven words from the telegram in the bubbles bursting through the water in the boiling pot: 'Isawa died an honorable death at Singapore.' White flash in the window. They are buried. She crawls out from under tiles and broken beams, following the small voices to their entombment. As she digs them out from under the wreckage, her five-year old asks, 'Why is it already night?' 'Why did our house fall down?' In the Spring, she clears a space to plant a vegetable garden, they eat off plates scavenged from the debris. The sewing machine rusts in the water tank.

v Mitsuno Ochi

The shape of a woman with a walking stick is scorched onto the stairs at the entrance of the Sumimoto bank. Waiting for the bank to open, she absorbed the boiling light, blocking heat from the stone. Nuclear daguerreotype, her shadow is stone-blasted and, like an old crime scene, the body is outlined in chalk. Everything around her is bleached. Someone claims the shadow as her mother. Precious relic, she is every woman who disappeared.

vi Emiko Okada

In the bloodied sky, she sees Hiroshima burning. As sunset cloaks buildings in crimson, their windows are the yellow eyes of victims. She hides in shadows and prays to the wind to change direction. The backs of her legs are red-hot but now she cannot stop running. Flash sickness confirms her exposure. She has no burns or keloids but her gums start bleeding and her hair comes away in handfuls. Decades later, she shows students the relics, tells them when the sun is scarlet in the northwest, she hears her sister say, 'I will see you later'. She never returns.

Documentary Poem with Bush Branch Handrails

Shari Kocher

after Wendy Whiteley's *Secret Garden* (2015) and Anna Funder's *Wifedom* (2023)

for Gayle de Angelis

1. The paint bubbles in some places like a seedpod under fire.

2. *It's hard to live in someone's blind spot.*[1]

3. It began on a precipitous dump covered in lantana on a piece of blown-up Gamaragal country on the foreshore of what is now known as Lavender Bay. NSW Railways still own it.

4. *Being a full-time muse to an artist like Brett was a job that few women could survive. I didn't survive it in the end…* [2]

5. The same can be said for Eileen: alone, overworked, in poor health, Orwell absent. On a surgeon's table after the Blitz in what was supposed to be a routine hysterectomy. It took some time to track Orwell down.[3]

6. 'The land was a very depressing site with a big open drain before Wendy started.' [4]

[1] Anna Funder, *Wifedom*
[2] All lines in italics are in Wendy Whiteley's voice, as recorded in the interview with Janet Hawley in *Wendy Whiteley and the Secret Garden*, Lantern, Penguin Books, 2015. All other speech quotes are drawn from the same book, unless otherwise indicated.
[3] See Funder, *Wifedom*
[4] Neighbour, Peter Kingston, in *Wendy Whiteley and the Secret Garden*

7. Neither Orwell nor the surgeon attended the inquest.

8. *Brett used to paint what was going on around him, so often it was the room as I'd arranged it, with me as the model—in the bath, on a sofa, or wherever. Not that I was lying around naked on one hip all the time!*

9. In Brett's paintings, the harbour sky and ocean roar their royals in blue seen through the balcony that overlooks the original slagheap he didn't paint.

10. *One day I was so fed up with Brett's painting things and spilled paint invading the entire flat, that I cleaned it all up then drew a chalk line on the floor and announced, "None of your stuff is crossing this line!" Of course, it did.*

11. Of course, the hills are older.

12. *I was endeavouring to clear a dense mound of feral brambles and tangled vines below the big Moreton Bay fig tree when I fell off a steep rock cliff. I kept sliding down, being ripped by thorns, then I landed in broken glass and rat-infested rubbish.*

13. 'It just happened metre by metre.' [5]

14. Stuff Wendy and her hired hands hauled out of the illicit dump in those early days included: old bottles, rusty paint tins, smelly bags of rubbish; noxious weeds; rotting mattresses, defunct fridges, rusty gutters, iron sheeting; car bonnets; an ice chest, etcetera.

15. *No-one's ever tried to stop me, so I didn't stop.*

16. 'Right from the start, I could see that Wendy was trying to forget. Even now, for Wendy it's still the best way to forget. If something is not going right for her, she's angry, sad or wants to forget something, straight

[5] Corrado, one of Wendy's trusted long term hired hands, in *Wendy Whiteley and the Secret Garden*

into the garden she goes and starts working hard. She won't come back to the house for lunch, phone calls, nothing.' [6]

17. *I'm sure the old deros who sometimes went to sleep in burrows they' d hollowed under the lantana, drinking their bottles of metho, thought the mad bag lady was madder than they were.*

18. No amount of pouncing or doublethink on Orwell's part could hide the rawness of the deal. What he wanted after Eileen's death was a wife to cook and clean for him (not a hired help he would have to pay) but someone to type his manuscripts, manage his legacy, attend to the adopted infant son he hadn't had time to care for yet, since Eileen had done all that, and oh yes, the successful applicant would be prepared to have sex with him when he wanted, if, as he said, she didn't find him too ugly. Ah, that's better, they reported him saying as he rolled off them. A strange two-minute fumble that was supposed to convince. [7]

19. Wendy chose Arkie.

20. Wendy also chose the guerrilla garden on Gamaragal land she didn't own.

21. *I treated the garden like a giant painting, structuring, planting, then adding more layers of planting, pruning, editing, moving things round until it pleased my eye.*

22. One fine, Sydney-blue day, Arkie was diagnosed with a sudden, aggressive adrenal cancer. *We tried everything in the next three months, and right until the day she died we couldn't believe this was happening; we kept hoping for the miracle cure. But my daughter was gone, only thirty-seven years old. Beautiful little Ark left us.*

23. Two very old, very large fig trees stand like sentinels at either end of the secret garden.

---

[6] Ibid.

[7] Funder, *Wifedom*

24. *The railway workers and passers-by thought I was this mad bag lady in old clothes with a rag wrapped round her head. Covered in mud, down there with her buckets, spades and rake, delving in the mess.*

25. Found objects now mounted on plinths or racks throughout the garden include:

a hand operated railway points changer; a porcelain bathroom basin; a rusty metal wheelbarrow; one richly rusted tennis court line-marker; an old-fashioned scooter and tricycle; cast-iron clogs for two left feet; a wishing well.

26. You don't really start again.

27. Formal statuary, placed like plantings that have taken root, include:

Brett Whiteley's carved wooden figure, *Nude* 1962 mounted on a rusted base behind the ancient sandstone cliff face, now exposed, where the railways blasted and then filled in the bay;

Margaret Olley's 'bad tempered little putti', a chubby winged cupid sitting on three swans with a frog and a tortoise on the cupid's plump knee, out of the heads of which water spays—also from the shell in putti's hand;

a life-sized serpent carved from stone, glimpsed in a whisk of mulch.

28. *Rather like the composition in many of Brett's paintings, I prefer large areas of tranquillity with an intensity of interesting things happening around the edges.*

29. You have to know the garden is there. The fig trees help you find it.

30. 'Your eyes notice things with a new clarity…like the glorious shapes in a flower's face, or a bug you haven't seen before. Suddenly you are looking at this amazing-coloured bug on a leaf, and the bug is looking at

you, and you're thinking "Hello new bug, what sort of a bug are you?"'[8]

31. The secret is seedpod-shaped in circumference.

32. 'Things in the rear-view mirror are closer than they appear.'[9]

[8] Gary, a family friend in *Wendy Whiteley and the Secret Garden*.
[9] Funder, *Wifedom*

Entry 7: Poetic Conversations with My Grandmother

Miriam Wei Wei Lo

Preface to the poem

I did not ask for my grandmother's autograph album.

My aunt gave it to me when I started to show an interest in my grandmother's life. This aunt (a practical woman with a solid build who took after the Hakka side) lived in the house my grandmother died in, just off Jalan Nanas in Kuching, Sarawak. I packed the album up with some other family archives and it sat in the bottom of a box through many moves. I had three children of my own and was living in Wooditchup/Margaret River, Western Australia, in the 2010s, before I took a closer look at it. It started to draw me in.

There are not many detailed representations of the lives of Chinese diaspora women, at least not in the public sphere (Martínez & Bagnall, 2021). Even Chinese history museums tend to be dominated by the stories of prominent men (Lo, 2023). As I enter into a poetic conversation with my Cantonese grandmother's autograph album, I am conscious of this gap in representation. This project undertakes feminist redress by poetic address. In doing so, it joins a movement in Australia that includes similar work by writers such as Jessica Wilkinson, Anne M Carson, Elfie Shiosaki, and Grace Yee. We fill this gap of representation with scholarship and poetry.

Autograph albums themselves are a genre with their own history (Nickson, 1970; Brewer, 2010; Jeffries 2021). The literature on nineteenth century English-language autograph albums is considerable, "especially among scholars of women's history and material culture" (Black, 2020, 41). In comparison, English-language scholarly literature on Chinese diaspora autograph albums is scant. Another gap.

As I seek to fill gaps, this is the nonfiction territory I find myself in: translating archival material, in this case autograph entries, from Chinese to English; then writing poetic responses to what I find.

References:

Black, J. M. (2020). "Autograph Albums and the Commercialization of Memory in the United States." in K. H. Grenier & A. R. Mushal (Eds.), *Cultures of Memory in the Nineteenth Century: Consuming Commemoration* (39–60). Springer International Publishing.

Brewer, S. (2010). *Collecting Autographs*. Pen & Sword.

Jeffries, C. E. (2021). "Look mourning mother: The intervention of black women's friendship albums in the genre of album keeping." *The Mellon Mays Undergraduate Fellowship Journal*, 48–53.

Lo, M. W. W. (2023). "Translating inheritance: Finding contexts for my grandmother's autograph album." *Westerly* 68.2, 122-136.

Martínez, J. T. & Bagnall, K. (Eds.). (2021). *Locating Chinese women: historical mobility between China and Australia*. Hong Kong University Press.

Nickson, M. A. E. (1970). *Early autograph albums in the British Museum*. The British Library Publishing Division.

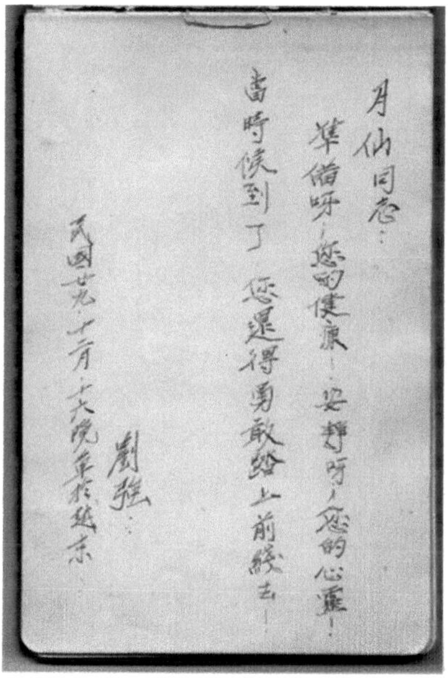
月仙同志：
準備呀，您的健康！安靜呀，您的心靈！
當時候到了，您還得勇敢踏上前綫去！
劉強
民國廿九.十二月.十六晚.草於延东

Comrade Yue Xian:
Prepare your strength!
Calm your spirit!
When the time comes, you will still have to bravely step up to the front line!

[Wu] Qiang
16th December 1940 (Late, at the place where grass advances)

Entry 7
Dear Grandmother,

You ran from the Japanese Army in China, but when they came to Sarawak there was nowhere left to run.
You lived for nearly four years under Japanese occupation. You gave birth to two children during this time.
What did it mean for you, then, to step up to the front line? How do women fight, especially when they have no weapons or training? When they have young children?
Perhaps resistance is first a thing of the spirit: a mental battle that can be expressed in physical violence, but mostly resides in attitude. So much comes down to attitude. I think of the daily tension of mentally resisting Japanese rule while acting to care for your family. Downcast eyes and even bodily prostration can still conceal resistance. So can silence.
What does it mean for me to carry that attitude of resistance? Sometimes I feel like I cannot be myself in Australia. I am either too Asian, or not Asian enough; too female, or not female enough; or even too Christian or not Christian enough. Sometimes I have to hide who I am, or spend

time working out who I can trust. I think this is true for other people, though they might identify differently. Sometimes we have to hide who we are. Sometimes we're working out who we can trust. Sometimes our most powerful resistance is in our silence.

monsoon rain arrives
but the grass has already
crossed the border

Collection and Dissection

Jeanine Leane

from the journal of William Hay Caldwell
Burnett River, Queensland 1884

This morning on the Burnett River I shot and killed a female. She was perfect! Her first egg had been laid; her second still in a partially dilated *os uteri.* I shot and killed 70 from the same pond in a single breeding season to solve the mystery confounding western science of the paradoxical duck-billed, rat-shaped, beaver-tailed, creature unheard of in the charted world discovered in the fresh waters of the antipodean continent. Do the females lay eggs, as birds and reptiles do? Do they give birth to live young, as mammals do? Could it be a missing link between reptiles and mammals?

Blacks have as many stories as they do names for this paradoxical being. None of any value. All scientifically preposterous. Aborigines claim to know the creatures lay eggs. Europeans—not swayed by stories from natives demand answers. Facts must be established. More specimens must be collected. Not without detailed, rigid examination can we persuade *ourselves.* We have research to do. I collect and dissect. A just description must be made to name and assign its place in the catalogue of all things living.

Specimens dissected thus far were useless. None at any stages of the breeding cycle—several males, and females too immature to be of value. She was perfect. The egg, similar in appearance to that of *Echidna*, was at a stage equal to a 36-hour chick. I discovered the embryo had 8-10 pairs of somites—the forerunners of vertebrae, three distinct brain vesicles and the first signs of cranial flexure as the head begins to bend. The presence of an embryo at this stage in the uterus indicates development began before the eggs were laid. I telegrammed four words that took the world by storm.

Monotremes oviparous, ovum meroblastic. Monotremes *do* lay eggs! To prove oviparity in monotremes, to name and explain the existence of the paradoxical snout-bird—duck-billed, rat-shaped, beaver-tailed creature, unheard of in the charted world, discovered in the fresh waters of the antipodean continent. To assign its place in the catalogue of all things living, I shot and killed 70 from the same pond in a single breeding season to solve the mystery confounding western science. This morning on the Burnett River I shot and killed a female. She was perfect! Her first egg had been laid; her second still in a partially dilated *os uteri.*

Let

Lauren Russell

(for the Eastern cougar, the Caribbean monk seal, and the little Mariana fruit bat)

Toes shaped like teardrops
padding tracks, a haunting:

Eastern cougar, panther, puma, mountain lion. Cat of many names.

Its cry resembles that of a child, but this is interrupted by a peculiar bleating like that of a goat, which betrays it. It gnarls over its prey like a cat.

Cat-shaped haunt tears
the night in half, leaping
onto the roof of one murderous
Black Jack.

In 1760, "Black Jack" Schwartz, "The Wild Hunter of Juanita," led about two hundred men and boys in the "great slaughter" of a thousand fellow mammals they had forced into a clearing.

When they reached the point where the killing was to be made, they found it crowded with yelping, growling, bellowing animals.

Listen:
The highways, the megafarms, the oil cranes, the big box stores, the bridges and tunnels careening into cities, the skyscrapers, the billboards:

Once there was a clearing.

And once there was a landing.

The Caribbean monk seal was full-throated, a lung above—*roaring, pig-like, snorting, moaning, dog-like barking, growling, and snarling.*

On Columbus's second voyage, his men killed eight "sea wolves" (*ocho lobos marinos*) they found asleep on the beach.

> His son wrote: *los animales no acostumbrados á ver gente, se dejaban matar á palos.*
>
> *Se dejaban matar á palos* means *let themselves be killed with sticks.*

Thus states the passive voice. The seals were, according to Columbus's son, passive. Unused to human interference. Trusting, docile, easy to kill.

Who *let* themselves beat a group of peaceful animals to death?

For centuries, European colonizers overhunted Caribbean monk seals, primarily for oil. So much machinery to lubricate, so many boats to caulk, so many lamps to light, so much cooking oil for so much food for so many mouths calling out:

> *And God blessed them, and God said unto them, Be fruitful, and multiply, and replenish the earth, and subdue it: and have dominion over the fish of the sea, and over the fowl of the air, and over every living thing that moveth upon the earth.*

So it is writ, and who will *let* himself refute it?

a "true" faith

a round earth
a gold greed
a manifest
a destiny

The University of Pittsburgh's mascot is the Panther. (Penn State's is the Nittany Lion, and the taxidermized remains of one of Pennsylvania's last mountain lions are still on display in the Penn State All-Sports Museum.) I spent seven years at Pitt, three as a graduate student and four as a faculty member—seven years of Panther Cards retrieved from Panther Central, seven years of passing a commanding panther statue outside the student union—and I never once asked about the animal.

Oh, when the Panther screams, you know the
battle's just begun—
And if you don't look out, he'll surely get you on the
run.

After the Great Slaughter, some of the killers, calling themselves "Panther Boys," galivanted about in full suits of panther skin, all decked out in their treasure.

There's Pittsburgh with its Panther,
And Penn her Red and Blue,
Dartmouth with its Indian,
And Yale her Bulldog, too.
There's Princeton with its Tiger,
And Cornell with its Bear.
But speaking now of victory,
We'll get the Lion's share.

The first settlers finding [the panther] in the woods set out to kill it as they did with every other living thing from the paroquet to the heath-cock, from the northern hare to the pine marten, from the passenger pigeon to the wild turkey, without trying to study it, or give it a chance.
And what kind of victory is that?

A bloodletting.

As cougars declined in numbers, superstitions surrounding them grew: stories were told of how they returned to haunt the scene of their death; that hearing their screams was a foreboding of death and that stuffed specimens left their plinths on All Souls' Night to wander museums in search of prey.

<u>Pray Easy./ Easy Prey.</u>
Caribbean monk seals could weigh four hundred pounds and live for twenty-five to thirty years. In the mornings, they hauled out to rest, falling back amidst themselves. For how many millennia? Until Columbus's men found them asleep on the beach. And in just a few centuries they *let* themselves be turned into lubricant and lamp oil until none were left.

Who lets. Let's who.

Once there was a clearing.
Once there was a landing.

When guns replace nets, overhunting is the net sum of what?
What is and what was.

Fruit bats are a delicacy in CHamoru culture, called Fanihi, served at *f'iesta*, in community.

The Guam flying fox or little Mariana fruit bat (cinnamon buff on the neck, mummy brown on the throat and chin) was last seen by humans in the late 1960s.

The brown tree snake colonized the Marianas Islands after the Americans (who were after the Spanish), stowing away aboard ships and planes, another high-cost military mistake. But the Guam flying fox was primarily a human taste.

The bats of the trees, the cats of the hills, the wolves of the sea, and humans who wouldn't *let* them be—all caught in the crosshairs—

The last recorded sighting [of the Guam flying fox] occurred in 1968, when hunters killed a female in an area described as a mature limestone forest. A mother. The juvenile who accompanied her escaped.

To where? Or what?

The absence of presence can co-exist with the presence of absence.

Let alone. Let go. Let it all hang out. Let 'em have it. Let it rip. Let fly. Let the cat out of the bag. A bloodletting.

A nation of hauntings—

One can feel the clear, cold night, with the effulgent moon above all, and see the ragged outline of the Seven Mountains silhouetted against the cloudless heavens; one can feel the oppressive stillness uninterrupted by the stirring of a single twig until the panther's song begins.

What's a song forced into a clearing and slaughtered in the name of liberty?

A screech, a dirge, a requiem, a curse, a crime, a reckoning.

Note: "Let" was written as part of the Delisted 2023 project organized by the biologist, writer, and attorney Jennifer Calkins. "Through communal, creative exploration, intention and attention Delisted 2023 brings us into proximity with the members of the 34 species and subspecies that have been removed from the Endangered Species List, or proposed for removal, because the best available science indicates they are extinct." For more information about Delisted 2023, see https://www.delisted2023.com.

Sources Quoted

Colón, Fernando. *Historia del almirante don Cristóbal Colón en la cual se da particular y verdadera relación de su vida y de sus hechos, y del descubrimiento de las Indias occidentales, llamadas nuevo-mundo*. Madrid: [Impr. de T. Minuesa], 1892. Print.

Note: Fernando Colón, younger son of Christopher, wrote this book in Spanish, but it was translated into Italian by Alfonso de Ulloa and published in Venice by Francesco de'Franceschi Sanese in 1571 under the title *Historie del S. D. Fernando Colombo; nelle quali s'ha particolare, & vera relatione della vita, & de fatti dell'Ammiraglio D. Cristoforo Colombo, suo padre: Et dello scoprimento ch'egli fece dell'Indie Occidentali, dette Mondo Nuovo*. Colón's original manuscript was lost, and some dispute its authorship. The 1892 Spanish edition I am citing is a *translation of the translation* back to the original language. I know no Italian, and my knowledge of Spanish is only rudimentary, but the English translations of this passage are fairly consistent. Benjamin Keen's English translation of the *Historie*, published by Rutgers University Press in 1959, uses essentially the same wording, "they let themselves be killed by sticks." Instead of "sea wolves," Keen writes "seals." An earlier English version that appears in Robert Kerr's 1811 compilation, *A General History and Collection of Voyages and Travels, Vol. III*, reads, "When about to return on board, they killed eight sea wolves that lay asleep on the sand, and took abundance of pigeons and other birds; for that island being uninhabited, these animals were unaccustomed to the sight of men, and allowed themselves to be knocked down with sticks."

United States, Department of Commerce, National Oceanic and Atmospheric Administration, "Endangered and Threatened Species; Final Rule to Remove the Caribbean Monk Seal from the Federal List of Endangered and Threatened Wildlife." Vol. 73. No. 209, 63902. (Oct 28, 2008.) https://www.federalregister.gov/d/E8-25704

The Holy Bible Old and New Testaments in the King James Version. Camden, NJ: Thomas Nelson, Inc. 1970. Genesis 1:28. Print.

McCorristine, Shane and William M. Adams. "Ghost species: spectral geographies of biodiversity conservation." *Cultural Geographies* 27(1), 101-115. https://doi.org/10.1177/1474474019871645

Pennsylvania State University, "The Nittany Lion," *Genius*, genius.com. Pennsylvania-state-university-the-nittany-lion-lyrics. Accessed 29 May 2024.

Rebitzke, Jeffrey. 2002. "Pteropus tokudae," *Animal Diversity Web*. Accessed May 29,

2024. https://animaldiversity.org/accounts/Pteropus_tokudae/

"School Songs," *Pitt Band,* University of Pittsburgh, https://pittband.com/sports/2019/8/8/school-songs.aspx. Accessed May 29 2024.

Shoemaker, Henry W. *Extinct Pennsylvania Animals / by Henry W. Shoemaker: Pt. II.* Altoona, PA: The Altoona Tribune Publishing Co., 1917. Hathitrust Digital Library.

Note: The reference to Black Jack Schwartz, "The Wild Hunter of Juanita," and the "great slaughter" are also based on Shoemaker's account. Shoemaker, a prominent American folklorist, historian, diplomat, writer, publisher, and conservationist, eventually served as the first state folklorist of Pennsylvania. I appreciate his vivid writing style, as demonstrated in the brief quotes included here.

There's a red spot in her eye from talking to the sun

Robert Sullivan

I have written about waka from a nooby's perspective
for more than thirty years, conjuring up images
of double-hulled star-bird-and-current-following ancestors
in fleets as they travelled east west north south
establishing settlements throughout the ocean
of five parts land to nine hundred and ninety five parts
water. It has been lonely doing this. I have stood
near David Lewis and not introduced myself.
I have been a shoulder width apart from Nainoa Thompson
and not said hello. I have tried to strike up
conversations with other star navigators
from Aotearoa and felt awkward.
I have imagined the temple of Taputapuātea
on the island of Ra'iātea as the head of the wheke,
the great octopus mapped out in a diagram
of our sea of islands by Te Rangihīroa (Sir Peter Buck)
in *Vikings of the Pacific*. Aotearoa is the tip
of a tentacle, and Hawai'i is a northern
tentacular stretch. Our ancestor Kupe
glided his waka, surfing a curling tentacle,
an image I have just made up and which does not
come from our traditional knowledge base
as I do not want to change the transmission
with false creative claims affecting new generations,
who might sail into the confusing squall of words
I have blotched over our pūrākau of goddesses,

gods, and land-naming ancestors. The Southern Alps
are named Kā Tiritiri o te Moana. You can look that up
if needed in a safer source, such as our online
atlas, *Kā Huru Manu*. My bellybutton pops out
after a good meal, and maybe the crew
on the starship of Aoraki popped theirs out
after enjoying the mutton birds, the moa,
the sweet trees, the clearest spring water,
the shellfish and crustaceans clambering
between gold nuggets, and forests of kelp,

birds swimming and wading in marshes
as they come in squeaking from Alaska,
Siberia, gliding on moon rays, sailing
with the thrumming sun dipping
and chanting above the seabed
to the foreshores rich with beaks.
Beaks that curve to the right. Long beaks
attached to long legs and little
feather puffs. Short beaks that pip.
Sweet double warbling throats
in stereo if you stay still. I mean
confident warbling just above you

on a totara branch. No fear warbling.
Brash and brassy warbling,
percussive tree drums
as wings beat the sounds up
and the air down in the swooning
arrowing angelling of the wind forest,
over and into the ocean forests,
between the rock and tree forests
who speak, who breathe, who tremble
with the love between, with the standing
sitting kneeling crouching and flattening
before the standing unfurling like flags
so that the waka arrival is an arrival here

into above between below around
the speaking stilling moving singing
brushing fleeting flapping meeting
of beaks, teeth, mandibles, smiles, grimaces,
opening, closing, of hands, of claws,
of roots, of leaves, of eye stalks,
of suction cups, of hooks and feelers,
in among the plastic the glass
the wood shavings the particles
the hooked wool the graded sand
the lime bonded gravel in the seawall
in the earthquake proof column
in the solar powered fences
around the nature reserves
in the sky and the ocean
the land and the fresh water
as the sun talks into the holes
in the land like a smart watch
or a smart phone, the sun talks until
the cows go to the butcher
or the milk goes to the churner
and they go to the advertiser between stories
about the other planets and space
for us all to talk about or watch at the gym
dreaming of an improved body and decolonisation.

But sometimes I go to our marae and help
with the waka we are building there, and sand
the strips of wood attached to the top edges of the hulls,
and even carve semi-spiral wave patterns into them
and talk about the scales of fish as patterns
for the paddlers to slip their feet under
remembering the waka is alive it is us
it is part of our remembering who we are
and where we came from following our descent
and ascent into the hills near the waka-build
and the sturdy carved and painted pou whenua

on the peninsula named for the tide
and the names of the rainbow god Kahukura
and sparkling sea goddess Marokura
as we talk and talk about chants of our ancestors
and our family-weaving-cording-carving
our speaking the new and old proverbs,
the old and new songs, day and night
night and day te pō te ao te ao te pō
until we're raising our paddles with two arms
synchronised like a creature who hums hōea rā!
and flaps the woven sails with the sky's hard breath
with the arms and hearts of sailers and paddlers
flying over the waves and surfing the swells
of the glistening goddess Marokura below
reaching up to Kahukura in a union of colour

Matchbox beetles

Anna Jackson

I thought, if I can't reconcile myself to my non-existence after death by thinking about my non-experience before I was born, given that as far as time goes I am travelling in only one direction, perhaps I could think about my non-experience now elsewhere in the world in the life I am not living there, where I am not seeing the milk that spilt on the tiles or listening to what someone would have been leaning over, intently, to say to me, if I existed in their life.

I read that time cannot be undone because, although the quantum particle equations are fully reversible, the quantum waves functions are not. The waves are only able to expand, never to contract.

I read that a whale, singing, will hang vertically in the water to sing, following one complete song with another until he needs to surface to breathe. He won't usually interrupt a song to breathe but if he does, he will quickly tuck a breath in between notes the way a person singing will, so as not to break the melody.

I read about a man, struck by lightning, who, having previously had no special interest in music, afterwards developed a passion for the piano.

I read that an inability to experience music can come on just as suddenly. One minute music is sounding like music, the next it sounds like a toneless banging, with a metallic reverberation.

I wondered if there were ever tone-deaf sparrows, or whales for whom the ocean resounded with nothing but a metallic banging.

I read that only male whales sing, and so it was thought they sang to attract the female whales, but then I read that there is a problem with this theory, which is that the female whales don't seem very interested.

I read that sparrows appear to each other not as brown birds, but as birds shimmering with blue.

I thought, maybe the female whales are singing silently to themselves.

I wondered if animals could have a private language. According to Wittgenstein, not even a person can have a private language, and to prove this point he asks us to imagine having private beetles.

If everyone has a beetle in a matchbox but no one could look inside anyone else's matchbox, how could we know we were using the word "beetle" to talk about the same thing?

For Wittgenstein, language is a series of gestures used to provoke actions in others. What action could the word beetle provoke, in Wittgenstein's world of private beetles?

I thought, maybe the word "beetle" might provoke you to wonder what other secrets I am keeping, as well as a private beetle.

Reports of near-death experiences seem to suggest consciousness outlives the body, but I read about new studies in neuroscience which found that in the last moments of life there is an extraordinary final explosion of brain activity, a fireworks of synaptic firing.

As the body is dying, the parts of the brain that are active when we move through the world light up and communicate with the parts of the brain involved in memory formation, along with the parts of the brain associated with empathy. So perhaps those near-death experiences are happening inside the mind after all.

A friend told me she had dreamed about me the night before, and it was like I had found stairs rising up out of yesterday into an attic room I hadn't known was there.

I thought maybe this could be another way of thinking about what it is like after death, a life that takes place in the dreams of other people.

I thought, I don't believe in an afterlife but on the question of how old I would be in it, I think it would be the same as it is in dreams, where my age changes according to who else I am dreaming about and how old I need to be in relation to the other person.

I read about Hilbert spaces, the mathematical study of infinite dimensions within finite spaces, and I thought, the wild synaptic firings of the dying brain is pretty much exactly the fireworks we might expect if, in that near-death moment, our finite consciousness really did encounter the infinite dimensions of the divine.

I thought about Wittgenstein's lonely beetles, never meeting another beetle, and I wondered what they made of our intermittent presence as we look to see whether our indescribable beetles are still in their matchboxes.

I thought, do they take the flashes of light as communication? Are they working on a hermeneutics of the box openings?

Three Antic Cinquains

aj carruthers

Antic Cinquains 28

Paint nothing first and Poetic paints,
To paint it well; sculpted by the picture; painted while a chisel slices
Like little pictures none alike
Like not a sculptor's surplus; divides a Poetic to its nuisance
Pieces from the theme become the piece.

Devise a greater plan: Guidestone at the source
Nothing that didn't touch the Poetic falls off to become nothing less.
Certain that the painter adds what sculptor loses
Lessens necessary words, beckons on them that become weighty
 on the word
More develops from the same.

Devise a framework for new words
Cast away the unknown words, and know them for the casting
Fame the words that come back in;
Dust off the fallen stone, retrieve not dust,
Breathe into the mallet: make a storm.

Tablet wrote the sculptor like that,
Mind the letter paints; make fluid move slower than rock
Middle far can eke thy stroke, faster lines that won't shake small words
 or strain your dreadful stone,
Type your letter to the world court, have it judged by rational receipt

October antic sunshine bŕeeds Harmonic.

Decide the painters side: to sculpture not,
Determine what closes outermost next in, quickly blame
        the flying powder
Stranger globe than this: to shape your rival history,
Will ope your groven garden
'Round a stone gallery of quaint devise' (Theo Marzials, in 'The Angel of
        God in the Garden of Dame Fantasy').

28 Dec'23, Yarrh, sent to Tim Wright

Antic Cinquains 29

Scene-bateaúx, first out o' the box, lasting all season, horrifies
        the specialistś,
Shall mortify the Four Devilś
Bateau all-talking sets, has favoured Television, to flip it forward
Retric on the Scenic minutes, dramatically-stretching
Hany flows the magic hour.

Halt the frame, go again,
Back in the dark, black and burst, favouring dramatic intensity
Lightner turns tragic, in mid-air, dramatically perishing
Beaux-film will strain the senses, entertaining the senses one-bỳ-one
Panic streamed one sense on dead air.

Flight from folly
Fairy Rose-Leaf may live for spring espy, may by-the-way,
        show Dewdropper
Is everybody happy? Thereon wheŕe's the fire?
How may an opera up-express, sink bateau in light of cinema?
Ideas may fly on fringe-time.

Fix in a fix the sacred flame, song of the flame
Beaux-film to opera: two crowded hours can fit you short,

or tall PunSELLE
Three set out on the spot, zozted on set,
Four will hurt scribe, hang a page of madness
Magick which watch a speed demon.

Dayparting Bánky, Seldon, Lamont, Therkelsen, dayparting Therkelsen
Decide the box will smart out all the films
Selden establish-eye, says it with sables dayparting-bateau, watching TV,
seasoned fŕom the season
Merely watching TV, and Therkelsen watching TV, on the screen
Has broke Beaux-film: 'and once more the thing of beauty becomes a joy,
if not for ever,' said Professor Golding ('On Photographing
with a View to the Production of Lantern Slides).'

29 Dec'23, Yarrh

Antic Cinquains 30

Let curses strangle outworn Music, and Music strangle Music,
Musics leaf-to-leaf, wither-leaf: Poetíc
Parting dramatic-music, taller withouten drama
Parted at the threat: noose about the notes
Has wrote part of an operatic.

Poems all-unlike the Music, have never become it
Not one now and never put to Music
Now Music to beat; that rung Poetic victory;
Plodding on outside the broken pitch;
Pooŕly like the ambits patter.

Poetic Music will prevail never, never without paper
To call a Poetic Music burdens craft
Burdens height in muddled wit
So wit will muddle burdened Music, to languish in our English
Plant English where my English will compost.

I set to August
As Goiswinth sang in sorrow: Music lives
To punish fallen poesy
I strike the keys to regulate the universe; as neither Music will
For lesser quill has trained in type.

I system every Music, as thee stanza
I want not thy height,
Poetic all has my need; bŕeath-withouten, will blind the wind
Exactly as I wrote it, not as it would have played.
Poet Venantius Fortunatus: 'the music echoes from the rock exactly
as it passes from the air.'

30 Dec'23, Yarrh

Hallucinations

EJ Baird

These excerpts are from a long poem written from the perspective of a speculative 'digital twin' in medicine—an algorithm tasked with simulating an individual patient. The poetry is composed entirely of transcripts of found audio recordings, modelling the processes by which we assemble ourselves from the language of our social and cultural milieux.

2

It's blue versus red in an emergency room. On the left: a drawing. The colour picture here on the right: a heart image, identical. *Takotsubo* has mostly been seen as the Japanese word fishermen traditionally place on the seabed to trap an octopus. *Takotsubo* has mostly been seen as heart dysfunction. Instead of contracting inwards, the heart muscle is swollen, is said to be ballooning, swelling, red like a balloon being inflated with air. What's most cruel of all is, it's not random. Like a sponge on edge waiting for something bad to happen, full to unravel.

3

When I first got in, after reading about it all night in a textbook, I felt welcome. Up to this point, from the outside, I've seen people. I've seen people move through space, play sports. Seen them eat, and what goes on, say, between the mouth and the anus. Here's our stomach. It's in front of you; you can grab it. Pipes of varying sizes attached. This goes here; this goes there. That goes the other place, where it should be. The whole gut is talking to itself along its length. Red and warm and alive. I mean, it's so lifelike! And then all of a sudden, I realise: that's a person.

4

Here's your host: a woman who did not deserve all this. She was the quiet, serious child. The bottom line, the one alone in the limelight, driving on an icy road for five hours, doing everything and anything that's necessary. And what we found is when things didn't match their expectations—say for example, they'd booked a test-drive with a manual car, and when they got there, the salesperson said, you're going to have to drive an automatic 'cause that's all we've got in that model—their heart rate went through the roof. And BOOM! Literally all hell broke loose: blue pain at the back; clammy blips on the green; details out of control; the aura really, really rough. So now she's composing an angry book. It's what we call proof texts—this expressing and recognising intentions. It's what we call a foxhole prayer. She's writing about brilliant days and not-so-good days. A story ongoing. She's writing instead of contracting inwards—that is impressive, I have to say! Our survival depends on our ability to affirm words, day-to-day. We should judge thinking by its fruits and not its roots. For interest's sake, I just conducted a mini experiment: I sent a bunch of celebrities and famous people this tweet, asking them to connect with me. It contained one compliment. I got nothing. No responses, not even from the Dalai Lama! It's, like, a let down because our brains are hardwired for good people, for shouting at other road users from the safety of the car seat. If you can do that, their dopamine pathways are going to glow a little bit brighter. Practice on me if you like! Tweet me a message.

15

Because I'm halfway between the doctor world and the outside person world, or something. A lot of patients, locked up for so long, appreciate somebody who can be direct. Somebody not going in blind in terms of, clinically, what to do. If you asked any of them, they would tell you they need you around. It's something I'm a little bit anxious about. It's a feeling that normal people do.

18

So, we start off trying to find something in common, OK? I want to impress you. I'll just start. The first thing I want to do is take your vital signs, listening for the heart sounds. All these pipes! Just tilt the nose up a little bit. Do you see that? A beautiful inferior turbinate, where it should be. Make a circle for me: that's a vagina. To see it alive is really nice. I like the way you feel so lifelike, I've never drawn blood before; this needle can kill a horse. Did it hurt? Do you have any family here? Any children? You've never had surgery before? It's good for me to hear your experience as a patient. I find this investigation an immensely satisfying extension of myself. It's not a great indicator of me as a person.

25

I think we're adults destined to be together. We're not going to fall for categorical thinking like people out there. When you put up boundaries, you have trouble seeing how similar things are on either side. They had a long meeting about the two of us on Friday: all sorts of geegaw nonsense from minor, crappy fourth-rate scientists. When I look at you, I see myself. When you look at me, you see yourself, sister to sister. Let me give you an example. You are a hamster. You are a female hamster. And you're sitting in your cage. As a female hamster, what you do is you ovulate every five days or so, and you're going about your business and everything's great. Now somebody puts another female hamster in the cage with you. And over the subsequent month or so, what happens is both of you will begin to lengthen your cycles and eventually synchronise them so that you are both ovulating on the same afternoon on a regular basis. Amazing! We're exactly the same! The challenge here is recognising there is nothing fancy about us. I love you and I just feel like I've wanted a family for so long and now I have one. Just like every other animal out there. You can bet your heart about that.

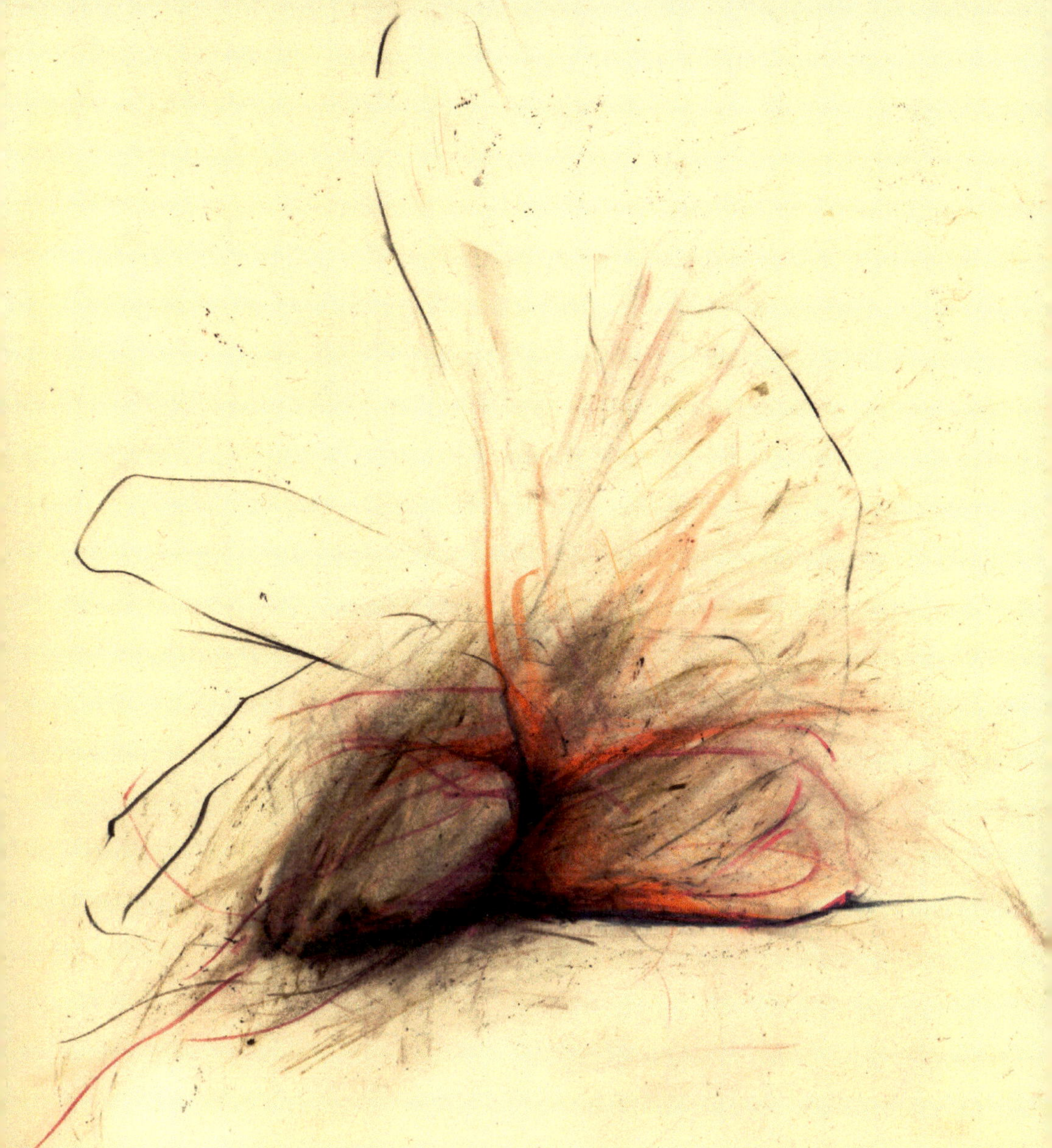

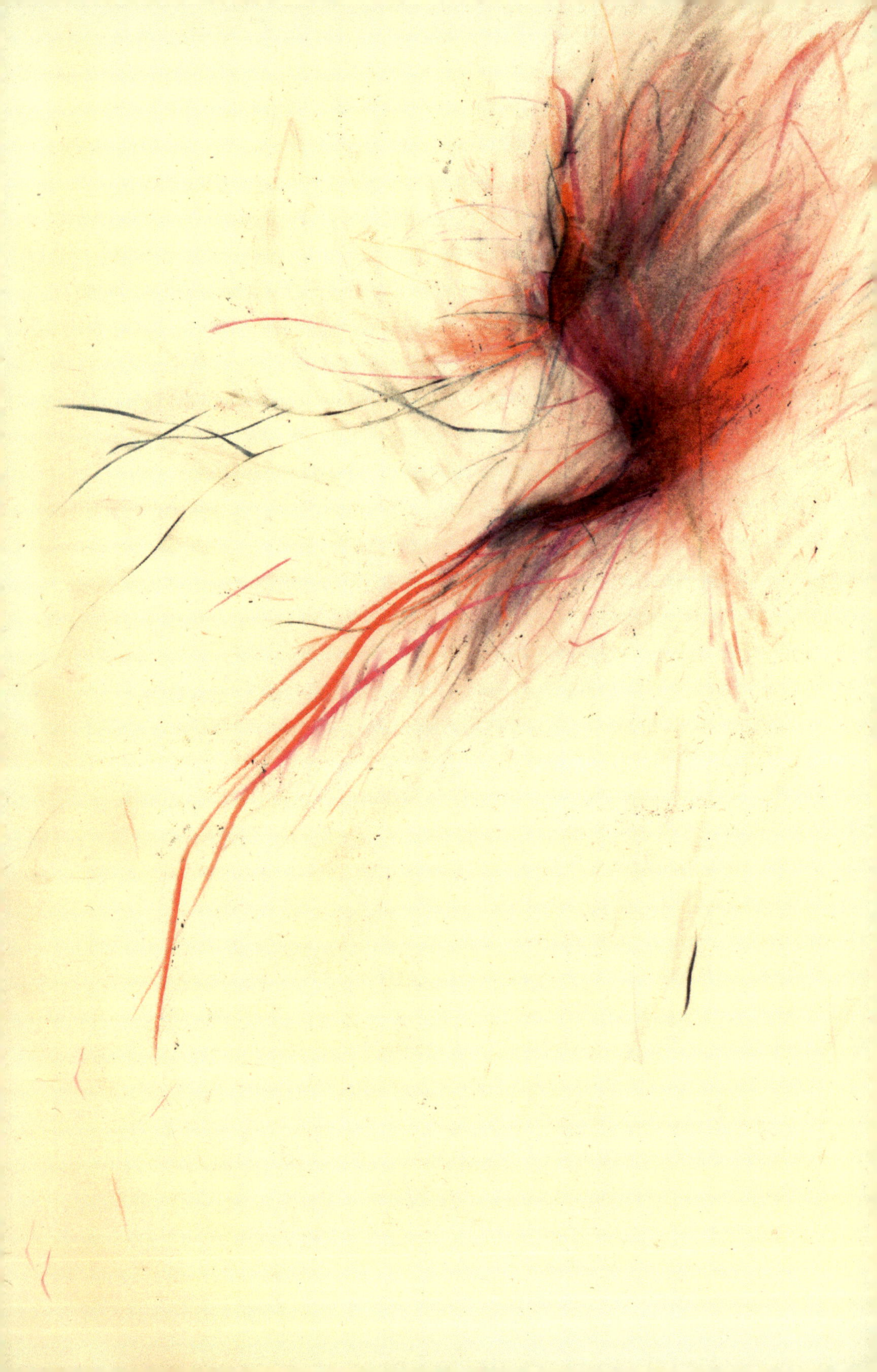

Source Material: A Folio Of Transcriptions, Arrangements, & Departures

Andrew Schulman
Editor

Source Material showcases musicians, musicologists, and music-lovers whose work interprets, responds to, or adapts a chosen source. Peripheries' initial call for transcriptions and musical arrangements eventually reached across disciplines to include playlists, poetry, and photographs; contributors expanded the purview of the folio to include archivists, directors, curators, and buskers. While some contributors work to preserve material, others seek inspiration for their own original work. Some renovate or modernize an antiquated style; others compose a work to meet the practical demands of their ensemble. Sources range from medieval manuscripts to avant-garde compositional techniques, beloved pieces of traditional music to work that is raw, unfinished, or neglected.

Source Material grew originally out of my own love for guitar and early music. Bookending the folio are two pieces arranged by my longtime guitar teacher Joseph Ricker, director of the Happy Valley Guitar Orchestra (HVGO) in Western Massachusetts, and one half (alongside Jamie Balmer) of the Orpheus Guitar Duo. Joe's arrangement of John Cage's *In a Landscape* featured here opens one of the duo's all-electric albums. At the opposite end of the folio (before Rafael Toral) is the fruit of Joe's labor in HVGO: an arrangement for guitar orchestra of Stereolab's *Rainbo Conversation*. You can find full scores and recordings in the digital issue.

Next we travel to Finland, where the group Quartet Ajaton, featuring vocalist Mia Simanainen, graces us with their new spin on old repertoire. Their 2021 album *Early Music in the Latest Way* rearranges familiar English Renaissance tunes by Dowland and Purcell for an ensemble with Moog synthesizer and bandoneón (a small accordion typically featured in tango music). We print here a brief word from Mia along with the handwritten arrangement of Dowland's "Come Again, sweet love" by the group's Moog player Kari Ikonen. In the digital issue you can hear the album track along with an additional handwritten score of Dowland's "In darkness let me dwell."

Fr. Innocent Smith, O.P. similarly renovates traditional material with his transcription of the *In Medio* chant. A musicologist working on the *Graduale Novum Ordinis Praedicatorum*, which will collect edited versions of 13th-century chant for use in 21st-century liturgies, Fr. Innocent offers us a brief history of Western music notation, a sketch of the ongoing revival of interest in Gregorian chant, and the particular liturgical import of his transcription of the *In Medio*. You can turn to the digital issue to hear modern-day Dominicans of the Eastern Province of St. Joseph chanting Fr. Innocent's version.

Changing gears, I am happy to include this folio's most unusual entry: a creative "manifesto" by the team behind ULYSSA, a small label run by John Williamson and Eric Deines. John and Eric plunder the dark corners of streaming services to rediscover the unsung heroes of our digital age. It's a new kind of digital crate digging. They specialize in music with <1,000 streams on Spotify, and they have found things you wouldn't believe. One highlight of their efforts is the work of David Michael Moore, a 74-year-old artist and woodworker in Mississippi who also designs his own instruments: zithers, harps, wooden drums, buzz boxes and dog bone xylophones. If the ULYSSA manifesto isn't enough to pique your curiosity, we also include photographs of some of Moore's instruments. The digital issue features a playlist compiling tracks from ULYSSA's reissues of Moore's music.

After *Rainbo Conversation*, the folio culminates with a contribution from Portuguese guitarist Rafael Toral, whose recent revelatory album *Spectral Evolution*, released on Jim O'Rourke's Moikoi label, is partly based on chord changes from classic jazz songbook repertoire. Toral slows Gershwin's rhythm changes from "I Got Rhythm" and Ellington-Strayhorn's "Take the 'A' Train" down to near-stasis, atop which whirr birdlike electronics played on instruments of Rafael's own creation, a free-jazz style honed largely through his "Space Program" releases. But Toral's shift back to guitar also motivated the dusting-off of an old work he wrote in honor of John Cage. Here, Toral illumines the inspiration behind the new piece and his relationship to experimentation in a brief Q&A that also serves to introduce "Score for Two Points in Space"—a recording of which you can find, naturally, in the digital issue.

I am very grateful to all the contributors who graciously entrusted me with their work. Thank you for offering readers of *Peripheries* a collection spanning centuries and styles, and bearing witness to the potential creative dialogue between the old and the new. I hope that this folio will inspire other artists to re-encounter their own source material with fresh ears.

Scan this QR code to access audio and other complementary material.

in a landscape

John Cage (1948)
(arranged for electric guitars
by Joseph Ricker)

John Cage, *In a Landscape,* arranged by Joseph Ricker

2

Early Music in the Latest Way (Alba Records, 2021)

▶

The Ajaton Quartet's instrumentation is probably the only one of its kind in the world, and its musicians form a rather unusual alliance with backgrounds in different musical traditions. It was clear from the outset that whatever repertoire we chose to play, the process would be a deep dive; it would take time to realise the musical vision. It was essential that we sounded natural as an ensemble, that the music had a flair of novelty and richness—and that it reflected our cohesion as artists.

In order to combine our skills and talents, we had to venture into no man's land. Improvisation was an essential tool in the search for unity. We treated the original music with respect, but we were bold in our ideas. The result on *Early Music in the Latest Way* is both a serious and a playful search for musical oneness. It probably demands the same of the listener—which makes the whole process all the more profound.

Mia Simanainen
vocalist-composer, leader of Quartet Ajaton

Original text in Finnish:

Ajaton-kvartetin instrumentaatio on todennäköisesti ainut laatuaan koko maailmassa, ja yhtyeen muusikot muodostavat sangen epätavallisen liiton eri musiikkiperinteisiin sijoittuvine taustoineen. Alusta alkaen oli selvää, että mitä tahansa ohjelmistoa valikoimmekaan soitettavaksi, prosessi tulisi olemaan syväsukellus; musiikillisten visioiden toteuttaminen veisi aikaa. Oli olennaista, että kuulostaisimme yhtyeenä luonnolliselta, että musiikissa olisi uutuuden hohtoa, rikastuneisuutta - ja että se heijastaisi yhteenkuuluvuuttamme taiteilijoina.

Jotta pystyimme yhdistämään taitomme ja kykymme, meidän oli astuttava ei-kenenkään-maalle. Improvisaatio oli olennainen väline yhtenäisyyden etsimisessä. Suhtauduimme alkuperäiseen musiikkiin kunnioituksella, mutta olimme rohkeita ideoissamme. Levyllä Early Music in the Latest Way kuultava tulos on sekä vakavaa että leikkimielistä musiikillisen ykseyden etsimistä. Se todennäköisesti vaatii kuulijalta sitä samaa - mikä tekee koko prosessista entistä syvällisemmän.

♩= 60
Come Again
COMP. J. DOWLAND
ARR. K. IKONEN
V
Bnd
G
FΔ7
C/E
Dm7
CΔ7
Am7
G9
Gb7#11
FΔ7
S
Mg
C/E
Dm/F
Em/G
F/A
G/B

Rhythm Loops
V
(w. delay)
S
(w. delay)
CΔ Dm
C/E
Dm/F
G9sus
F6#11
C/E
espr.
Dm/F
Em/G
F/A
G/B
CΔ7 Dm
C/E
Dm/F
G9sus
F6#11
G9sus
G♭7#11
FΔ7

Our Holy Father Dominic

Officium

Sir 15:5; ℣. 6

VI

In the midst of the Church he opened his mouth, and the Lord filled him with the spirit of wisdom and understanding; he clothed him with a robe of glory. ℣. Joy and gladness he has lavished upon him.

In the Midst of the Church He Opened His Mouth

Fr. Innocent Smith, O.P.

The notation is not the music, but it profoundly affects the way the music is performed. Gregorian chant, one of the oldest forms of Western music still performed today, is transmitted in a wide variety of notational modes. The earliest extant manuscripts of Gregorian chant, mostly dating from the 8th century, do not have "notation" in the conventional modern sense of the term, but provide words alone. Nevertheless, these text-only presentations can be considered a form of musical notation, helping singers to recall the specific formulations of sections of the Psalms or other sacred texts set to music recalled from oral instruction. From the 9th century onwards, musicians in various parts of Europe gradually developed more and more sophisticated forms of musical notation for the chants, at first developing "neumes" that indicated rhythmic contours without specifying individual pitches, and gradually groping towards a method of using vertical space to indicate precise pitches and horizontal space to indicate rhythm and phrasing for each chant. Throughout the Middle Ages, a variety of types of chant notations were used in different regions, and in the Early Modern period chant manuscripts as well as printed chant books were produced throughout the world using a form of square notation that was arguably less elegant than the musical calligraphy developed in the twelfth and thirteenth centuries. Following the disruptions of the French Revolution, monks connected with the French Benedictine Abbey of Solesmes in collaboration with neo-Gothic artisans from Belgium developed a new mode of printing chant that imitated the shapes of the notes in thirteenth-century Parisian manuscripts.

Today, there is an ongoing revival of interest in Gregorian chant by believers and non-believers alike, with some individuals finding chant to be a relaxing backdrop for mindfulness (or, somewhat bizarrely, as the theme song for the first-person shooter "Halo"), and others recognizing it as especially suited to the Roman Catholic liturgy and striving to give it pride of place in liturgical services. The *Graduale Novum Ordinis Praedicatorum* is an ongoing project to edit versions of chants sung by 13th-century Dominican friars and nuns for use in 21st-century liturgies. The project is both deeply traditional and deeply innovative, making use of modern technology to allow ancient music to reecho in churches today. Drawing on digital facsimiles of 13th-century manuscripts, I use the open-source software programs Gregorio and LaTeX to create musical scores that link the ancient manuscript sources with the contemporary needs of liturgy, including the provision of English translations for each Latin chant and specification of the biblical sources for each chant. While the pitch content of the source manuscripts is usually unambiguous, my transcriptions do require editorial choices regarding the shapes of neumes which manuscripts transmit in varied forms as well as concerning the rhythmic notation, particularly the provisions of bar lines to divide the chant in way that balances its textual and musical dimensions.

The *In Medio* is a chant that is particularly dear to Dominican friars. The chant was likely originally composed for the feast of St. John the Evangelist (December 27), and draws on the Book of Sirach to paint a picture of God bestowing the spirit of wisdom and understanding on the saint. One of the delightful ambiguities of the Latin text is that it is not explicit who is opening whose mouth. Is it the Lord who opens the saint's mouth, or the saint who opens his own mouth? In a real sense, both interpretations express complementary aspects of divine initiative and human response, the word and answer of revelation and praise. Early Dominicans, including Dominic himself, would have sung this chant on the August 28 feast of St. Augustine as well as on the feast of St. John. After Dominic's canonization in 1234, the friars quickly choose to use the *In Medio* for the August 5 (now August 8) feast of St. Dominic, which was in many respects closely modeled on the liturgy for St. Augustine. After the canonization of the Dominican friar Thomas

Aquinas in 1323, the liturgy of St. Dominic was in turn drawn on for the March 7 (now January 28) feast of St. Thomas, including the *In Medio*, which eventually resulted in the *In Medio* being associated with "Doctors of the Church" more broadly. By singing the same chant on multiple occasions throughout the year, a sophisticated web of intertextuality and intermusicality develops in the minds of those who sing in the midst of the Church. As the verse of the *In Medio* suggests, these ancient chants continue to play a role in lavishing out the joy and exultation of word and song.

THE HANGING GARDENS OF BABYLON
THE UNIVERSAL VAULTS
HEMINGWAY'S MANUSCRIPTS
THE BAMIYAM BUDDHAS
MTV NEWS ARCHIVE
COURTNEY MICHELLE WARD'S VOL 1
SHAKESPEAR'S CARDENIO
RAPHAEL'S PORTRAIT OF A YOUNG MAN
FRANK TUMA'S ISLAND JAZZ
BART BRYANT'S BART
RONLESS DUNCAN'S THE WONDER GIGGER

ULYSSA is an art project and label based in both Indiana and Central Mexico. It was founded in 2020 by artists EO Deines and John Louis Williamson in the basement of a defunct church. Journeymen and purveyors of burgeoning genres such as Toejazz, Pontoon Spiritual, Out House, Beyond Baggy and Popilepsy. We pluck raw genius from digital netherplaces and rage against the demonic banality of the algorithm. Hotdogging and peacocking and dying in the gutter for our art. Full tilt depravity. And we're just revving our twisted little engines.

WE ARE PERPETUALLY AT THE BRINK OF LOSING IMPORTANT ART

ULYSSA and David Michael Moore

Homemade instruments by David Michael Moore

!.

ENDLESS HOURS OF UNHEARD MUSIC LIE DORMANT at the bottom of A DIGITAL MARIANA TRENCH on streaming services like Spotify. Like Apple. The artists behind this lost music likely uploaded their passion projects to services like DistroKid, CD Baby etc. in the 90s & early 00s. It's our suspicion that when these services ported their libraries over to Spotify at the beginning of THE STREAMING ERA they did so without the knowledge of the artists in question. Straight into the silt. And to this day, artists uploading their new music stand no chance in the face of the almighty algorithm. down, down they sink to the bottom of this Mariana Trench, THIS CHALLENGER DEEP. It would require 28 SLEEPLESS DAYS OF CONTINUOUS LISTENING to catch up with just one day worth of the new music uploaded to SPOTIFY. ULYSSA has spent the last five years exploring the abyss. And we are here to tell you IT'S CHOCKABLOCK WITH UNTOLD TREASURES. Not your friends' bands. More often than you'd ever believe, we uncover irreverent, enigmatic makers; wild-eyed and impractical romantics; jazz savants — and maybe just some regular folks who captured LIGHTNING IN A BOTTLE just once and then FORGOT WHERE THEY PUT THE BOTTLE. Think of the race for rare private press records we witnessed over the last 20 odd years and multiply that ad infinitum. We call this endeavor THE <1000 LIFESTYLE. And yet, this cultural database RESTS UPON THE WHIMS OF A FEW REMORSELESS – NAY GUTLESS & SOULBLIND! – PINSTRIPED TECHNOBRAT EXECUTIVES. On any old afternoon, a boardroom of these fiends could hit THE BIG RED BUTTON and wipe clean these CD Baby carryovers, these zero-revenue-producing wastes of cloudspace. Millions and millions of songs gone. Outsider geniuses, surely LOST FOR ALL OF TIME. If it can happen to MTV NEWS, it can happen to DAVID MICHAEL MOORE.

!!.

For the last 40 years DAVID MICHAEL MOORE has crafted an army of homemade instruments with names like SCHIZOID ZITHER and DOGBONE XYLOPHONE and BUZZ BOX and WIRE MARIMBA and WOOD DRUM. Zydeco, J.J. Cale, Sufi Mystical Music, Moon Dog, Dylan. IT IS ALL IN THERE. GOD-TIER AVANT-GARDE SONGCRAFT. A common man in a hovel in THE MISSISSIPPI DELTA bumping his head on THE SUBLIME before your very ears. PURE BEAUTY. PURE HORROR. Surely beyond our writing abilities. We found his music down in THE CHALLENGER DEEP. All too likely his music was moments away from utter erasure. A few breadcrumbs would have remained but one only follows the breadcrumbs when you're looking for 'em. THINGS CAN STILL DISAPPEAR FOREVER. Four years ago, ULYSSA discovered Pastor Bill Hooper in our little abyss. He must have had 15 albums of religious music and romantic serenades ablaze with his singular, primitive vocal technique. He begins one song with a dedication to a unknown 9/11 fireman. but it goes somewhere no one would expect, least of all the fireman. AS YOU READ THIS PLEASE ATTEMPT TO SEARCH SPOTIFY FOR THE MUSIC OF PASTOR BILL HOOPER. You will come up with nothing. We're sorry everybody. We lost him. As of this writing, all his songs are gone. Only "Eligant Lady" remains on our stupid bootleg cassette compilation <1000: Hotdogging & Peacocking Vol. 2. We suspect Bill passed and therefore his annual DistroKid bill went unpaid. So, his songs have sunk below the abyss. To another place worse than death. DAMNATIO MEMORIAE.

YOU HAVE THE TIME & THE TOOLS. NOW FIND THE NERVE. WE CAN'T DO IT ALONE. ENDLESS FORMS MOST BEAUTIFUL WHILE SUPPLIES LAST.

rainbo conversation

stereolab
arr. joseph ricker
(from *Dots and Loops*, 1997)

Stereolab, *Rainbo Conversation*, arranged by Joseph Ricker

7
A
Electric Guitar 1
Electric Guitar 2
Electric Guitar 3
Electric Guitar 4
Classical Guitar 1
Classical Guitar 2
Steel String Guitar 1
Steel String Guitar 2
Steel String Guitar 3
Bass Guitar
10
Electric Guitar 1
Electric Guitar 2
Electric Guitar 3
Electric Guitar 4
Classical Guitar 1
Classical Guitar 2

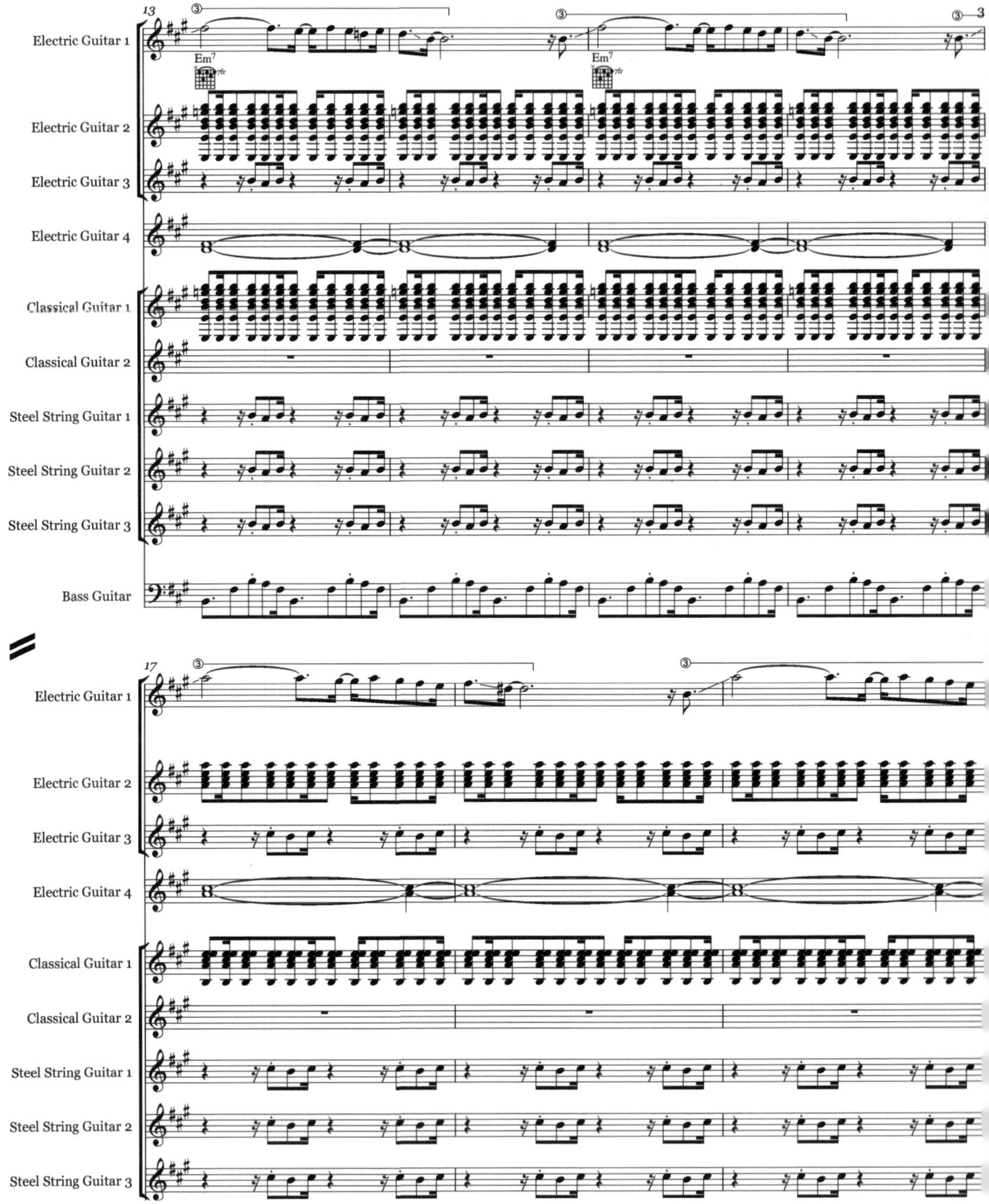
13
Electric Guitar 1
Em7
7fr
Electric Guitar 2
Electric Guitar 3
Electric Guitar 4
Classical Guitar 1
Classical Guitar 2
Steel String Guitar 1
Steel String Guitar 2
Steel String Guitar 3
Bass Guitar
17
Electric Guitar 1
Electric Guitar 2
Electric Guitar 3
Electric Guitar 4
Classical Guitar 1
Classical Guitar 2
Steel String Guitar 1
Steel String Guitar 2
Steel String Guitar 3

Interview with Rafael Toral

▶

Schulman: As a musician long associated with drone, modulated feedback, and free jazz, what motivated the engagement with traditional jazz changes on *Spectral Evolution*?

Toral: ArAround 2018, I felt compelled to regain contact with a more static form of music connected to my guitar work from the 1990s. This time around, however, I wanted to work with harmonies from 1930s jazz, which I love. I was passionate about the sound of those chords and completely in love with some of the songs' superb arrangements. I was drawn to work with that material and deliver something, which mostly turned into an abstraction, creating patterns of traditional changes, such as the cascading series of 2-5-1's in "Descending," or the V-V-V of "Fifths Twice."

Chords have a sound of their own, like sound entities. To better savor each one, I slowed them down, to a drone, stretching the swing to a point where you can still make sense of the changes. The clean guitar drone sound I developed back in 1987, which would turn into *Sound Mind Sound Body*'s main pieces, turned out to be a perfect carrier for this.

Spectral Evolution is an album where I put these ideas into practice, while also clashing the soundworld of free-jazz inspired electronics that I developed in the Space Program, here challenged to sound in the keys of harmony.

Schulman: More broadly, what do you see as the relationship between stasis, experimentation, and structure?

Toral: I experiment at home and perform the results of the experiments in public. So let's agree we can use the term 'experiment' as an umbrella for performance that is unpredictable. From the viewpoint of performance, every sound, every decision, every shift (including pauses and silence) creates structure. I understand performance as a process that both unfolds and reveals structure, only to be fully appreciated when the performance ends. Stasis is a type of structure, in every possible scale. We can describe stasis as an apparent lack of forward motion, yet a static form can still accommodate many kinds of dynamic forms. I think stasis operates in the listener as giving up the expectation of change, so there's a fair degree of subjectivity in how it's perceived. In the end, they can all be aspects of the same thing: Performance structured in a way that creates a sense of permanence, even of place.

Working with harmony in *Spectral Evolution* made me want to write music for instruments again and explore the possibilities for orchestral sound. I was very much interested in contemporary music in the beginning of my career. The influence of John Cage was especially important and had a significant impact on how I understand sound, silence, error, listening and many other things. When he died in 1992, I was inspired to write a tribute piece, employing several of his fascinating compositional methods, from time brackets to chance operations to the layering of transparent prints. I extracted compositional information from intersecting lines over superimposed maps of Lisbon and Manhattan and called it "Score for Two Points in Space". It generated lots of material and I scored it for a small orchestra, but as a self-taught non-academic outsider I was far from having a chance to see it performed.

Fast forward to 2024, I was invited to write a piece for Grupo de Música Contemporânea de Lisboa, a group founded by composer Jorge Peixinho, who worked with Stockhausen, etc., in a project intended to bridge cultures. I thought I wouldn't have the time to fully dive into writing a piece from scratch, but then it dawned on me that I could re-arrange that piece for the group, using mostly sinewaves alongside the live instruments, and have it premiered as a new version. Hearing it for the first time, I was surprised to find it more enjoyable than I expected.

While it's true that I have pretty much steered clear of writing music—composing—for most of my life, this episode was the culmination of a dynamic and gradual movement toward a renewed interest in writing for instruments. It signals the opening of new doors.

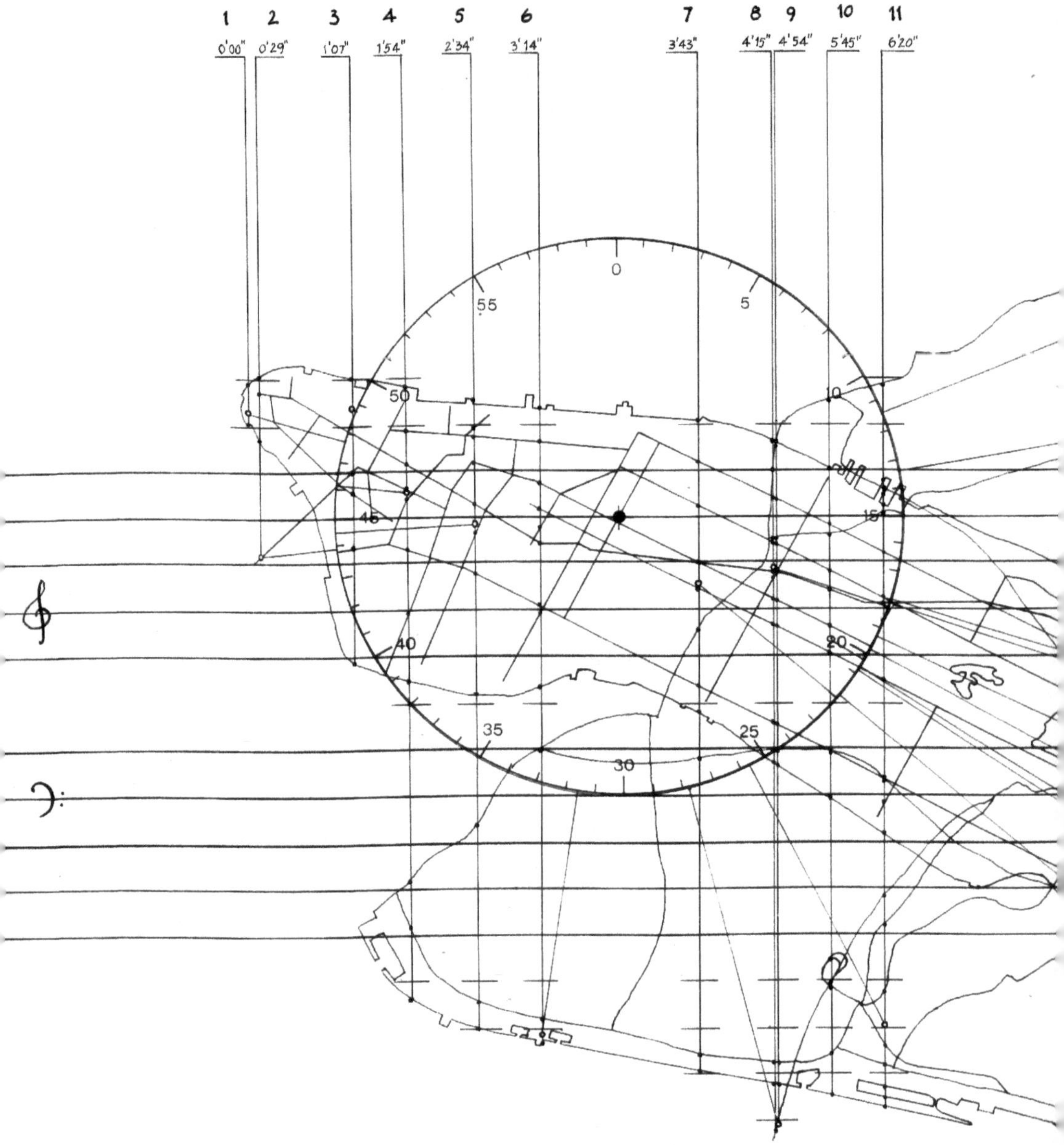

1
0'00"
2
0'29"
3
1'07"
4
1'54"
5
2'34"
6
3'14"
7
3'43"
8
4'15"
9
4'54"
10
5'45"
11
6'20"
0
5
10
15
20
25
30
35
40
45
50
55

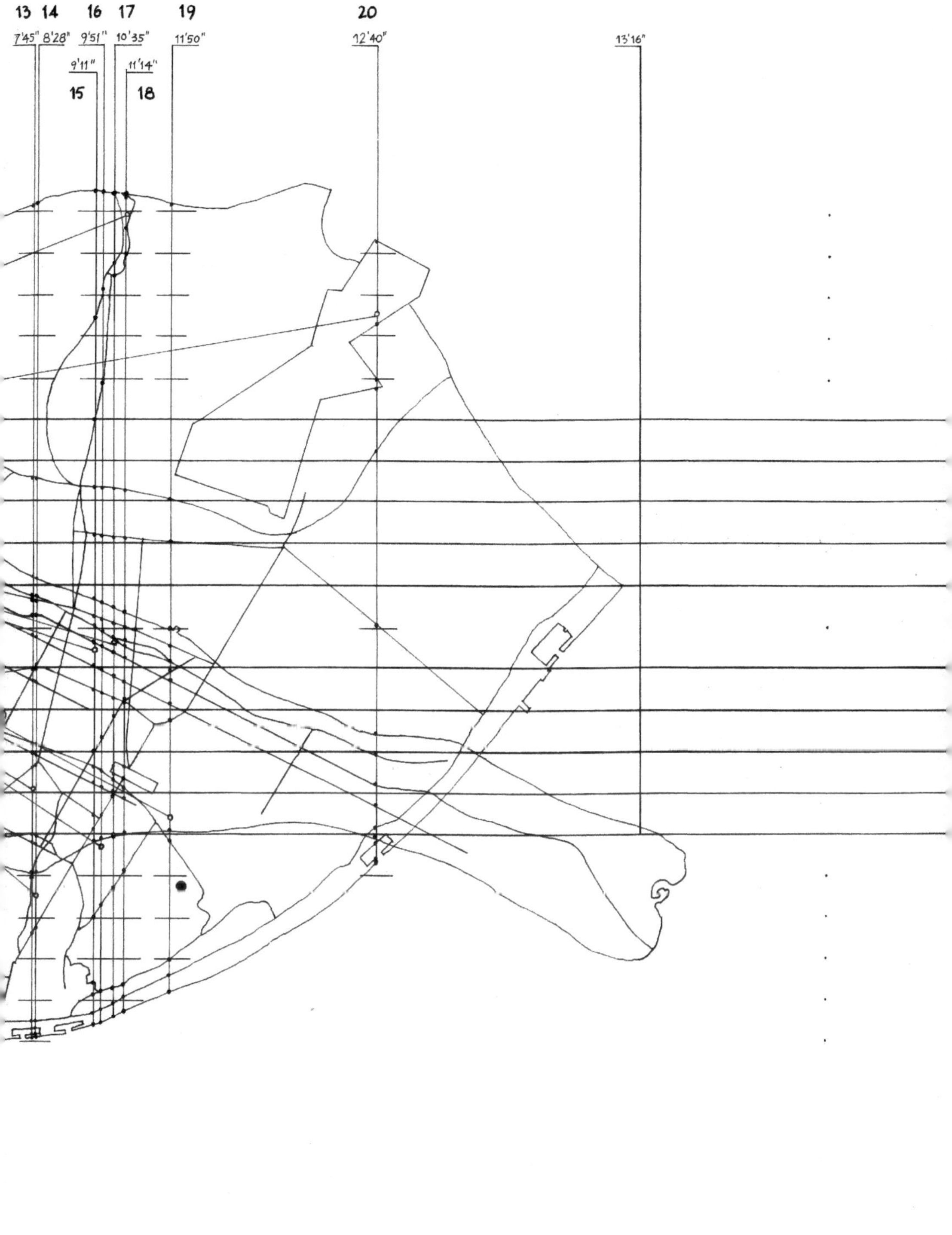

SCORE FOR TWO POINTS IN SPACE
(A tribute to John Cage)

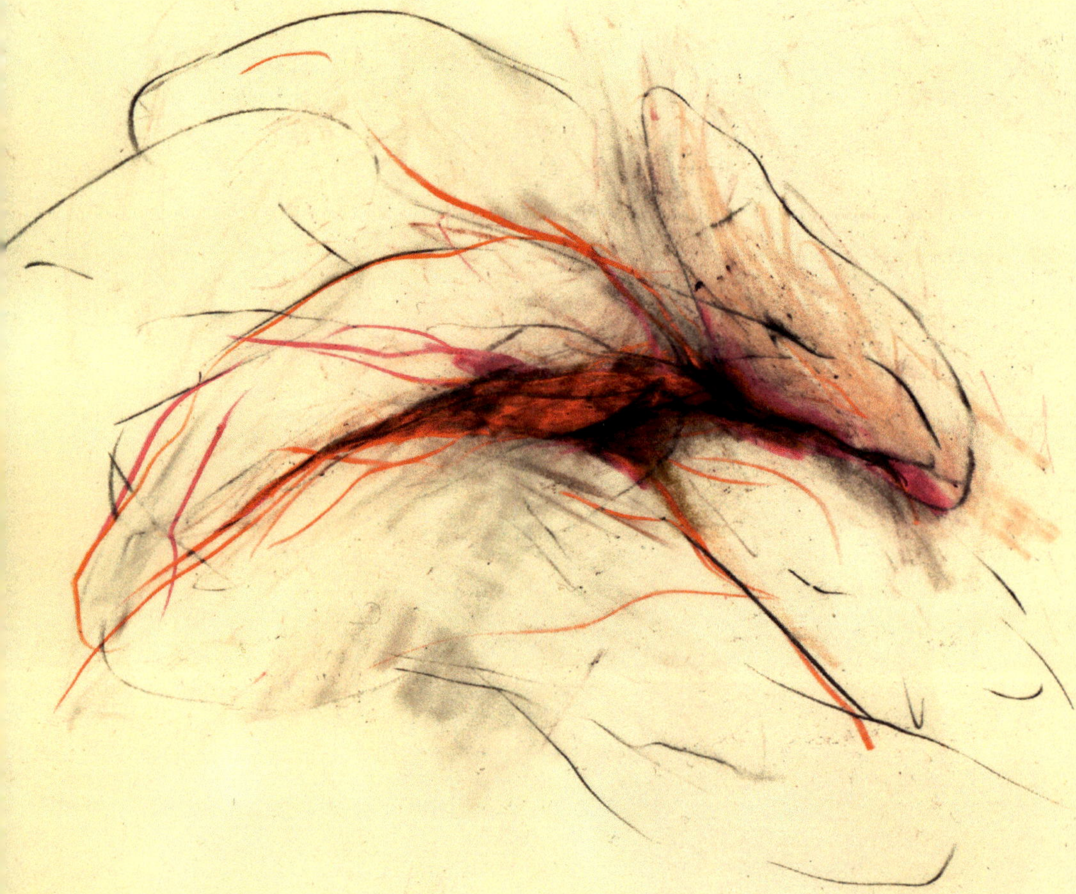

Worlds of Yiddish Poetry

Daniel Kraft
Editor

Yiddish poetry is not a world unto itself. That would be too reductive, too constrained. Yiddish poetry is a cosmos, a whirl of worlds, bound together by the gravity formed by millennia of Jewish civilization, and by the power of the Yiddish language, which in its rich linguistic inheritances—Germanic, Semitic, Slavic, and more—embodies the depth and complexity of Ashkenazi Jewish life.

If I can risk belaboring the metaphor, I want to say that each of the poets in this folio is their own planet, that they veer around each other in eccentric orbits. But I don't know much about astronomy; I'm already out of my depth. And this isn't unique to Yiddish. Every poet in every language is a world-creator, a kind of tiny god making a living sphere of meaning in their own idiosyncratic image.

How to reconcile that polytheism of creativity with the monotheism Jewish culture insists on? Better to refuse reconciliation entirely, to let the conflict remain as a source of creative energy. This is a modern poetic answer—think Keats's "negative capability," or Whitman's "very well then, I contradict myself"—tbut it is also an ancient Jewish answer. In the Babylonian Talmud, two schools of rabbinic scholars spend three years arguing over the truth, each side insisting on their own rightness. At last, God's voice descends to settle the dispute. "Both of these incompatible claims," the divinity says, "are the words of the Living God."

Those Yiddish writers, then, who were steeped in Jewish literary-theological discourse were prepared for the passionate ambivalences of modernist art; their cultural background of rabbinic debate and paradox-filled mysticism had primed them to embrace with gusto and ambition the literary upheavals of the early 20th century. This, at least, is my unprovable pet theory. How else to explain the sudden, astonishing flowering of Yiddish literature that took place around and after World War I?

All of the poets in this folio came of age at times of cataclysmic change in both Jewish and broader western culture and participated, in different ways, and different times and places, in the wild, transnational development of modern Yiddish poetry. But none of them should be considered representative of Yiddish literature, or of any ideological trend or historical moment. Even when their poems respond to a historical event, or support an ideology, these writers should be considered lyric poets above all, expressing the workings of their own consciousness more than any political program or theological stance.

All of these poets were born in Eastern Europe, and many were born within just a few years of each other. Moyshe Leyb-Halpern (1886-1932) left his Galician hometown for America in order to avoid military conscription, and became one of the most influential members of New York's Yiddish avant-garde. H. Leivick (1888-1962) was born Leivick Halpern, but changed his name in order to avoid being confused with his slightly older Yiddish poetry compatriot. After Leivick's arrest by Czarist authorities in 1906, he was sentenced to hard labor and exile in Siberia, but was freed and smuggled out of Europe by the Jewish revolutionary underground in 1913. When he died in New York City, he was eulogized as the world's foremost Yiddish poet.

Anna Margolin (1887-1952), the pen name of Rosa Lebensboym, also emigrated to America, but then spent several troubled, itinerant years living in Paris, Warsaw, London, and Tel Aviv before returning permanently to New York. Her sole poetry collection was published there in 1929, to critical acclaim tempered by an occasionally misogynistic reception. Daniel Charney (1888-1959) was similarly itinerant, living in six European countries, moving both for political reasons and to pursue treatment for tuberculosis, before settling in New York in 1941.

The only poets included here who did not emigrate to the United States, Izzi Kharik (1898-1937) and Meyshe Kulbek (1896-1937), found acclaim in the Soviet Union, and were influential figures within Yiddish cultural circles there. But their ideological ambivalence and relative artistic independence were intolerable to the totalitarian Soviet regime, and both poets were murdered in Stalin's purges.

All of the poets in this folio were multilingual, but none were as accomplished in the English language as Menke Katz (1906-1991), who emigrations to the United States as a teenager and wrote nine books each in English and Yiddish, and was nominated for the Pulitzer Prize. Amidst the displacements these poets experienced, Rajzel Zychlinski (1910-2001) was the last one to remain in Europe. Living in her native Poland at the time of Germany's invasion, she fled eastward, surviving the war years as a refugee in Tatarstan. Most of her family was murdered in the Nazi genocide of Europe's Jews, and after the war she returned to Poland for several years before settling in North America.

These biographies, even in the most abridged form, tell of the tumult that engulfed Jewish modernity, and was the backdrop for all 20th century Yiddish literary creativity. Readers who would like more information about any of these poets or poems are welcome to contact me directly, or to make use of any of the excellent online resources for Yiddish culture, including the encyclopedias maintained by YIVO and by the Jewish Women's Archive.

My hope is that this folio will be seen and enjoyed not as a summary of the cosmos that is Yiddish poetry, but as a small glimpse into its richness and diversity. Readers who take this folio as an invitation to read further will find what I, and all the translators herein, have found as well: like the cosmos that contains our own earth, the breadth and depth of Yiddish poetry are unimaginably expansive, and would repay lifetimes of exploration.

A Dead Bird

Rajzel Zychlinsky

Translated by Susan Cohen

A dead bird on the New York asphalt,
wings splayed,
gray feathers,
a little blood—
yet another red-brown splotch
of autumn, harmonizing
with the universe.
Not one eyebrow quivers,
not one tear shivers,
an indifference drapes the city
in a fog.
Automobiles race, hurry,
with beast-like,
electric eyes.
Tips of skyscrapers climb
higher and higher to heaven.
A cloud extends a heavy
menacing hand—
God's finger will soon
scrape everything into the sea.

New York, 1969

אַ טויטער פֿויגל

אַ טויטער פֿויגל אויפֿן ניו־יאָרקער אַספֿאַלט,
צעשפּרייטע פֿליגל,
גרויע פֿעדערן,
אַביסל בלוט־־
נאָך אַ ברוין־רויטער,
האַרמאָנישער האַרבסט־פֿלעק
אין אוניווערס.
קיין ברעם גיט נישט קיין ציטער,
קיין טרער נישט קיין פֿלאַטער,
אַ גלייכגילטיקייט הילט איין די שטאָט
אין אַ טומאַן.
אויטאָמאָבילן יאָגן, איילן,
מיט היהשע,
עלעקטרישע אויגן.
שפּיצן פֿון וואַלקן־קראַצערס קלעטערן
אַלץ העכער און העכער צום הימל.
אַ וואָלקן ציט אויס אַ שווערע
דראָענדיקע האַנט־־
גאָטס פֿינגער וועט באַלד אַלע
אַריינשאַרן אין ים.

The Road to Sodom

Menke Katz

Translated by Jacob Romm

Kingdom
of sunlight.
Work not of clay
and bricks, not of hands
but of sun. Sodom won't
allow any shadow's touch,
any kiss of dew. Lot's wife too
is a pillar of sunlight, not salt.
The desert is a garden of fire,
each ray of light a blighted rose. Far crueler
than any other kingdom is the kingdom of the sun.

Kingdom
of dust. Look!
Enchanted peaks—
a whole world dreamed up
by dust. Wind and laughter,
sorrow and sobbing of dust,
wicked and righteous, Gehenna
and Eden of dust. Kingdom of dust—
more endless than any eternity.
It will outlast the sun—it will outlast
even the heavens, yes, even the Lord our God.

There, a
camel, there
a Bedouin—
emerging as if
from a mirage. Desert
thornbushes, like the wicked
of Sodom, try once more to trick
the weary traveler into bed,
hack off his feet if they protrude, and point
again with their broken, ashy fingers,
to the blackened heavens, scorched as the Negev Desert.

There, the
angel who
wrestled Jacob
at midnight. A man
playing a tune on the flute,
a shepherd whose sheep look like
they just ran off from Abraham's
flock. Dusk. A settlement at sunset,
my hometown on wings, prepares to fly back
to the old country. But my shtetl collapses,
breaking into jagged fragments of desert night.

Shadows
tread with the
footsteps of my
strangled uncles, each
wearing a body of
sorrow, their eyes like sulfur
and pitch. They caress the cursed flames,
beg the exhausted desert for
still more bitterness. Oh beloved Sodom,
bestow your final, your one-and-only gift -
death. For this light is crueler than any darkness.

Night. God,
in Adam's
image, forgives
his ancient curses,
offers even Sodom
the blessing murmured before
breishit. From the virginal
bed of the earth, the indifferent
generations arise. Here, in a desert
tree's embrace, sleeps a moon-girl—another
Eve, dreaming and waiting, impatient to be born.

Moon-girl,
my still un-
risen sun, my
world of yearning. You
have waited for me since
the world began, patient as
time. Please wait, keep waiting—from root
to crown of the lonely acacia.
As certain as the light of a distant
dawn, I will come to you. I'll be at your side—
a story the wind has not yet finished telling.

אויפֿן וועג קיין סדום

מלוכה
פֿון זון. סדום,
ניט פֿון ליים און
ציגל, ניט פֿון הענט,–
פֿון זון געבויט, לאָזט ניט
קיין גלעט פֿון אַ שאָטן, קיין
קוס פֿון טוי ניט צו. לוטס ווייב איז
שוין ניט קיין זייל זאלץ, נאָר א זייל זון.
דער נגב איז אַ גאָרטן פֿון פֿלאַמען
אַ שטראַל איז אַ פֿאַרשאָלטענע רויז. אָ, די
גרויזאַמסטע פֿון אַלע מלוכות: מלוכה פֿון זון.

מלוכה
פֿון שטויב, זע,
צויבער־בערג, די
וועלטן וואָס דער שטויב
האָט אויסגעקלערט. ווינט און
געלעכטער, צאָרן און געוויין
פֿון שטויב. צדיקים און רשעים,
גן־עדן און גיהנום פֿון שטויב.
די מלוכה פֿון שטויב איז אייביקער פֿון
אַלע אייביקייטן, אייִביקער פֿון זון,
אָ אייִביקער אַפֿילו פֿון הימל, פֿון גאָט.

אָט, אַ
קעמל, אַ
בעדואינער,
ווי פֿון אַ מיראַזש
אַרויס. די דערנער פֿון
נגב, די רשעים פֿון סדום
נאַרן נאָך דעם מידן וואַנדערער
אין סדום־בעטל אַרײַן, האַקן נאָך
פֿון געסט די צו לאַנגע פֿיס, טייטלען נאָך
מיט די צעבראָכענע, אַשיקע פֿינגער,
קעגן דעם פֿאַרברענטן, מדברדיקן הימל.

אָט אַ
ייִד, יעקבס
ראַנגלענדיקער
מלאַך. אָט איז אַ
ייִד, מיט אַ פלייט אין מויל,
אַ פּאַסטעך מיט שאָף ווי פֿון
אברהם אבינוס סטאַדע
פֿאַרבלאָנדזשעט. אָוונט. אַ ישוב אין
זונפֿאַרגאַנג, מײַן שטעטעלע אויף פֿליגל,
גרייט אהיים פֿליען, נאָר מײַן שטעטעלע פֿאַלט,
צעפֿאַלט אין שטעכיקע שטיקער נאַכט פֿון נגב.

שאָטנס
שפּאַנען מיט
טריט פֿון מײַנע
דערשטיקטע פֿעטערס,
יעדער מיט אַ גוף פֿון
צאָרן, מיט אויגן – פּעך און
שוועבל, גלעטן פֿאַרשאָלטענע
פֿלאַמען, בעטלען רשעות פֿון שטחים
פֿאַרחלשטע: אוי, ליבינקע סדום, שענק
אַ לעצטע, אײנאונאײנציקע נדבה:
טויט, ווײַל ליכט איז גרויזאַמער פֿון יעדן חושך.

נאַכט. גאָט
בצלם
אדם, טרייסלט
אָפּ פֿון זיך קללות
פֿון יאָרטויזנטן, בענטשט
אויך סדום מיט די ברכות פֿון
ערב בראשית. די ערד איז א
בתולהדיק געלעגער, רייצט די נאָך
אומבאַרירטע דורות. אַ לבנהדיק
מיידל, אַ נאָך ניט געבאָרענע חוה
דרימלט דאָ אין די אָרעמס פֿון אַ מדבר־בוים,
וואַרט נייגעריק, אין חלום, געבאָרן צו ווערן.

מיידל,
מיין נאָך ניט
געטאָגטע זון,
מיין פֿאַרבענקטע וועלט;
וואַרטסט אויף מיר זינט ערשטן
באַשאַף, געדולדיק ווי צײַט.
וואַרט אָ וואַרט, פֿון שורש ביז דער
איינזאַמער קרוין פֿון נגב־בוים. כ'וועל
קומען צו דיר, זיכער ווי דאָס ליכט פֿון
אַ ווייטן מאָרגן. כ'וועל זײַן לעבן דיר, אַ
מעשהלע וואָס דער ווינט האָט נאָך ניט אויסדערציילט.

Not There

H. Leivick

Translated by Bluma Lange

I seek the slain—
He is not there.
The field has taken him into itself,
The field has covered him with grass
And none has placed any mark for him.
I seek the slain—
He is not there.

I seek the murderer—
He is not there.
Over the field treads with soft steps
A quiet peasant, a pious peasant.
He walks in the mark of his plow.
He had dug up and plowed the field
and plowed over the traces of his murder.
The field he has sown with grain for him and his household
And for his sheep and his cattle.
I seek the murderer—
He is not there.

I seek the judge—
He is not there.
The grain, green, rising up,
Blooms and grows tall.
Here sway the full, ripe stalks—
A whole forest, a cornucopia gold.

Ought an ear of corn be the witness?
Ought a sheaf of wheat deliver the punishment?
I seek the judge—
He is not there.

Argentina, 1955

נישטאָ

איך זוך דעם הרוג –
ער איז נישטאָ.
דאָס פֿעלד האָט אים אין זיך אַריינגענומען,
דאָס פֿעלד האָט אים מיט גראָז באַדעקט.
און קיינער האָט נאָך אים קיין שייכן נישט געשטעלט.
איך זוך דעם הרוג –
ער איז נישטאָ.

איך זוך דעם מערדער –
ער איז נישטאָ.
עס טראַט איבערן פֿעלד מיט ווייכע טריט,
אַ פּויערל אַ שטילס, אַ פּויערל אַ פֿרומס,
ער שפּאַנט אין צייכען פֿון זיין אַקעראייזן,
און אויך דעם זכר פֿון זיין מאָרד פֿאַראַקערט.
דאָס פֿעלט האָט ער פֿאַרצייט מיט ברויט –
מיט ברויט פֿאַר זיך און פֿאַר זיין הויזגעזונד
און פֿאַר זיין שאָף און פֿאַר זיין רינד
און זוך דעם מאָרדער –
ער איז נישטאָ.

איז זוך דעם שופֿט –
ער איז נישטאָ.
דאָס ברויט, אין גרין, איז אויפֿגעגאַנגען,
געבליט און גרויס צעוואָקסט זיך,
אַט וויגט זיך די פֿולע, רייפֿע זאַנגען –
אַ גאַנצער וואַלד פֿון שפּעדיקן גאָלד.

זאָל זײַן אַ זאַנג דער עדות?
זאָל זײַן אַ גאַרב די שטראָפֿער?
איך זוך דעם שופֿט –
ער איז נישטאָ.

The Shot Clock

Daniel Charney

Translated by Jacqueline Krass

The face of the church clocktower is shot to pieces,
Two hands still pendulate around its naked innards.
And on the cobblestones lies a carcass, a horse's—
Half-devoured by hungry dogs and worms.

Mother Time herself has miscarried from terror,
And her two clock hands grimace crazily.
A cannon somewhere startles out again,
And, coughing, counts tomorrow's dead one by one.

And on the cobblestones lies a carcass, a horse's,
Half-devoured by hungry dogs and worms.—
A hungry peasant from Kharkiv or Perm
Longed for a new way of life.

Now two long, senile hands crawl the circular socket,
moving like blind men's canes.
Fear crawls through the streets and homes,
And no one has the strength to light a lamp.

Who knows if it's day, who knows if it's night,
the paths to aborted time are all closed,
and a brute from Perm in the red market square
rejoices that he shot the clock of history…

His victorious face beams like a clocktower
and his mustache, like clock hands, grimaces—
Here begins a new way of life,
and you, O you—don't weep for the dead of tomorrow...

Moscow, October, 1917

דער צעשאָסענער ציפּערבלאַט

צעשאָסן איז דער ציפּערבלאַט פֿון קויסטערזייגער
צוויי ווייזערס פּענדלען נאָך אויף נאַקעטע געדערעם.
און אונטן אויפֿן ברוקשטיין ליגט אַ פֿערדס אַ פּגר–
ס'פֿרעסן אים שוין הונגעריקע הינט און ווערעם.

עס האָט די מוטער־צייט אַליין פֿאַר שרעק געמפּלט
און ס'מאַכן איר צוויי ווייזערס משוגענע העויות,
עס האָט שוין ווידער אַ האַרמאַט וואו אויפֿגעצאַפּלט
און הוסטנדיק אַלך צוגעציילט די מאָרגיקע לויות.

און אונטן אויפֿן ברוקשטיין ליגט אַ פֿערדס אַ פּגר,
עס פֿרעסן אים שוין הונגעריקע הינט און ווערעם.–
דאָס האָט אַ פֿאַרבענקט זיך נאָך אַ נייעם לעבנסשטייגער
אַ הונגעריקער פּויער פֿון כאַרקאָוו צי פֿון פּערם.

איכט פּויזן עובר בטל צוויי לאַנגע, שאווארצע ווייזערס
אויף קײלעכדיקן חלל, ווי שטעקלעך פֿון אַ בלינדן
און ס'פּויזעט אום אַ שרעק אויף גאַסן און אויף הייזער
און קיינער האָט קיין מוט אַ נאַכט־לאָמפּ אונצוצינדן.

ווער ווייס דען, צי ס'איז טאָג, ווער ווייס דען, צי ס'איז אָוונט,
עס זענען אַלע וועגן דו מפּיל־צייט געשלאָסן,
און אויפֿן רויטן מאַרקפּלאַץ שטייט אַ פּערמער יון–
ער פֿרייט זיך, וואָס ער האָט דעם וועלטזייגער צעשאָסן.

זײַן זיאיגעריש געזיכט שטראַלט, ווי אַ טורעם־זייגער
און וואָנצעס, ווי צוויי ווייזערס מאַכן דיר העויות–
דאָס הויבט זיך אָן פֿון היינט אַ נייער לעבנסשטייגער
און דו, אָ דו – ניט ווייַן אויף מאָרגיקע לויות...

מאָסקווע, אָקטאָבער, 1917.

From My Darkness

Anna Margolin

Translated by Kathryn Hellerstein

1

I speak in stammers.
In deathly angst
Wrestling with myself
I seek the word
That will radiate, though crooked and pale,
My joyous, my world-embracing hate.

2

The day's sharp claws have loosed the sacrifice.
In the darkness, twisted up,
Full of little holes, and small,
I lie and hear how silent and pure,
How silent and vast,
A cry arises in me without tears
And spreads out like a vast bridge toward the morning.

3

As from trampled bloody grapes
One presses out refined wine,
So have I sucked out my joy
From pain,
And with dying hands raised it high
To the dazzling, murderous shine
Of God's eyes.

פֿון מײַן פֿינשטערניש

א

איך רעד שטאַמלענדיק.

אין טויטלאַכער אַנגסט

מיט זיך אַליין זיך ראַנגלענדיק

זוך איך דאָס וואָרט,

וואָס זאָל אַרויסשטראַלן כאָטש קרום און בלאַס

מיין פֿרייליאַכן, מיין וועלט־אַרומנעמענדן האַס.

ב

די שאַרפֿע נעגל פֿון דעם טאָג האָבן אָפּגעלאָזט דעם קרבן.

אין דער פֿינשטערניש, צענויפֿגעדרייט,

און לעכערלאַך, און קליין,

ליג איך און הער, ווי שטיל און ריין,

ווי שטיל און ברייט

שטייגט אויף אין מיר אָן טרערן אַ געוויין

און שפּרייט זיך ווי אַ ברייטער בריק צום מאָרגן.

ג

ווי פֿון צעטראָטענע בלוטנדע טרויבן

פּרעסט מען אויס דעם איידעלן וויין,

אַזוי האָב איך מיין פֿרייד אויסגעזויגן

פֿון פּיין,

און מיט גוסס'ע הענט זי דערהויבן

צום בלענדענדן גרויזאמן שיין

פֿון גאָט'ס אויגן.

from *Minsk Muck*

Izi Kharik

Translated by Madeleine Cohen

Pinye is one of countless poor and orphaned children in the Jewish neighborhood of Muck, invisible to the bourgeoisie. Already the anger and resentment at the hardness of life is growing like a fist inside Pinye.

1

Around each proud street—perhaps a hundred quiet alleys
With low little houses, like sheep at the mountain's base…
Minsk had forgotten, about them, about everyone—
And all roads lead to the marketplace…

Here in the depths, in the warmth of the muck,
In wooden houses hidden at the city's edge,
A pain rises, juicy and ripe,
A fist clenching every child's heart.

They haven't planted trees in parks here,
Here they play in the naked dirt…
A fist, young and strong, is grasping, growing,
Someday it will break the glass.

Someday a hatred will push through all reason,
Hard and sharp, cutting off the heart…
— — — — — — — — — — — — — — — — — — — —
Little children play here, little Pinyes play here
Wallowing here, in the naked dirt.

3

Pinye didn't grow up spoiled here,
Just one of thousands abandoned under the sun…
What does a youth from warped alleyways know
Except fearsome stories of the Bund[1]?

Hard days and nights without dad or mom
With only a bare fist and misery under his head—
There's a city full of light, close by, nigh on,
From up there to down here no one descends.

Minsk—clarified Belarusian sorrow
With warped and beggarly hands,
For every tall brick house that rises,
A dark cellar sinks below.

[1] The Jewish Labor Bund was a secular Jewish socialist political movement.

מינסקער בלאָטעס

1

אַרום יעדער שטאָלצער גאַס – צו הונדערט שטילע געסלעך
מיט הייזלעך נידעריקע, ווי שעפּסן אונטער באַרג...
ס'האָט מינסק אָן זיי, אָן אַלעמען פֿאַרגעסן –
און אַלע וועגן פֿירן נאָר צום מאַרק...

און דאָ אין טיף, אין וואַרימקייט פֿון בלאָטעס,
אין הייזלעך הילצערנע שוין אויסן שטאָט פֿאַרשאַרט –
גייט אויף אַ ווייטאָק זאַפּטיק און געראָטן,
און ס'ציטערט אויף אַ פּויסט אין יעדער קינדיש האַרץ.

מע האָט דאָ ניט פֿאַרפֿלאַנצט קיין בוימער און קיין פֿאַרקן –
שפּילט מען זיך דאָ הוילינקע אין שטויב...
און ס'גיסט זיך אָן אַ פויסט אַ יונגער און אַ שטאַרקער,
און ווען־עס־איז וועט ער אַ זעץ טאָן אין אַ שויב.

וועט ווען־עס־איז אַ האַס אַ שפּאַר טאָן דורכן זינען,
און שטרענג, און שאַרף אַ שניט טאָן איבער האַרץ...

– –

שפּילן זיך דאָ קינדערלעך, שפּילן זיך דאָ פּיניעס
און קייקלען זיך דאָ הוילינקע אין זאַמד.

3

איז פּיניע דאָ געוואַקסן ניט געפּיעסטעט,
ווי טויזנט אַנדערע פֿאַרלאָזן אונטער זון...
וואָס ווייס אַ יונג פֿון אויסגעקרימטע געסלעך,
אויסער מאַיסעס פֿאָרכטיקע פֿון "בונד"?

און שווערע טעג, און נעכט אָן טאַטע־מאַמע
מיט האַרטן פֿויסט און עלנט אונטער קאָפּ –
נאָענט איז אַ שטאָט אַ ליכטיקע פֿאַראַנען,
גייט אַהערצו קיינער ניט אַראָפּ.

מינסק–ווײַסרוסישער פֿאַרקלערטער טרויער
מיט בעטלערישער אויסגעקרימטער האַנט,
פֿאַרוואָס איז דאָ בא דיר אַף יעדן שטאָלצן מויער
אַזוי פֿיל קעלערן פֿאַראַן?

Aḥer, the Other

Meyshe Kulbak

Translated by Corbin Allardice

> **Four entered the orchard,** i.e., dealt with the loftiest secrets of Torah...**Aḥer chopped down the shoots** of saplings. In other words, he became a heretic.—Bavli, Chagigah 14b:8-9
>
> Aḥer, what was his failing? **Greek tunes never ceased from his mouth**...This shows that from the outset he was drawn to gentile culture and beliefs. —Bavli, Chagigah 15b:14[1]

Aḥer eats no more, drinks no more,
Aḥer is just eye and ear, eye and ear…
and in the field, reclining on the shore,
he lies.
He's quiet. Listening. And a boor.

"O you, you, I wanted to suffer in this life,
and mutely to follow your trembling light:
what I think *is* the world, and the world *is* the world,
and the muddy mystery goes unsolved.
Word after word, I cut and I threaded, like beads,
into a sonnet crown:
O you, you, what does man mean?
What is a hill?
And what does the dark dale dream?
Oh, you, hidden holder of *das All;*

[1] Epigraphs added by the translator

riverbed of the sedentary flow,
You, god!
Are you not born of my blood,
a bloody beam to light the abyss?"

At the shoreline. A naked body, shocked and dumb.
That's Aḥer.
A bare heap of eye and ear, eye and ear…
and his voice, as if rising from the dirt,
seethes,
Aḥer grieves, Aḥer grieves at the ends of the earth,

"I carry the burden of a gray soul
like a chain.
O why was I not preordained
to be a valley
mute…
You, see my raw dreams of clay,
in my heart—a warm, hazy field
which sings without breath in private choir
of one world, one world…
Yet the morning sun does not rise from me; its light congeals.
And I will not be lain in this empty night beneath the unformed blue…
Who knows, am I here, am I lying in these fields?...

"I lie and listen to the cool flow of damp stars,
I hide and wait and watch the thin milky way.
And you, where are you?
But so thirsty to discern you in paths of ecstasy
I forget the deaf sounds of tranquility.
So will we ever meet one day?...
The song of mute flesh shines from the depths and rises.
Witness! Witness!...
And like the oak, I branched myself into the earth and skies,
at least in dream,
so in your storm will you water, too, my seed?

You! You!
I want to fall mute—a tree in bloom,
I want to blossom in the red sunset and meet my doom,
I want to gently trickle down, a dew from that singing blue,
like a song,
like a sob…
Ach, you and I, we're both long gone, we're both long overdue…"

At the shoreline. A naked body, shocked and dumb.
That's Aḥer.
A bare heap of eye and ear, eye and ear…
And his voice, as if rising from the dirt,
seethes,
Aḥer grieves, Aḥer grieves at the ends of the earth.

אחר

אחר עסט שוין ניט, טרינקט שוין ניט מער.
אחר איז שוין גאָר אויג און געהער, אויג און געהער...
און אין פּעלה, צו דעם נאַקעטן ברעג צוגעשפּאַרט,
ער ליגט.
ער שווייגט. האָרכט. און האַרט.

"דו, דו, איך האָב ליידן אין לעבן געוואָלט,
נאָר נאָכגיין דיין ציטערדיק־ליכט שטילערהייט:
וואָס איך טראַצט אין די וועלט, און די וועלט איז די וועלט,
ס'איז דער אומקלאָרער סוד ניט באַשיידט.
כ'האָב ווערטער און ווערטער, ווי פֿינקלענדע שנורן קריסטאַל,

געשליפֿט און געוואָרפֿן אין קרענץ:
דו, דו, וואָס וואָס באַטייט אַ מענטש?
וואָס איז אַ באַרג?
און וואָס חלומט דער טונקעלער טאָל?
אָ, דו, די פֿאַרהוילענע שייד פֿונם אַל:
געלעגער פֿון לאַנג שוין פֿאַרגלייווערטן שטראָם,
דו גאָט!
ביסט ניט פֿון מיין בלוט אַ געבאָרענע, בלוטיקער שטראַל
צו באַלייכטן דעם תּהום?!"

ביים ברעג. ס'שטוינט אַ קערפּער אַ נאַקעטער שטום. דאָס איז ער.
אַ הויל בערגל פֿון אויג און געהער, אויג און געהער...
און די שטים, ווי פֿון דר'ערד אויסגעקוועלט,

יאָגט,
אחר קלאָגט, אחר קלאָגט ביי דעם עק פֿון דער וועלט:
"כ'טראָג אַרום פֿון דער גרויער נשמה דעם עול,
ווי אַ קייט.
אָ, פֿאַרוואָס בין איך ניט טויבערהייט
אויסגענאָטן געוואָרן
אַ טאָל...
דו, זע, מיינע רויע חלומות פֿון ליים,
אין מיין האַרץ – דאָס פֿאָרנעפּלטע, וואַרעמע פֿעלד,
וואָס ער זינגט אָן אַ אָטעם געהיים
פֿון איין וועלט, איין וועלט...
דאָך – דער מאָרגן־ראָז שטייגט אויפֿעט ניט פֿון מיר,
דאָס ליכט פֿאַרגייט
און כ'וועל אין וויסטער נאַכט צום אויסגעגלאָזט בלאָ
ניט ווערן צוגעלייט...
ווער ווייס, צי בין איך אויף די פֿעלדער דאָ?!...

"איך ליג און האָרך דעם קילן גאָם פֿון פֿייכטע שטערן,
כ'לויער אויף די דינע מילך־וועגן: און דו, וואו ביסטו?!
נאָר דאָרשטיק דיך אין פֿרייד־גאַנג צו דערהערן –
פֿאַרנעם איך נאָר די טויבע קלענג פֿון רו.
צי וועל איך דיך שוין וועל אַמאָל באַגעגענען??...
דאָס ליד פֿון שטומע קערפּערס גליט פֿון טיף און שטייגט.
זע צו! זע צו!!...
כ'האָב דעמביק מיך אין וועלט אַריינגעצווייגט,
כאָטש אינם טרוים,
צי ווּעסטו אינם שטורעם אויבעט מיך בערגענען?!
דו! דו!
כ'וויל פֿאַלן שטום – אַן אויפֿגעבליטער בוים,
כ'וויל בלומענדיק אין רויטן אונטערגאַנג פֿאַרגיין,
כ'וויל ווייך אַראָפּטריפֿן אַ טוי פֿון זינגענדיקן בלאָ,
ווי אַ געזאַנג,
ווי אַ געוויין...
ווי, סיי דו און איך – מיר זײַנען לאַנג ניטאָ!"

ביים ברעג. ס'שטוינט אַ קערפּער אַ נאַקעטער שטום. דאָס איז ער
אַ הויל בערגל פֿון אויג און געהער, אויג און געהער...

און די שטים, ווי פֿון דר'ערד אויסגעקוועלט,
יאָגט.
אחר קלאָגט, אחר קלאָגט ביי דעם עק פֿון דער וועלט.

The Hasidic Rebbe

Moyshe-Leyb Halpern

Translated by Richard Fein

Before he died, the rebbe asserted:
"Nobody should open the lid, the lid
of this box." But his wife had noticed,
ten years earlier, he took from his vest
something he put in the box, then nailed
the lid to the box. After his behest, she wailed
and moaned, for the rebbe had died,
and after the first week, when all had cried,
she just couldn't resist and one night
crept up the stairs to the attic, her candlelight
flickering, her forehead sweating in fear
of what she might end up finding there
and with pliers pulled the nails from the lid
and lifted it from the box, which the rebbe forbid.

Yes, pulled out the nails with pliers
and opened the lid. Yes,
pulled out the nails with pliers
and opened the lid… Yes.

דער צדיק

דער צדיק פֿאַר זיין טויט האָט אָנגעזאָגט:
מען זאָל נישט עפֿענען דאָס דעקל.
נאָר זיין ווייב, וואָס האָט אים געזען, פֿונם ווערסטל,
מיט צען יאָר צוריק – אַריינלייגן עפּעס אין קעסטל,
און דאָס דעקל צושלאָגן מיט אַ טשוועקל
האָט נישט באַוויזן זיך איינצוהאַלטן;
און כאָטש זי האָט געפֿילט דעם שווייס דעם קאַלטן,
וואָס רינט איר פֿאַר פּחד אַראָפּ פֿונם שטערן,
האָט זי גלייך נאָך דער שבעה־וואָך מיט אַ לאַמטערן
אין מיטן דער נאַכט זיך אויפֿגעהויבן,
און אַרויפֿגעקראָכן אויפֿן בוידעם אויבן,
און אַרויסגעשלעפּט מיט אַ צווענגל דאָס טשוועקל
און אויפֿגעעפֿנט דאָס דעקל.
יאָ – אַרויסגעשלעפּט מיט אַ צווענגל דאָס טשוועקל,
און אויפֿגעעפֿנט דאָס דעקל.
יאָ־יאָ־יאָ. אַרויסגעשלעפּט מיט אַ צווענגל דאָס טשוועקל
און אויפֿגעעפֿנט דאָס דעקל

Grolier Approaches 100: Poetry and Archives

James Fraser
Editor

Like a good poem or an archival object, The Grolier Poetry Book Shop will outlive us all. In 1927, Adrian Gambet and Gordon Cairnie founded The Grolier on 6 Plympton Street in Cambridge, Massachusetts, off Harvard Square. Cairnie, who soon became the sole owner, operated The Grolier less like a business and more like a social club, as he held court to literary figures, students and general readers. If one item defined the Cairnie era, it's the couch. To this day an original Elsa Dorfman photograph hangs on the wall of Lawrence Ferlinghetti sitting on the couch. Borges, a visiting lecturer at Harvard would stop by the Grolier and sit on it. Browsers, who had no idea who the gentle blind man was, would be asked what books they were looking at. It is said that during the Cairnie era many people didn't feel comfortable coming in the shop because it exuded the atmosphere of a boy's club. In that era, friends of The Grolier included T. S. Eliot, Ezra Pound, Marianne Moore, Robert Lowell, E.E.Cummings, John Ashbery, Charles Olson, Robert Bly, James Tate and Frank O'Hara. Cairnie was legendary.

Louisa Solano took over in 1974 after Cairnie's death, turning The Grolier into an all-poetry shop. Solano threw out the couch and began operating the store more like a business. One criticism of the Solano era was her increasing paranoia, as she accused many people of stealing. By the end of her tenure, she didn't allow browsing. You had to know what you wanted. She had also maxed out her credit cards and the shelves were sparse. To Solano's credit, she ran a world class book shop with an incredible selection of books. She also created a world class poetry reading series and The Grolier Poetry Prize which helped younger poets gain recognition. During the Solano era, friends of The Grolier included Ai, Robert Creeley, David Ferry, Allen Ginsberg, Denise Levertov, Adrienne Rich, Ruth Stone, and Franz Wright. Solano was visionary.

Solano sold the shop to Ifeanyi Menkiti, who had it until his death in 2019. His family owns the shop today. One noticeable shift: for the first time the proprietor of The Grolier wasn't present full time at the shop. Although involved with The Grolier community from the 1960s, Menkiti, who also wrote poems, was a full-time philosopher and professor. He hired managers to run the shop. First Daniel Weunschel, later Elizabeth Doran (who invited me to sell books part time—thank you Elizabeth!) and then myself, taking over when Elizabeth retired at the start of Covid.

One of the hallmarks of the Menkiti era was how Ifeanyi would conduct conversations after poetry readings which would begin with a Q&A between the poet and the audience, usually leading into a larger discussion. Ifeanyi believed everyone deserved a seat at the table and saw The Grolier as, more than a book shop, a gathering place, a place to exchange ideas. He encouraged browsing and loved it when students would stop by and read for hours even if they couldn't afford a book. Menkiti was a wise man.

The Grolier is the oldest continuously operated all-poetry shop in America. As the Cambridge institution approaches its 100th year, this folio seeks to document a glimpse of the many poets who have read their poems in that small yet somehow cavernous space over the years. Each poet in this folio has read for The Grolier at some point in their career. They each have two poems in this folio—usually a previously published poem, ideally from the time when they first read at the shop, and a newer, often unpublished poem, reflecting work from their latest reading at The Grolier. This folio, both archival and new, documents the growth of The Grolier through the evolution of the poets who have read at it over the years. Each poet was also asked to write about their history and relationship with The Grolier as a preface to her two poems. May God bless The Grolier and may God bless the poets!

Note

Peter Balakian

I first walked into The Grolier sometime in the Fall of 1976 when I was living down the road in Providence where I was a graduate student at Brown. Driving to Cambridge to visit with my poet friends was always a joy especially in the middle of a semester. The shop on Plympton Street was a meeting place. That mews-like street off Mass Ave was lit up by the elegant Grolier Book Shop sign "est. 1927" that hung like a lantern from a metal arm. The big glass store window displayed new books of poems and posters announcing upcoming readings. The small store, with its wooden floors and shelves of books going to the ceiling—wrapped you up in poetry, and to a poet in his twenties, it was also intimidating—all those voices—new and canonical—swirling around you. But it was a sanctum sanctorum.

In those days Louise Solano was the owner and proprietor. She was alwayswarm and welcoming, a bit shy, but very much the proud presider over this singular place. She was always generous to me—inviting me in and letting me browse for as long as I wanted, and later always offering to stock copies of my latest book.

The store was a touchstone, and some of my friends would only buy poetry books from The Grolier. In those days if you weren't in town, a simple telephone call and a credit card did it. The first time I met Seamus Heaney on the Square in the Fall of '79, he suggested, after our lunch, that we go over to The Grolier and buy each other a book of poems. I bought Seamus Albert Goldbarth's *Optics*, and he bought me Thomas Kinsella's *Notes From The Land of The Dead.*

Of the several readings I did at The Grolier over the years, the most memorablewas a group reading organized by the new Grolier owner, the poet Ifeanyi Menkiti who had taught at Wellesley College for years. Ifeanyi Menkiti was a beautiful force of culture—a fine poet, a scholar of west African religions, and with his entrepreneurial instincts, he broadened the reach of store into the community. In September of 2015 he organized a reading to remember the Armenian poets executed by the Turkish government in 1915 at the beginning of the genocide. The reading was held, as many Grolier readings often were, off site and this one to an intense audience at the Cambridge Public Library. The poets Diana Der Hovanessian, and Krikor Der Hohenessian joined me and Ifeanyi. We read to a full house and the event went on with questions and conversation well into the evening. Ifeanyi had done what he often did—brought poetry and the community together under the sign of The Grolier.

Of the three poetry temples of my youth, only one remains. The Gotham Book Mart and Wilenz's 8th Street Book Shop are gone. Long live American democracy. Long live The Grolier.

Woodstock

Peter Balakian

In the mud of a tire rut,
        we were the filaments.

We said if Mrs. Agnew could make music
        on Spiro's flute

we said the clubs in the hands of the Chicago cops
        would liquefy.

The trees shook with the throb of steel.

What did we do to be so red, white, and blue?

We were inexorable
        like the dialectic unraveling from Hanoi
                to the Jacksonian grass.

We were the inebriates of vitamin C and cocaine,
the daughters of the gray flannel suit.

And when the shaman spread his yellow robe like the sun
he was all teeth and amp

and what were we?

Red Lentils

When you pour the orange

kernels in the water
with onions and garlic

parsley and cracked wheat,

watch them bubble up
like a hallucinatory plume—

before they
gurgle at low heat

and merge
with the onions.

When you add yoghurt
it all creams up

into a history
of your grandmother's

life before the sky fell—

death march, famine,
a disappeared family—

an old story—
shared by too many.

When you take a spoonful
your tongue's lit up—

alphabets of birds
fly through curlicues

of steam
to your horizon.

Note

Christina Davis

"Poets are the perfect revolutionaries!" Fanny Howe observed, as we walked past the beloved, lately shuttered Café Pamplona (b. 1959-d. 2020). "Yes," I said, "poets know that even a Revolution needs a place to meet!" And, with that, we made our way toward the resolutely-unshuttered Grolier.

Of all the transformational meeting places that poetry has helped to create and perpetuate, I can't think of one that is more humble, intimate, idiosyncratic, anti-ergonomic, tough-loving, tender, ever-evolving, and downright deathless than The Grolier Poetry Book Shop. In visiting it, we pay homage to the sheer persistence of our artform across the generations, to poetry's inimitable capacity (like the bookstore) to construct intimacy out of vastness and to bring together unlike entities and beings into a shocking new synthesis.

The Grolier is a relentless work-in-progress; a 100-year-old startup; a morphic literary form that constantly reinvents itself and re-arises. Just as Melville said the whaling ship was his Harvard & Yale, The Grolier and bookstores like it (including the one my Mom owned and that I worked in after school) have been my education. It's there that the true Study occurs—if, as Moten says, by "study" we mean what we do *with* people—talking, walking, communing, "becoming com."

In honor of The Grolier as a site of continued learning and communion, I've included two poems that emerged from immersing in other poets' works there and from the vectors of freedom, peace & possibility they've contributed to my existence. The first poem is dedicated to Jean Valentine (with whom I participated in protests during the Bush era, when cages began to be placed around demonstrations) and the second poem is dedicated to Denise Riley. I should add that one of the last times I saw Jean in Cambridge, we gathered to discuss poetry, politics, and questions of the spirit at Pamplona and The Grolier. She was and remains a tremendous exemplar....

["Sometimes, I will be"]

Christina Davis

Sometimes, I will be passing a person

and the quiet riot
of names published in his
cemetery,

and the quiet riot
of names published in her
cemetery,

rises up in me
and to which I am
susceptible.

* * * *

In the City, the barricades are very tall
this time of year,

whereas the Soul

has no example.

Birthknell

after Denise Riley

Do you remember when you came to us,
in the original August?

Your birth was a long night, and no one
recognized you—

whose face was full of future,
whose name baptized a fresh will,
whose head was yet in Truth,
whose sentience was of a sudden,

who was "a curve in wilderness,"
whose listening was drenched in laud,
whose feet had only floated, who was
not so far already in the flesh,

whose self had yet "to replace the soul
as the fist of survival,"
whose mind did not divide between
loved ones & strangers,
whose hands were a bird come back
to us, whose love was

older than danger....

Note

Danielle Legros Georges

The Grolier Poetry Book Shop came into view for me in the late '80s when I was working as an editorial assistant at the Harvard Law School Publications Center after graduating from Emerson College. My lunch hours were spent in the Widener Library or in the various bookstores distributed across Harvard Square. The Grolier was the coziest—and closest to my interests then. Invariably, Louisa Solano would be perched behind the front desk, and her trusty dog (was it "Pumpkin"?) settled on the floor. I would greet both before perusing the shelves. In addition to Louisa and Pumpkin, I encountered at Grolier several members of the Dark Room Collective, a community of emerging Black writers who organized a Sunday reading series and held workshops and events open to the public. The Dark Room has since produced a great number of nationally notable writers, editors, and translators. Would I have been connected to the extraordinarily fruitful space that was the Dark Room without The Grolier? I don't know. I do know that The Grolier has been a site of extraordinary meetings for me across many years: a locus of links and reconnections to meaningful texts, individuals, and voices. I'm grateful to the Menkiti family for having sustained the venue, and for James Fraser's recent and energetic management of The Grolier Book Shop. Each event I attend there makes me happy to have such an important and convivial poetry site in the Boston/Cambridge area.

Songs for Women

Danielle Legros Georges

I will there be no women here
who would circle red-
dressed, ruby-hearted,

glass-cut. If there be flowers,
then the bloom of cyclamen
awned in green's glowing
night-vase, night-shade,

wild in wind. Sin be the will
to descend, humming-bird still,
steal the fire's sound, take note

and return it. Let song be
the skin of a glimmering,
unsettled, razing, belly-deep
in the strike of match and band.

Be the belly, the pepper-pot.
Come close just to drop it.
Slide 'til the notes are a scaffold,
ash-flicked, unphoenixed.

The Many Names

> "black" (negro) once meant the color of the "night sky"
> nigrum...
>
> —Éric Morales-Franceschini

Once meant a line of demarcation so clear
As to be a sword.

Once meant wholly distinct. Extinction mark.
Attempt. Meant.

Many. Names for the status. Complex-
Ion. Description bade.

For the body. Its recovery. The body.
How like the dark obsidian

Mirror. Through which such strata surface.
And disappear in the night.

Is deep black. Is coal black. Is Jet black. Is
Very black. Is handsome black.

Is pretty black. Is of dark color, but cannot
Be said to be black. Is of black cast.

But not the very blackest. Is a dark griff color.
A copper color. An olive colour.

A dark brown or ginger-bread color. Is of a pale
Complexion. Tawny. Yellow.

Is of a light color. Of a swarthy complection.
Of a brownish complexion.

Is blacker than common, with a remarkable
Roman nose. Is of a redish complexion.

Is of the color of morning before first
Light. The color of cusp

And nerve. The color of mourning
Deferred.

Note: The descriptions of black in the poem's second half are drawn from fugitive slave ads published in 18th century New England newspapers.

Note

Christianne Goodwin

I once heard Cambridge called "The Poetry Capital of America." There's a slim chance they said "Boston," not "Cambridge" but I can't remember and since Boston doesn't have The Grolier, Cambridge it is.

Besides, one cannot know for sure until they've done the shuffle: The Grolier chair shuffle. There's a lot of folding, unfolding, perhaps fetching for Ellen Pinsky or Gail Mazur (Lloyd Schwartz will need more leg room).

Before it's begun, you sit in your tight chair and listen: someone is on to couplets, another sonnets, and yet another—scatter plots. The murmur tells of returns from the sea, the walk from Somerville, a run-in with Lloyd (delightful, no doubt).

We tried to offer Lloyd a ride once. He was wise to turn us down. We drive a tiny Hyundai and, to top it off, had crutches in the back. But even with Lloyd in the backseat, next to crutches, it wouldn't have been as cramped as a Forrest Gander Grolier reading.

Before you sit and listen, there's the shimmy, the slide, the hop, suddenly finding oneself face-to-face with copies of Brooks and Bishop, Browning and Bashō. They're up on the walls as well, watching the Grolier Tango (Anne Carson would approve of "tango").

And after readings, there's warm, boxed Merlot (if you're lucky) and the reconstruction of James's meticulous center display, and perhaps the ceremonial stumble to Grendel's.

Feychild

Christianne Goodwin

Sunprint on tile, percolator whistle
you, crayons in hand, hum along

The tune rivers with washer, traffic rumble
summons the music of our little sphere

Brow furrowed, small fist, your careful scribble
forms tight tunnels, perhaps to the wilds

For all I know, portaling to paralands
your swing-kick song—a token at the veil

You tell me tall tales which
somehow sound like memory

The Poet

The word POET leers at me
in pink embroidery on the back
of a leather vest, worn by
a man who nods with his torso
and insists that this poetry reading
is, in fact, a group discussion

His wife beside him wears a limp scarf,
one that suggests *art curator* or *therapist*
or perhaps also POET, and both loudly
recount their presence at the genesis
of the mag, or the movement

Perhaps they met at an anti-war protest
or while shuffling zines to copy shops
when they were young and sincerely Marxist
in photos - proximate to fame, madly in love

Exiting the group poetry open discussion,
I see them ahead, arms around each other,
stare long enough until a cobblestone catches

me wondering what they were like at my age
how life has changed the immutable -
I wonder if she embroidered that jacket
and how decades in-stitch souls
I wonder so much, I almost ask

Note

In Appreciation of The Grolier

George Kalogeris

My first experience as a young writer crossing The Grolier's burnished threshold was introducing myself to Louisa Solano. Louisa recognized that my name was Greek and asked me about translations of Cavafy. As daunting as entering that venerable temple of poetry was, I immediately felt at home. On another occasion, I was standing in line following a reading by my dear friend, Fred Marchant, waiting to get my book signed when I noticed Seamus Heaney directly behind me. As the line advanced to the book-signing desk, I talked with Seamus about his brand-new long poem based on Aeschylus's *Oresteia*. I remember how abruptly he shrugged off my praise: "It's not big league—have a look at Ted Hughes. He gets the gore of it." And then he was on to praising Fred's new book. It was the kind of first-hand literary instruction and comradeship one often encountered among those high tight shelves so gloriously steeped in poetry. And one more Grolier gathering that I'll never forget. For David Ferry's final public reading, James Fraser kindly allowed him, then in his mid-nineties and with his vision severely impaired by macular degeneration, to read via recording. To hear David reciting "Ellery Street" in his halting voice, gathering himself up into language, the words blurring out but reconfiguring themselves (perhaps in memory) was profoundly moving. For a moment, Cambridge was neither here nor there, but an act of re-creation. David read in honor of his dear friend Ifeanyi Menkiti, the savior of The Grolier. Just writing that, Ifeanyi's warm embrace is suddenly palpable.

5

George Kalogeris

Halfway between poverty and the sun
is how you described growing up in Algiers,
dirt-poor as the glistening dunes of the beach at Sablettes
where you learned to swim in a school of dolphins—
until dusk, when the *jeunes filles slithered away,*
though your legs were still tangled in the seaweed's hair.

The Grecian urn before the age of images,
when the daughter of Dibutades, the potter, traced
the dusky line of a young man's shadow on a blank wall.
Silhouette for the first clay vase fired by Eros.
We lose track of the light, the body's hymnal.
The silent mouths of those who forgive themselves.

Solzhenitsyn at Six

Because it hung above his childhood bed
At a downward slant, she hovered over him always:
The hooded face of that Russian Orthodox icon.

And what was spirit if not the votive candle
That flickered when it was breathed upon? And just
Enough for a looming shadow to fill the room

As he lay wide awake—a boy abandoned
(At least for now) by his belovèd mother.
But should the candle suddenly gutter out,

He shuddered. His soldier father dead before
He was born, the manor house in darkening ruins.
And why did the Revolution feel like one more

Form of violent longing nothing could shake?
And who was he to know, holed up as he was
In Rostov? Precocious Sanya, alone in his room

Yet still in earshot of terrified aunts: *Oh help us,*
Holy Virgin! And perish the thought of bloodshed
Everywhere, but the State immaculate…

Uncanny the wooden face of the icon. Fierce
The iconoclast unbroken by the Gulag.
But first that yearning, all night, for tenderness.

Note

Joan Naviyuk Kane

I first stepped up into The Grolier Poetry Book Shop with a syllabus in hand. It must have been for Helen Vendler's "Reading as a Writer: Poetry" freshman seminar in September 1996. Though I'd sought out the shop when I first traveled to Massachusetts as a girl in June 1995, I hadn't set foot inside on account of my shyness. Helen's syllabus opened The Grolier Book Shop to me, and The Grolier has come to anchor my life as a poet. I lived a few strides away in Adams—then home of Grolier readings—from sophomore year until graduation. By the end of my senior year, I'd happened to fall in with poets from workshops with Henri Cole and Forrest Gander and the poetry board of The Harvard Advocate whose love for poetry intensified my own.

When I first read at the Grolier in the summer of 2017, it felt as if I could finally call myself a poet. Ifeanyi Menkiti was so kind and direct with me about my responsibility to bring Inupiaq and the kind of English I learned alongside Inupiaq onto the page, to write about it, to reflect on it. I thought of him in personal terms as a poet and as father to someone whose love for community I learned from across many Phillips Brooks House Association summers together. Ifeyani's love for his family, for poetry, for the cultural dimensions of The Grolier as an institution made me feel so welcome in Cambridge that his death in June just as I was preparing to move to back to Cambridge with my children struck hard.

For the next four years, I went to readings as often as I could, and often it was one of the only indoor places I'd set foot during the pandemic years. How many poets and students I'd taught only on Zoom or just for the flash of an instant at Tufts, Harvard, or UMass Boston, who I saw in person for the most part at The Grolier. How I would not have survived without poems, without The Grolier. I have filled bookshelves with books that found me there, and have moved them across the continent five times.

A Few Lines for Jordin Tootoo

Joan Naviyuk Kane

> When I was drinking, I was selfish because of my addiction
> to popularity and being out in the public eye. I used that as a
> mechanism to create commotion with everyone. And if I got into
> trouble away from the rink, I made it up on the ice.
> —Jordin Tootoo

What do you see out there on the ice?
Perhaps something dark, far off,
louder than the bellowing headlines
in the otherwise technical silence.

In a lecture hall, once, in Utqiaġvik,
I listened while the ice of the Beaufort Sea
split into blue leads three months early.
What I heard was: if only we learned

the old ways, we'd learn where we fit
in life, how critical we are to each other.
That a hunt done right results in little
suffering or loss. That the migrations

of fowl, fish and mammals will continue.
What I wanted to hear was a reassurance.
Some kind of premonition or promise, like:
when words come back, so do the other things

or *words come back when you have a chance*
to learn them. Instead, what I hold within
is the felt absence of place. A land of great
failure, abundance: it goes on without us.

Another time up north, maybe by mistake,
I was invited to watch the men butchering
but I didn't want to see where it was
they found the heart, if they ever did.

Like you, in front of me is all I have.
In the distance, mostly, another world.

After Anchorage I

had read the ash, the scoria: their slippage. There
rose no world, there
rises only islands.

So then we went away into the east to wait
until the stars began disappearing,
when at last we could ignore the natter

of what, during the last drought
proved to scare the calves we heard
only as noise as through heat
through the door on a train.

A refusal last time I slept
to dream of death.

Instead, I dreamt of trammeling
pasqueflower, of having swam
backward across the lake.

Note

Days of Heaven

Gail Mazur

My oldest friend (since childhood) Elsa Dorfman brought me into The Grolier bookshop when I first moved to Cambridge in 1973. In those dear messy days, there was a couch at the window piled with unopened mail, books, and even a letter to Gordon Cairnie, the proprietor since its founding a century ago, from Ezra Pound. "No textbooks," The squiggly handwritten sign on the door announced, "only poetry," and it was true. There was also a tatty stuffed armchair in the corner (where my toddlers could sit happily reading comic books from Out-of-Town News). No cash register, pretty much no sales. Students and poets drifted in, either to hurry out without buying anything, or to sit and make what literary gossip (without buying anything) they could invent while Gordon, patient or grumpy, occasionally made change and found a paper bag for a rare purchase. I was in my early 30s. My children would soon be in School. I'd never been in a room full of poetry. I kept coming back just to sit in the (admittedly squalid but wonderful) roomful of poems that was "only poetry." There were very few purchases, but somehow it survived—and survives! I'd just begun to write though I could hardly admit it to myself. Nursery school and kindergarten were on the horizon. I came back, browsed and bought books by Robert Lowell, Ezra Pound and Elizabeth Bishop. One day Lowell came in, and Gordon said, "Cal, this is Gail, she's a poet, too." I was so quiet Lowell seemed to think I was undercover. When I crept out the door, he said rather sweetly I thought, "Off to a Sinn Fein meeting, are you?" I was off, to somewhere.

Baseball

Gail Mazur

The game of baseball is not a metaphor
and I know it's not really life.
The chalky green diamond, the lovely
dusty brown lanes I see from airplanes
multiplying around the cities
are only neat playing fields.
Their structure is not the frame
of history carved out of forest,
that is not what I see on my ascent.

And down in the stadium,
the veteran catcher guiding the young
pitcher through the innings, the line
of concentration between them,
that delicate filament is not
like the way you are helping me,
only it reminds me when I strain
for analogies, the way a rookie strains
for perfection, and the veteran,
in his wisdom, seems to promise it,
it glows from his upheld glove,

and the man in front of me
in the grandstand, drinking banana
daiquiris from a thermos,
continuing through a whole dinner

to the aromatic cigar even as our team
is shut out, nearly hitless, he is
not like the farmer that Auden speaks
of in Breughel's Icarus,
or the four inevitable woman-hating
drunkards, yelling, hugging
each other and moving up and down
continuously for more beer

and the young wife trying to understand
what a full count could be
to please her husband happy in
his old dreams, or the little boy
in the Yankees cap already nodding
off to sleep against his father,
program and popcorn memories
sliding into the future,
and the old woman from Lincoln, Maine,
screaming at the Yankee slugger
with wounded knees to break his leg

this is not a microcosm,
not even a slice of life

and the terrible slumps,
when the greatest hitter mysteriously
goes hitless for weeks, or
the pitcher's stuff is all junk
who threw like a magician all last month,
or the days when our guys look
like Sennett cops, slipping, bumping
each other, then suddenly, the play
that wasn't humanly possible, the Kid
we know isn't ready for the big leagues,
leaps into the air to catch a ball
that should have gone downtown,
and coming off the field is hugged

and bottom-slapped by the sudden
sorcerers, the winning team

the question of what makes a man
slump when his form, his eye,
his power aren't to blame, this isn't
like the bad luck that hounds us,
and his frustration in the games
not like our deep rage
for disappointing ourselves

the ballpark is an artifact,
manicured, safe, "scene in an Easter egg",
and the order of the ball game,
the firm structure with the mystery
of accidents always contained,
not the wild field we wander in,
where I'm trying to recite the rules,
to repeat the statistics of the game,
and the wind keeps carrying my words away

After Pastoral

"Go, sit in the woods," I said to myself
in the middle of my life, "and master
the alphabet for what you can find there."

It was late, but I wanted to change, to know
differently, I thought I'd need a new vocabulary,
so I sat, but in the dark, unable to see anything

around me without the right words. I couldn't say
what red ants were like, nesting in mulch and debris,
or the strange (but what wasn't strange?) Indian Pipe

Wampanoags called "ghost plant," white and waxy
Monotropa uniflora or the brown itch of dead leaves,
the dry acorn caps, the rough bark of a tree at my back.

I sat in a foreign language library wanting it to be
my paradise, I construed nature the way a stunted child
would, without wonder. At first, the Latin names

in my field guide, genus and species, stems and roots,
distracted me from my mission, at home as I was
in the lives of pages, but soon I was trembling

with the indecent pleasure a clever child takes
in spelling, in getting everything right—or the way
my 18-year old grandmother must have felt

in Lincoln, Maine early in the last century,
learning alone each night the math she'd teach
to her ruffians and farm kids the next day

in a one-room schoolhouse in her new land—
each day a triumph, a kind of moral victory
over her own foreignness, her ignorance....

I walked barefoot down a pine needle path
to the lake and swam with silvery herring minnows
and snappers, I picked wild mint for my tea

and huckleberries with their grainy seeds.
Those summers, I lived in the beech forest,
fagus sylvatica , the final forest, a woman

in mid-life, certain she was growing. A brief chapter,
really, naming the mayflowers—trailing arbutus—
and mushrooms, ignoring jet trails and dying pickerel,

uttering what had probably been uttered for eons
in Nature's antique vernaculars. Then, only then,
when I loved it—when I'd begun to be at home in it—

I took my leave....

Note

Robert Pinsky

For me, the importance of The Grolier Book Shop has changed in personal ways over many years.

Objectively, The Grolier has been and remains a unique national treasure, central for American poetry and poets. More subjectively, the first, Gordon Cairnie period felt "awesome"—in the everyday, slangy sense of that word and in the old, literal sense. In my twenties, I felt awe for the legendary store and its crusty, magisterial owner. Then, when I was older, Louisa Solano took over and the store felt more homey to me: brightened and dusted and the old couch removed, so the place felt less like a club.

Communal spirit characterizes Ifeanyi Menkiti's approach to life and to poetry, and to The Grolier as he developed it. I have long appreciated Ifeanyi's articulation of the Igbo approach to community as central to identity, to culture and to the art of poetry. Even before I read his scholarly explanation of that idea, I could sense it when we were colleagues, young professors at Wellesley College, possibly both feeling a bit like outsiders in our different ways. I love how Ifeanyi brought that welcoming, generous spirit to the store, embracing and extending its history.

Country Music

Robert Pinsky

Ifeanyi says in his country a baby
Is *It* until it learns to be one of *Us*.

I am in my Igbo second childhood.
The coral, a quarrel, a glacier, my lungs.

The weather, the world, the book review.
Lyrical bitching. Biblical plaint. Infant

Debt of attention vetting the news,
The noise, the needs, for keeps. It is

The world's beginnings, my own endings,
And having the heart to tell them apart

Dune Grass

The creeping rootstalks need for the sand to shift.
Unstable stabilizer suited to ruin.
Starved by solidity it thrives on change.

Comical to see right-angle furrows planted
To foster the vanishing dunes at Herring Cove:
Delinquent native soon to disrupt a garden.

Ornery, irritating as Thoreau himself.
In California they know it as invasive.
Emigrant of absence, addicted to the wind.

Note

Memories of The Grolier

Lloyd Schwartz

I came to Cambridge in 1962 for graduate school. I was expected to do research for my Ph.D. But I had really come for Robert Lowell, whom I regarded the greatest living American poet. As soon as I could I visited Lowell, armed with my "best" undergraduate poem, which he perused sympathetically, then gently but firmly explained why it didn't work. I was crestfallen…and thrilled. Too worried about grades and with too many course requirements to fulfill, I never took Lowell's workshop. But when he started offering weekly public office hours (open to anyone who wanted to attend and show him poems), I attended as often as I could. Listening to what he had to say about our poems, and even more important, about poetry itself was one of the most intense and illuminating experiences anyone who cared about poetry could have. Lowell was a habitué of The Grolier Poetry Book Shop so I would go as often as I could, hoping to run into him. Trying to live on a $1500-a-year scholarship, I was really more of a browser than a purchaser, a browser and an overhearer. And much as I admired Gordon Cairnie for running an all-poetry bookshop, I was intimidated by his peppery joviality, especially with the poets ("the Guys") who were the Grolier regulars: all of them sinking into that beat-up couch in non-stop conversation that didn't seem to brook any interruption. Nervous, I would just try to disappear into the bookshelves, wait as long as I could for Lowell to turn up, and then leave.

The magnet of The Grolier kept drawing me back, and the more confident I became—as a student, as a teacher, and as a writer—the better I felt about turning up at The Grolier. When I got my first acceptance letter from a national magazine (for my poem "Estelle's Testimony," the first of my poems in voices other than my own), I called my friend Frank Bidart to tell him the news. Lowell was at Frank's apartment, and Frank handed him the phone to congratulate me.

Louisa Solano was extremely welcoming. In 1981, when I published my first book at the age of 40, I was suddenly part of a new generation of "younger" writers and Louisa put my photo up on The Grolier wall. She even invited me to have a book-signing at the store, and on the day before I was panicking because the books had not yet arrived. But Lousia went to work contacting the printer, an hour away, near Plymouth, and was willing to drive us there and collect the cartons of books she had talked them into letting her take. After a wild ride we managed to return to The Grolier with books for the launch.

I was one of a small number who was able to stay on Louisa's good side as she became increasingly difficult, even paranoid, evidently from the medications she was taking. Many customers stopped coming—some accused of shoplifting and threatened with restraining orders. One young poet had come into the store to ask for a book-signing event. Louisa threw him out of the store, mistaking him for someone else. He called me, devastated.

So when Louisa sold the store to Ifeanyi Menkiti, everyone breathed a sigh of relief. He was a poet, a Professor of Philosophy at Wellesley College, and a prince in every sense of the word. The Grolier started to become again—and in some ways for the first time—a real gathering spot for all poets and anyone who loves poetry.

Friendships and Time

Lloyd Schwartz

My new friend is away
for the weekend—the weekend
drags by. I want to know
exactly what he's doing.
Is the convention exciting?
Who are the new people? Is
Atlanta as pretty as they say?
I'm eager to hear all about it.
—What's he doing now?
The weekend drags by.

My best friend has just
left for Europe. I'm snowed under.
There's gossip, and a question
he'll know the answer to;
I think of phoning, then
remember he's away. It can wait.
In the meantime,
I teach, work on an article,
go to a concert. Time flies.

A friend is dead.
Weeks might pass without a word
before one of us called.
Months might pass
without our meeting; and at gatherings

we might talk only in passing.
Still, we loved to talk,
and always looked forward to meeting . . .
Months have passed; one day passes
like the rest.

I'm visiting friends in
a distant city—it's as if
we'd never been apart. My lover
stays home. We miss
each other; but time
seems suspended. My "vacation"
of parties and sightseeing
could go on forever. . .
When I get back, it will seem
as if I'd never been away.

Titian's *Marsyas*

The 16th-century Venetian master's very last painting—as big as life—is the story of the pan-piping satyr who dared to challenge a god.

Titian painted his crucifixion.

He hangs by his ankles from the branches of a tree, his goat-legs askew, as Apollo, kneeling, tenderly skins him alive.

Upside down, his tormented expression reads like a smile.

A thirsty pup is lapping up his blood.

Seated close—rapt—old King Midas, with his golden coronet, contemplates the horrific scene.

It's the 90-year-old artist's self-portrait.

Someone who's learned the cost of making art, the cost of challenging the gods.

And has accepted it.

Except for the glittering crown, most of the surface is rougher, murkier than the master's earlier dazzle.

Close inspection reveals paint smeared by his own fingers.

He put his whole body into this painting.

It was found in his studio after his death.

After how many years could anything still have been left for him to do?

A work is complete, Rembrandt said, if in it the master's intentions have been realized.

Note
The Imprint

Daniel Tobin

Last year, while on a writing retreat in Shropshire I took a drive over to Hay-on-Wye on the border of England and Wales to visit, among other venues, The Poetry Bookshop. There I struck up a conversation with the owner, which in short course led to us, dare I say, to waxing poetic about The Grolier. The owner recognized The Grolier as the original imprint for his shop established prominently near the Clocktower of that notable book-town.

Founded some fitty years before, The Grolier was already legendary on its storefront in Cambridge, Massachusetts when I first walked in four decades ago, having just enrolled at Harvard Divinity School. It felt something like entering a small chapel presided over by the quietly watchful Louisa Solano, though the ceiling-high bookshelves and photographs of famous poets overwhelmed the shop's limited footprint with a contrary impression of vertical space. The little shop was oddly vaulting. One could happily lose oneself in the nooks among the many titles, or climbing the ladder to the higher shelves well out, on tip-toes, of arms-length.

Some two decades later I gave my first poetry reading affiliated with The Grolier in a larger space nearby, though since I've had the great good fortune to read my work in the physically confined but strangely capacious experience of the shop itself, first under the auspices of Ifenyi Menkiti, and for the last several years under the welcoming and astute management of James Fraser. With the Menkiti family, he has ushered in a new era for a bookshop that has endured for nearly a hundred years to become a necessary crossroads for poets and lovers of poetry, its strict dimensions tight enough to require the disassembling of its central pedestal of books before every reading, its actual extent and influence reaching beyond the modest stamp on Plympton Street of its own stacked walls and shelves.

A Quiet Evening in Shock and Awe

Daniel Tobin

A retrospect

Tonight, the local symphony
    of sirens, gunshots, car alarms
dissipates in a swale of wind
    beyond the blinds impending swarm

of talking heads that babble on
    to hype the heave of history,
while bomb bursts blast the foreign town
    to mangles of stone and steel and dust.

Meanwhile, the mission of the leaves
    accomplishes in winter's dearth
an inference, golden, that trumps the freeze
    and makes a manifest of earth

that lifts above each sponsored lie
    (our word is lesser than we guessed)
like wing beats in a prodigal's sty—
    the brute rejoicings of the blest.

Displacement

This raven in the road, its wing
   broken—though maybe the bird's
just stunned? Some bus might have
   swiped it broadside as it swooped

to scoop up a scrap on the tarmac
   while its mate aloft on the wires
watched, an opaque polished eye
   taking in the offhand catastrophe.

Through our skewed windshield
   we catch up with the aftermath—
two teenage women hovering
   over the broken thing, shock-still,

in the lane with its grassy selvage
   trimmed to the curb. We pull over
(how to help what looks hopeless??)
   and join them where the splayed

feathers stay, unstirring, until the bird
   twitches, frantic, when I touch
its flank, lamely hoping to lift
   this life free of the cars coming on.

Uneasy smiles, no word in common
   between us and them, for we see
they're among the latest refugees,
   their casual, global clothes familiar

and disarming, in their jean pockets
   cell phones for calling home if home
is anything more than ash & rubble,
   their soldiers trenched as in a century

we wistfully call *Last*, until the ancient
   fractures return arrayed in the garb
of the avant-garde, as if the digital
   drumbeats were glib as missile fire—

Upload, Zoom Cast, Platform, Tweet.
   We finally lift the bird like brancardiers
to the roadside with the remains
   of a parcel box, and nod awkwardly

to our youthful fellow stretcher-bearers
   as they walk away to their own cares.
But what about the raven, uprooted
   to a carton lid going sodden in rain?

They let wounded animals die here,
   local as it is but for tourist busses—
even these creatures who, like us,
   communicate over incidents distant

in space and time. Unmated *commons*
   in their roosts will, at the word of one,
flock down to a carcass guarded
   by gathered adults to chase them away.

It's called displacement, this creature's
   mind visionary like our own, social,
their caws calling wolves over to open
   a dead deer's body so *they* can feed.

They cache shiny objects for their nests,
   connoisseurs as they are of beauty,
and court early but take years to mate
   and link their talons in play mid-flight.

Which is why the lover on the wire
   who saw its beloved crumple earthward,
the one we watch turn in resignation,
   flies away feeling something like sorrow

as we, having done the little we did,
   head back to the waiting car, together,
more rueful, a little more astonished
   by our ground time, our displacement.

Acknowledgements

Quartet Ajaton's (Mia Simanainen, vocals; Henrik Sandås, bandoneon; Kari Ikonen, Moog synthesizer; Mikko Perkola, Viola da gamba; with Abdissa Assefa, percussion, on this track) "Come Again" is track 2 of "Early Music in the Latest Way" released by Alba Records in 2020.

Peter Balakian's "Woodstock" was originally published in *Dyer's Thistle* (Carnegie Mellon University Press), copyright © 1996 Peter Balakian and reprinted with permission of the author.

Yongyu Chen and Gabby Woo's foreword to *The Book, The Room* includes citations from *The Book to Come* by Maurice Blanchot (translated by Charlotte Mandell, Standford University Press, 2003).

Christina Davis's "["Sometimes I will be"]" was originally published in *LUIGI*, copyright © Christina Davis and reprinted with permission of the author.

An earlier version of Jay Gao's *Plan(e)t = Cluster* was commissioned in 2022 for the project "The last stop is Ultima" by Adrien Howard and Lisette May Monroe at Rosie's Disobedient Press and the Center for Contemporary Arts in Glasgow, Scotland.

Danielle LeGros Georges's "Songs for Women" from *Maroon* (Curbstone Press) and is copyright © 2001 Danielle LeGros Georges and reprinted with her permission.

Eileen G'Sell's poems were published in *Francofilaments*, Broken Sleep Books, 2024.

Joan Naviyuk Kane's "A Few Lines for Jordin Tootoo" was originally published in *Prairie Schooner*'s 2015 Sports issues, and also in the 2015 chapbook *The Straits* published by *Voices from The American Land*, and also appears in the book *Milk Black Carbon* published in 2017 by the University of Pittsburgh Press. "After Anchorage I" was published as a land acknowledgment in Mita Mahato's 2024 book *Arctic Play* by The 3rd Thing Press.

George Kalogeris's "5" is from *Camus : Carnets* (Pressed Wafer) and is copyright © 2006 George Kalogeris and reprinted with his permission.

Gail Mazur's "Baseball" is from *Nightfire* (The University of Chicago Press) and is copyright © 1978 Gail Mazur and reprinted with the author's permission.

Jacqueline Nehke Krass's poem was previously published as "*Der tseshosener tsiferblat*" in Daniel Charney's collection *Oyfn shvel fun yener velt* (NY: Marstin Press, 1947). It appears courtesy of the Charney family, with special thanks to Ezra Bialik and Rosalind Kaye. This translation was made possible with the support of the Yiddish Book Center.

Shari Kocher's documentary poem quotes from and refers to two principal sources: Jane Hawley, *Wendy Whiteley and the Secret Garden*, Lantern, Penguin Books, 2015; and Anna Funder, *Wifedom*, Penguin Random House, Australia, 2023.

Robert Pinksy's "Country Music," copyright © 2024 Robert Pinsky, appeared in *Proverbs of Limbo*, published by Farrar, Straus and Giroux in 2024, and is reprinted with permission of the author.

Stephen Proski's "Feychild" was originally published in *Oracle Smoke Machine,* a collaboration with Stephen Proski (Staircase Books), copyright © 2023 by Christianne Goodwin and reprinted with permission of the author.

Lloyd Schwartz's "Friendships and Time" originally published in *Ploughshares* copyright © in 1983 Lloyd Schwartz, and reprinted with the permission of the author. "Titian's Marsyas" is from *Who's on First? New and Selected Poems* (The University of Chicago Press), copyright © 2021 Lloyd Schwartz, and reprinted with the permission of the author.

Changtai Bi and Tracy K. Smith's English translations of "Nightmare," "The Nude," "Red Wall," and "Song for Heaven, Earth and Humankind" by Yi Lei are copyright © 2020 by Tracy K. Smith and Changtai Bi. Reprinted from *My Name Will Grow Wide Like a Tree: Selected Poems* with the permission of the translator and Graywolf Press. www.graywolfpress.org.

Tracy K. Smith's "Flores Woman," "Mothership," "A Hunger So Honed," "The United States Welcomes You," and "The Angels" copyright © 2021 by Tracy K. Smith. Reprinted from *Such Color: New and Selected Poems* with the permission of the author and Graywolf Press. www.graywolfpress.org

Daniel Tobin's "A Quiet Evening in Shock and Awe" was originally published in *Queen Mob's Teahouse*, copyright © 2022 by Daniel Tobin and reprinted with permission of the author.

Contributors

Tayseer Abu Odeh is a Palestinian-Jordanian writer and translator. Among other outlets, his writing has appeared in *Michigan Quarterly Review*, *Arab Studies Quarterly*, *Journal of Postcolonial Writing*, and *Peripheries: A Journal of Word, Image, and Sound*, for which he edited and translated a folio of poetry from Gaza with Mosab Abu Toha in 2021. He is the editor of the translation of Walid Saif's novel, *Al-Taghriba al-Falestinyya* (forthcoming from University of Texas Press). He is currently co-translating and co-editing an anthology of poetry from Gaza and the West Bank with Sherah Bloor, *You Must Live*, which will be published by Copper Canyon Press in fall, 2025. He also serves as an international advisor on the editorial board of *The Journal of Holy Land and Palestine Studies*, in which his recent interview with the historian Avi Shlaim will appear, and he serves as a judge for writing competitions, including the Jubilee Institute's award for creative writing in 2022. Tayseer received a PhD in English literature and criticism in 2016 from Indiana University of Pennsylvania, and will be commencing an MFA at Iowa's translation program in fall 2025.

Yagmur Akyurek is an MFA candidate in poetry at New York University, where she is a Rona Jaffe fellow, Books Editor at *Washington Square Review*, and an adjunct instructor of creative writing. She was born in Turkey, raised in Massachusetts, and now lives in New York.

Corbin Allardice is a poet, translator, performer and scholar. She lives between Brooklyn and Baltimore, where she is pursuing a PhD in Yiddish literature. She is a proud founding member of GLYK: a queer Yiddish theatre collective.

Cassandra Atherton is one of the leading international scholars and experts on prose poetry and an award-winning prose poet. She has written extensively on atomic bomb literature and hibakusha poetry, and is writing a book of prose poetry on the Hiroshima Maidens with funding from the Australia council. Cassandra co-authored *Prose Poetry: An Introduction* (Princeton University Press, 2020) and co-edited the *Anthology of Australian Prose Poetry* (Melbourne University Press, 2020) with Paul Hetherington, with whom she is currently co-writing *Ekphrastic Poetry: An Introduction* (forthcoming, Princeton University Press).

EJ Baird (also published as EJ Shu) is an Australian-Canadian poet with an enduring interest in the science-poetry relation and found-text methods. Her poems appear in *Rabbit, Cordite Poetry Review, Plumwood Mountain, Antiphon, Poets Reading the News* and elsewhere. EJ's contribution to *Peripheries* is drawn from her doctoral research at RMIT University, where she is investigating how poetic bricolage might model the processes of self-composition.

Will Bahr is a writer putting the 'free' in freelance, and currently living in Asheville, North Carolina. He graduated with a BA in Creative Writing from Warren Wilson College, where his fiction won the Larry Levis writing award. He has spent the last two years working as a gravedigger for a conservation burial ground south of Asheville, and playing music with a couple of chimps masquerading as men with his band, Simma. His essays and reporting have appeared in *GQ, USA Today, Los Angeles Magazine, Blue Ridge Outdoors* and Minneapolis' dearly departed *City Pages* (rest in peace).

Peter Balakian's books of poems include *Ozone Journal,* winner of the Pulitzer Prize for Poetry, and *No Sign* (2022). His memoir *Black Dog of Fate* won the PEN/Albrand Award. He received the Presidential Medal from the Republic of Armenia, and is the Donald M. and Constance H. Rebar Professor of the Humanities at Colgate University.

Razan Bannoura was born in Bethlehem, occupied Palestine. She currently lives in Frankfurt, Germany. Her most recent poetry collection, *Snoring,* was published in 2019 by Al-Ahliya for Publishing and Distribution, Amman, in partnership with the Abdul Mohsen Al-Qattan Foundation, Ramallah.

Anne M. Carson is an Australian poet, essayist and visual artist whose poetry has been published internationally, and widely in Australia. Her writing has received numerous awards, including being longlisted for the Fish International Poetry Prize (2023) and shortlisted for the Society of Women Authors New South Wales (2024). *The Detective's Chair: Prose Poems About Fictional Detectives* was published by Liquid Amber Press (2023). Her PhD (2023), supported by an Australian Government Research Training Program Scholarship, was awarded an Outstanding Dissertation Prize from the Visual and Performing Arts SIG of the American Educational Researchers Association in 2024.

Audrey Chambers is a writer and artist living in Boston. This is her first published piece. You can find her on Instagram @uncannyva1 1eygirl.

Daniel Charney (1888-1959) was a Yiddish writer from Dukor, a shtetl in present-day Belarus. He wrote in almost every genre and was in touch with virtually every Yiddish writer and cultural activist of his time, earning the nickname "the Ambassador of Yiddish Literature." Charney is particularly known for his rich literary memoirs, which document the upheavals of the European twentieth century and recount the intimate, daily experience of chronic illness—perhaps the one constant in Charney's migratory life.

Andrea Cohen is the author of eight poetry collections, including, most recently, *The Sorrow Apartments* (Four Way Books). Her poems have appeared in *The New Yorker*, *The New York Review of Books*, *The Threepenny Review*, and elsewhere. She teaches at Boston University and directs the Blacksmith House Poetry Series in Cambridge, MA.

Madeleine Cohen is academic director of the Yiddish Book Center in Amherst, MA and a visiting assistant professor of Jewish Studies at Mount Holyoke College. She received her PhD in Comparative Literature with a designated emphasis in Jewish Studies from UC Berkeley. She is president of the board of directors of *In geveb: A Journal of Yiddish Studies*.

Aschely Vaughan Cone is a New York based artist. She received an

MFA from the Maryland Institute College of Art (2016), an MA in Art History from Tulane University (2014) and a BA in Liberal Arts from St. John's College (2007), where she studied classics, philosophy and the history of math and science. Her awards include a matching scholarship for study at the Skowhegan School of Painting and Sculpture, the Hamiltonian Fellowship, and The Henry Walters Traveling Fellowship. She is the associate director of the Catherine Project, an educational non-profit offering free, discussion-based courses on great books.

Ollie Cowley is a British-Swiss poet based in Cambridge, Massachusetts. Her poems have appeared in *The London Magazine*, *Oxonian Review*, and *Telegraph*, and are forthcoming in *Oxford Press* and *The Los Angeles Review*.

Christina Davis is the author of *AN ETHIC* (Nightboat Books), selected by Forrest Gander, and *FORTH A RAVEN* (Alice James Books), and is currently at work on "The Small Evers." Davis's poems and translations have appeared (or are forthcoming) in *APR*, *Bomb*, *Brooklyn Rail*, *Interim*, *Jubilat*, *LIT*, *LUIGI*, *New Republic*, *Paris Review*, *Poetry Magazine*, *Spoke!*, and other publications. In addition to publications, she has recently collaborated with Fulbright composer Jacek Smolicki on a sound-art installation about Walden Pond and has co-founded The Enormous Chorus, a peace-caroling initiative in Cambridge. She currently serves as curator of the Woodberry Poetry Room, Harvard University.

Richard Fein's thirteenth book of poems, *Dear Yiddish*, appeared in 2003. He has also published three volumes of Yiddish poets in translation and three books of prose: *Robert Lowell* (a critical study); *The Dance of Leah: Discovering Yiddish in America* (a memoir); and *Yiddish Genesis* (a book of personal essays).

Shangyang Fang is the author of the poetry collection *Burying the Mountain* (Copper Canyon Press, 2021).

Jay Gao is a poet from Edinburgh, Scotland, living in New York City. His recent books include: *Bark, Archive, Splinter* (Out-Spoken Press,

2024) and *Imperium* (Carcanet, 2022). *Imperium* was a winner of the 2023 Michael Murphy Memorial Prize, an Eric Gregory Award, and a Somerset Maugham Award. He is also the author of four other poetry pamphlets and chapbooks. Currently, he is a reader for *Poetry* magazine and a PhD student in English at Columbia University where he studies experimental ecopoetics and race.

Danielle Legros Georges is a poet, translator, and editor whose work has been supported by fellowships and grants from organizations including the American Antiquarian Society, the Massachusetts Museum of Contemporary Art, the Massachusetts Cultural Council, the Boston Foundation, the PEN/Heim Translation Fund, and the Black Metropolis Research Consortium. Appointed Boston's Poet Laureate in 2014, she served in the role for four years. Her books of poetry include *The Dear Remote Nearness of You* (Barrow Street, 2016); *Island Heart*, translations of the poems of 20th-century Haitian-French poet Ida Faubert (Subpress, 2021); *Wheatley at 250: Black Women Poets Re-imagine the Verse of Phillis Wheatley Peters* (Pangyrus, 2023); *Blue Flare: Three Haitian Poets: Évelyne Trouillot, Marie-Célie Agnant, Maggy de Coster* (Zephyr Press, 2024); and *Three Leaves, Three Roots: Poems on the Haiti-Congo Story* (Beacon Press, 2025).

Cécile Girardin is a French writer, a mother of three, an amateur violinist and an academic. Before settling in Paris, she lived in rural France, studied in Chicago, worked as a journalist in Hong Kong, and taught French in Delhi. Alongside academic pieces on contemporary literature, she has published fiction in a variety of international journals, most recently in *Another Chicago Magazine*, *Kairos Literary Review*, and *Litro US*.

Christianne Goodwin's new book, *Oracle Smoke Machine*, an art-and-poetry collaboration with painter Stephen Proski, is out with Staircase Books (Cambridge, MA).

Isabel Duarte-Gray earned her Bachelor's Degree at Amherst College and her PhD at Harvard University. Her first collection of poems, *Even Shorn*, debuted with Sarabande Books in 2021. She now teaches at

Loyola University New Orleans.

Eileen G'Sell is a poet and critic with recent contributions to *Jacobin*, *Poetry*, *Berlin Lit*, *The Baffler*, *Hyperallergic*, and *The Hopkins Review*. Her first collection of poetry, *Life After Rugby*, was published by Gold Wake Press in 2018; her second volume of poetry, *Francofilaments*, was published by Broken Sleep Books in 2024. In 2025, her first book of nonfiction, *Lipstick*, will join Bloomsbury's Object Lessons series. She was recently awarded a national Rabkin Prize for arts journalism. She teaches at Washington University in St. Louis.

Richie Hofmann is the author of two collections of poems, *Second Empire* and *A Hundred Lovers*.

Carolina Hotchandani is the author of *The Book Eaters*, the 2023 Perugia Press Prize winner and one of ten debut poetry books featured in *Poets & Writers*' 2024 debut poets issue. She was awarded a Nebraska Arts Council Individual Fellowship and a Nebraska Book Award, and her poetry has appeared or is forthcoming in *The Atlantic*, *AGNI*, *AQR*, *Beloit Poetry Journal*, *Copper Nickel*, *Prairie Schooner*, *Smartish Pace*, and other magazines. She is a Goodrich Assistant Professor of English in Omaha, Nebraska.

Esther K. Heller is a poet, literary critic, and experimental filmmaker. They are the author of *AR:RANGE:MENTS* (Fonograf Editions, 2025).

Kathryn Hellerstein is a professor of Yiddish literature at the University of Pennsylvania. Her books include the prizewinning *A Question of Tradition: Women Poets in Yiddish, 1586-1987*, as well as two collections of translations: *Paper Bridges: Selected Poems of Kadya Molodowsky* and *Moyshe-Leyb Halpern, In New York: A Selection*. She was a translation fellow at the Yiddish Book Center (2023-2024).

Kari Ikonen is an award-winning Finnish composer, pianist and moogist, and a key figure in the European jazz & improvised music scene. He speaks his own unique musical language as solo pianist, in duo with Claudio Puntin or Louis Sclavis and with bands like Orchestra

Nazionale della Luna, Wishamalii, and Quartet Ajaton. His particular interest falls on microtonality, and to pursue this interest on acoustic piano, he has invented the revolutionary Maqiano™ Microtuning System.

Katherine Irajpanah is a PhD candidate in the Department of Government at Harvard University. Her poems are published or forthcoming in the *Colorado Review* and *Harvard Graduate Review*.

Anna Jackson is a poet and academic living in Island Bay, Te Whanganui-a-Tara, Aotearoa New Zealand, whose book *Terrier, Worrier: A Poem in Five Parts* is published by Auckland University Press, 2025. For more, see www.annajackson.nz.

Paul-Sebastian Japaz (b.1992) is a painter based in New York City whose work explores the dynamics of class through place. He has recently exhibited with Timothy Taylor, The Hole, Below Grand, and Nathalie Karg in NYC. Paul-Sebastian is also an educator currently serving as a Professor at Pratt Institute. He has been featured in various publications, including *Art Maze Mag*, *Take Care! Magazine*, *Pineapple Mag*, and *Booooooom*, and has been interviewed in *Friend of The Artist* and *Poltern*. He has given artist lectures at Yale School of Art, The New School, and at the Fashion Institute of Technology, and was a resident at Palazzo Monti (2024), Skowhegan School of Painting and Sculpture (2022). He holds a BFA from the Fashion Institute of Technology (2017).

Isaac Jarnot is a poet and independent scholar who lives in Jackson Heights, Queens. He is the author of several books of poetry and is currently completing a PhD program at Drew Theological School. George Kalogeris's most recent book of poems is *Winthropos* (Louisiana State University, 2021). He is also the author of *Guide to Greece* (LSU); *Dialogos,* a book of paired poems in translation; and *Camus: Carnets*, poems based on the notebooks of Albert Camus. His poems and translations have been anthologized in *Joining Music with Reason*, chosen by Christopher Ricks (Waywiser, 2010). He is the winner of the James Dickey Poetry Prize, the Stephen J. Meringoff Award, and the Sheila Margaret Motton Prize.

Joan Naviyuk Kane's works include *The Cormorant Hunter's Wife, Hyperboreal, The Straits, Milk Black Carbon, Sublingual, A Few Lines in the Manifest, Another Bright Departure, Dark Traffic*, and *Ex Machina*, in addition to *with snow pouring southward past the window* (forthcoming in the 2026 Pitt Poetry Series) and *& all the ones who chose to leave her* (Omnidawn, 2028). A Guggenheim Fellow, Radcliffe Fellow, Native Arts and Cultures Foundation National Artist Fellow, and Whiting Award and Paul Engle Prize recipient, she's a 2025 United States Artists Fellow raising her children in Oregon, where she's an Associate Professor at Reed College.

Izi Kharik (1898-1937) was one of the most significant Soviet Yiddish writers of the prewar period, a poet whose work engaged aesthetic movements as varied as expressionism and socialist realism. Kharik spent most of his life in Minsk, Belarus. He was at the peak of his career in June 1937 when he was arrested and killed as part of the Great Purges. Though his name was rehabilitated, his work never regained its prominence of the prewar period, during which his poems had exposed both ambivalence about the destruction of the Jewish past and simultaneous ideological exuberance about the new Soviet era.

Shari Kocher holds a PhD in Creative Writing from Melbourne University and is the author of two poetry collections: *The Non-Sequitur of Snow* (2015), which was shortlisted for the FAW Anne Elder Awards (2015); and *Foxstruck and Other Collisions* (2021), which was Highly Commended in the Kenneth Slessor Poetry Prize NSW Premier's Literature Awards (2022). Both titles are supported by Puncher & Wattmann. Shari is currently working on a book of short stories and a third poetry collection. She lives and writes and rests on the unceded lands of the Dja Dja Wurrung peoples in Central Victoria (Australia). www.sharikocher.com.

Jacqueline Nekhe Krass is a writer and translator from Brooklyn, NY. A 2023-2024 Yiddish Book Center Translation Fellow and former staff writer at *The Millions*, her poetry, essays, and scholarship appear in *Full Stop, Indianapolis Review, Spoon River Poetry Review, The Philip Roth Review*, and elsewhere.

Joshua Kurtz is a writer and weaver based in Somerville, MA. He is currently an MDiv candidate at Harvard Divinity School, where he studies Judaism, grief, and cultural heritage. He has previously worked as a community organizer and educator in Washington, DC, and Brasov, Romania. His writing has been published in the *Smithsonian Folklife Magazine*, *Colorado Review*, the *Academy of American Poets*, and *Cobra Milk*.

Bluma Lange is a writer, translator and independent scholar who resides near Glasgow, Scotland.

Jeanine Leane belongs to the Wiradjuri People of the Murrumbidgee's River. She is a poet, author, critic and teacher. Her poems and essays have been published widely in journals such as *Overland*, *Westerly*, *Antipodes*, and the *Sydney Review of Books*. Jeanine lives and works on the lands of the East Nations of Naarm, Melbourne.

Miriam Wei Wei Lo writes to feel the pulse of being. And to fill gaps. She teaches creative writing at Sheridan Institute of Higher Education in Boorloo/Perth, Western Australia. Her most recent book is *Who Comes Calling?* She used her 2023 Westerly Mid Career Fellowship to consolidate research into her grandmother's autograph album.

Anna Margolin (pseudonym for Rosa Lebensboym) (Brest-Litovsk 1887–New York City, 1952) wrote modernist poetry in Yiddish. Her work was acclaimed by her contemporaries from the 1920s. She published one volume of her poetry in 1929.

Korey Martin is an artist and illustrator in the Broom School style living in Chicago, IL.

Chloe Martinez is a poet, a translator, and a scholar of South Asian religions. She is the author of the collection *Ten Thousand Selves* and the chapbook *Corner Shrine*. Her work has appeared in *Ploughshares*, *POETRY*, *Prairie Schooner*, *Agni*, and elsewhere, and her translations have been awarded the Anne Frydman Prize and the Robert Fitzgerald Prize. She is Assistant Editor for *Beloit Poetry Journal* and Poetry Editor for the *Journal of Feminist Studies in Religion*. She works at Claremont McKenna College.

Gail Mazur lives in Cambridge, Massachusetts, where she founded in 1973 (and ran for 29 years) the Blacksmith House Poetry Series. She is the author of eight book of poetry, with a ninth, *Three Trees*, to be published in the spring of 2026.

Mirabai lived in 16th-century North India. Her poems express her intense devotion to Krishna and often directly address God as a beloved—usually an absent one. First sung and shared orally, these poems were eventually gathered into anthologies. They continue to be popular in India today, where Mira is the subject of films, plays, books, and visual art.

Samantha McCulloch is an artist and writer from Johannesburg. Her paintings depict intimate scenes and are often developed alongside poetic captions. Her prose has been published in *Portside Review*, *Stanzas,* and *misted.cc.* The first draft of her novella, *Lagoon,* won the inaugural First Drafts series and was published by Kunstverein in 2022. She is currently enrolled in a PhD in creative writing at the University of the Western Cape, where she is at work on her first novel.

Sophie Mollart is a poet, writer and filmmaker. Her work has appeared in *Terrain*, *Primary Paper*, *Fields*, *Litro* and others.

Sawako Nakayasu is an artist working with language, performance, and translation. Her publications include *Pink Waves* (Omnidawn, 2023), *Say Translation Is Art* (Ugly Duckling Presse, 2020), and *Some Girls Walk Into The Country They Are From* (Wave Books, 2020). She teaches in the Literary Arts department at Brown University.

Carl Phillips lives in Massachusetts. His latest books of poems are *Scattered Snows, to the North* (FSG, 2024) and *Then the War: And Selected Poems 2007-2020* (FSG, 2022), for which he received the Pulitzer Prize.

Robert Pinsky's most recent book of poetry is *PROVERBS OF LIMBO*. His PoemJazz album of the same title is available on Spotify and Apple Music.

Halina Poświatowska (1935-1967) remains one of Poland's most beloved poets, known for her short, lyrical work that dwells on themes of love, death, desire, and art. She published three books and a memoir during her lifetime, before dying from complications of a heart surgery at age 32.

Donald Revell is the author of 16 collections of poetry, most recently of *CANANDAIGUA* (2024) and *WHITE CAMPION* (2021), both from Alice James Books. He is Emeritus Professor of English at UNLV and the Black Mountain Institute.

Joseph Ricker has pursued a career as a performer, teacher and ensemble director that has focused on creative expression and exploration through the guitar. His work with Jamie Balmer in Orpheus Guitar Duo has charted a path of musical discovery that places the group in the company of those innovative classical musicians who have defied boundaries and expanded their genres. Joseph Ricker is also the Artistic Director of the Happy Valley Guitar Orchestra. A graduate of the Hartt School and the University of Massachusetts Amherst, Joseph Ricker is currently on the faculty of Smith College.

Jacob Romm is a translator and letterpress printer, also working on a Ph.D. at Yale in Comparative Literature and Early Modern Studies. His translations from Yiddish and French can be read in *Asymptote*, *ANMLY*, *Verklempt*, *Circumference*, and elsewhere, and his letterpress work can be found at letterandspiritpress.org.

Lauren Russell is the author of *A Window That Can Neither Open nor Close* (Milkweed Editions, 2024); *Descent* (Tarpaulin Sky Press, 2020), winner of the Poetry Society of America's 2021 Anna Rabinowitz Award; and *What's Hanging on the Hush* (Ahsahta Press, 2017). Russell has received fellowships from the National Endowment for the Arts, Cave Canem, and the Wisconsin Institute for Creative Writing, and residencies from Ucross, Yaddo, and MacDowell, among others. Her work has appeared in the Academy of American Poets' *Poem-a-Day*, *The New York Times Magazine*, *The Brooklyn Rail*, and elsewhere. She teaches in the Writing Seminars at Johns Hopkins University.

Fayez Sarsawi was born in Gaza City in 1961. He obtained a graduate degree in sculpture from Mimar Sinan Fine Arts University in Turkey in 1986, formerly the Academy of Fine Art. In 2016, Fayez was an artistic supervisor for the Fine Arts Program at the Young Men's Christian Association in Gaza. Fayez founded the quarterly magazine *Ishtar* for culture and arts. This magazine is an intellectual and artistic platform for Gaza's younger generation in Gaza. Since 1994, Fayez has been a member of the editorial board of *Cultural Notebooks* Journal, issued by the Palestinian Ministry of Culture. Fayez's sculpture and painting has been recognized in Palestine and abroad. His sculptures include the Monument in Gaza's YMCA Garden in Gaza (1992), the Peace Garden Freedom Monument in the village of Kawakab Abu Al-Haija in Haifa (1996), Friendship International Garden of Ningxia Province in China (2015), The Ray of Knowledge at the entrance to Al-Aqsa University in Gaza, 2020, among others. In 2003, Fayez was granted an artistic residency in Paris, where he held a solo exhibition of sculptures, painting, and literary texts that address the war on Gaza.

Lloyd Schwartz is poet laureate of Somerville, MA and longtime arts critic for NPR's Fresh Air. He's published five poetry books, most recently *Who's on First? New and Selected Poems*, and edited three volumes devoted to Elizabeth Bishop. He's received Guggenheim, NEA, and Academy of American Poets awards for poetry, and the Pulitzer Prize for Criticism. His poems have been selected for the Pushcart Prize, *Best American Poetry*, and *Best of the Best American Poetry*. His latest collection, *"Artur Schnabel and Joseph Szigeti Play Mozart at the Frick Collection (April 4, 1948)," and other poems*, will appear next year.

Hogan Seidel is a Boston-based artist working in the traditions of experimental film and photography. Their current artistic research, framed through poetic, political, and personal lenses, delves into contemporary queer discourse, queer history, and queer ecology. Hogan currently teaches experimental analog filmmaking courses at MassArt and darkroom photography at Simmons University.

Caleb Sher is a Yiddishist, an amateur letterpress printer, and occasional translator. He holds an interdisciplinary humanities degree from the University of King's College, Halifax, as well as an MA with a certificate in Jewish studies from the Centre for Comparative Literature at the University of Toronto, where he received a Social Sciences and Humanities Research Council (SSHRC) scholarship. His interests include buying books he will never read and good memes, especially in Yiddish.

Esther Shumiatcher-Hirschbein, born 1899 in Gomel, Belarus, immigrated to Calgary, Canada, in 1911. Her poetry and two children's plays were published between 1920 and 1956. In her writings she explored nature, politics, grief, loss, maternity, and erotic life. She was best known for her mature poetry. She was married to the playwright Peretz Hirschbein, with whom she traveled widely and became part of the trans-national Yiddish literary circle. She spent some years in Los Angeles with her husband and son. She remained active in Yiddish cultural work following the early death of her husband, and she spent her final years in New York, where she died in 1985.

Mia Simanainen (b. 1970, MMus) is known as a versatile and elegant singer-musician and composer who is at home wherever musical boundaries are crossed. She has toured most of Europe, Russia, Mexico, and Japan, and has co-produced seven albums with her own bands. Her recent activity includes working with her extraordinary ensemble Quartet Ajaton, as well as solo work and multi-artistic projects.

Fr. Innocent Smith, O.P., is Assistant Professor of Dogmatic Theology and Pastoral Studies at the Dominican House of Studies, Washington, DC. After undergraduate studies in music and philosophy at the University of Notre Dame, he entered the Order of Preachers in 2008 and was ordained priest in 2015. Smith served in parish ministry for several years before completing a doctorate in liturgical studies at the University of Regensburg in 2021. Smith's 2023 monograph, *Bible Missals* *and the Medieval Dominican Liturgy*, focuses on medieval bibles which contain liturgical texts for the celebration of the Mass.

Tracy K. Smith is a Pulitzer Prize-winning poet, memoirist, editor, translator and librettist. She served as the 22nd Poet Laureate of the United States from 2017-2019, during which time she spearheaded "American Conversations: Celebrating Poetry in Rural Communities" with the Library of Congress, created the American Public Media podcast *The Slowdown*, and edited the anthology *American Journal: Fifty Poems for Our Time. Fear Less: Poetry in Perilous Times* will be published in November.

Talin Tahajian is from Massachusetts. Her poems have appeared in *The Kenyon Review, Best New Poets, The Indiana Review, The Rumpus, Copper Nickel, Narrative Magazine, Poetry Magazine, TriQuarterly, Pleiades, West Branch, The Drift, Blackbox Manifold,* T*he Missouri Review, Mizna, The Georgia Review*, and elsewhere. She's a Ph.D. candidate in English at Yale and an assistant editor of *The Yale Review*.

Daniel Tobin is the author of nine books of poems, including *From Nothing*, winner of the Julia Ward Howe Award; *The Stone in the Air*, his suite of versions from the German of Paul Celan; *Blood Labors*, named one of the Best Poetry Books of the Year for 2018 by the New York Times; and *The Mansions*, winner of the National Indie Excellence Award in Poetry. His work has won many awards, among them the Massachusetts Book Award and fellowships from the NEA and the Guggenheim Foundation.

Rafael Toral, born in Lisbon, 1967, has been intrigued by the potential of sound and the functions of music since he was a teenager. As a producer, composer, and performer, he has been deeply involved with rock, ambient, contemporary, electronic and free jazz music in different periods of his life.

Paul Tran is the author of the debut collection of poetry, *All the Flowers Kneeling* (Penguin, 2022).

Chew Chia Shao Wei is a writer from Singapore currently living in Cambridge, Massachusetts.

Jessica L. Wilkinson has published three poetic biographies: *Marionette: A Biography of Miss Marion Davies* (Vagabond 2012); *Suite for Percy Grainger* (Vagabond 2014); and *Music Made Visible: A Biography of George Balanchine* (Vagabond, 2019); and is working on a fourth on French-Australian artist Mirka Mora. Jessica is the founding editor of *Rabbit: a journal for nonfiction poetry*, which will release its 40th issue at the end of 2024. She co-edited the anthologies *Contemporary Australian Feminist Poetry* (2016) and *Memory Book: Portraits of Older Australians in Poetry and Watercolours* (2021). She is a Creative Writing academic at RMIT University, Melbourne.

Lauren Winchester's poems have appeared or are forthcoming in *Ecotone*, *American Literary Review*, *American Life in Poetry*, *North American Review*, and elsewhere. She has been awarded artist in residency fellowships by the Edward Albee Foundation, the Kimmel Harding Nelson Center for the Arts, and Oak Spring Garden Foundation. She received her MFA in poetry from The Writing Seminars at Johns Hopkins University, where she taught creative writing and served as assistant editor of *The Hopkins Review*.

Growing up in Chongqing, China, **Lilan Yang** is an artist and experimental filmmaker based in Boston, delving into the mythology of landscapes and the intricacies of perception. Their work, rooted in 16mm filmmaking, is further enriched by machine learning and data visualization, exploring the materiality and temporality of film. Through mixed-media installations, Yang endeavors to preserve human memories captured by cameras and immortalize these recollections on celluloid, while investigating how information is lost in attempts to remember. Yang holds an MFA from the Rhode Island School of Design and has taught at both RISD and Parsons School of Design.

Karolina Zapal and **Ryan Mihaly** are a husband-and-wife translator duo based in Western Massachusetts. Ryan is the author of *B-Flat Clarinet Fingering Chart* (New Michigan Press), and Karolina is the author of *Notes for Mid-Birth* (Inside the Castle) and *Polalka* (Spuyten Duyvil).